The

"Pete Boardman was the strongest climber that I have ever been privileged to climb with."
—CHRIS BONINGTON

When Peter Boardman and Joe Tasker disappeared May 17, 1982, high on the Tibetan side of Mount Everest, the entire world mourned the passing of two of Britain's foremost climbers. It had been a heroic attempt: two climbers, at 27,000 feet, setting off on their final assault from the unclimbed northeast ridge, alone, without oxygen, aided only by two men in support. And it had seemed a fitting challenge for the two men who had successfully concluded a two-man lightweight expedition up the supposedly unclimbable West Wall of Changabang six years earlier—the feat described in this suspenseful, utterly unromanticized narrative, now being published for the first time in the United States.

Joe contributes a second voice throughout the story, which starts with acclimatization by night in a frozen-food cold-storage plant and progresses through three nights of hell suspended midair in hammocks on the Wall during a storm, to moments of exaltation at the variety and intricacy of this punishingly difficult rock and ice climbing. It is a story of how climbing can become an all-consuming goal; a story of the tensions and mutual separateness inevitable in forty days of isolation on a two-man expedition carried out on a Himalayan scale. It records the moment of joy when they reach the summit ridge, and also tells briefly of defeat—when they descend by fearful night abseiling to find an American climbing team has perished, and set out to find the bodies.

The Shining Mountain

TWO MEN ON CHANGABANG'S WEST WALL

PETER BOARDMAN

with material by Joe Tasker
Epilogue by Chris Bonington

E. P. DUTTON, INC.   NEW YORK

Published in the United States by E. P. Dutton, Inc.,
2 Park Avenue, New York, N.Y. 10016

Library of Congress Catalog Card Number: 83-70379

ISBN: 0-525-24186-8 cl.

10 9 8 7 6 5 4 3 2 1

Contents

1 From the West   11

2 The Rim of the Sanctuary   (22nd August–7th September)   27

3 The First Stone   (8th–20th September)   50

4 The Barrier   (21st–27th September)   67

5 Survival   (28th September–2nd October)   87

6 Recovery   (3rd–8th October)   101

7 The Upper Tower   (9th–13th October)   118

8 Beyond the Line   (14th–15th October)   138

9 Descent to Tragedy   (15th–19th October)   150

10 The Outside   (20th October–1st November)   170

Epilogue *by Chris Bonington*   182

GLOSSARY   185

INDEX   190

Sixteen-page gallery of photographs follows page 130

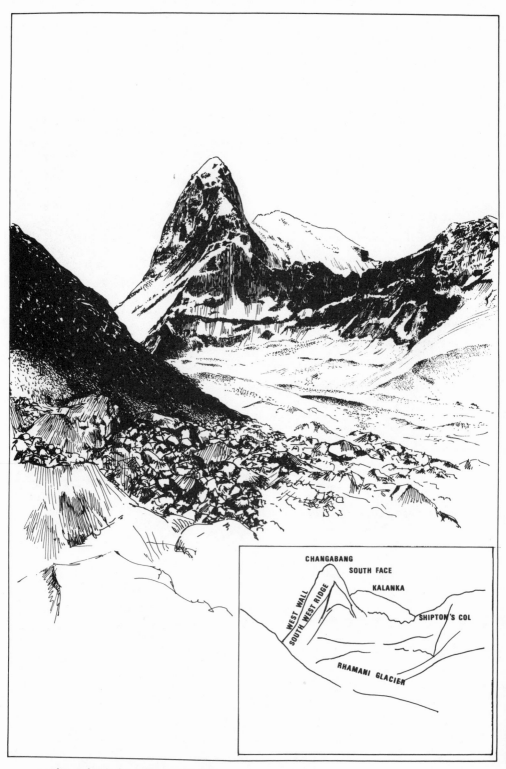

Changabang from the south-west

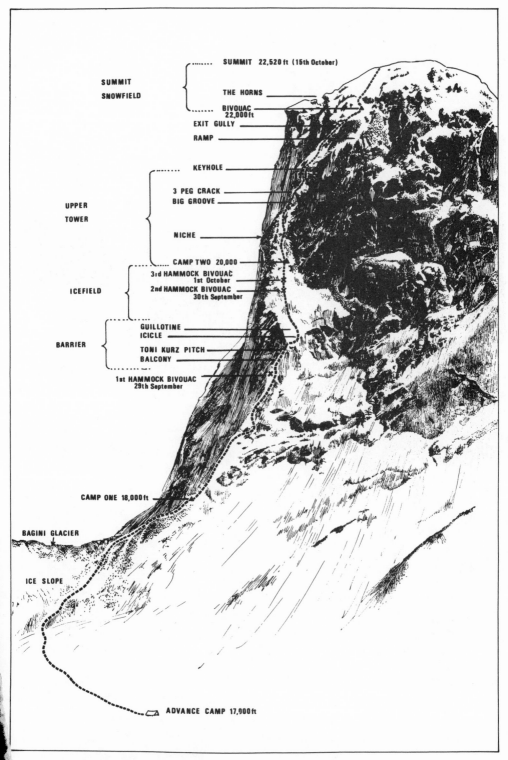

The route up the West Wall

CHAPTER ONE

From the West

"SITTING HUDDLED BENEATH A DOWN JACKET, SHELTERING FROM THE sun, my back against a rock, I drank some liquid for the first time in four days. I was going to live. The photographs I took were purely a conditioned reflex; I would want one picture of this view, just as a reminder of the ordeal I had endured. The glacier, spread about before me like a white desert, was peopled by my imagination and over it hung the massive West Wall of Changabang, a great cinema screen which would never have figures on it."

Joe Tasker had survived Dunagiri and had returned to life to the west of the Shining Mountain.

Autumn days passed; meanwhile I was in the western world.

"Have you seen this letter?" asked Dennis Gray across the office of the British Mountaineering Council in Manchester, where we both worked. "What a fantastic effort," he added. I picked it up. It was from Dick Renshaw, who had just been on an expedition to the Garhwal Himalaya with Joe Tasker. The magnitude of their achievement jumped out from its few words:

Dear Dennis,

   We climbed Dunagiri. It took us six days up the South-East Ridge. When we reached the summit, we ran out of food and fuel to melt snow into water. The descent took five days and we suffered. I got frostbite in some fingers and shall be flying home soon from Delhi. Joe's driving the van back.

                    Yours,
                    Dick.

P.S. Congratulations to Pete on climbing Everest.

I sat down, filled with envy. Dennis was already on the 'phone to the local press. "Incredible feat of endurance . . . Just the two of them . . . Tiny budget . . . 23,000-foot mountain . . . Far more significant than the recent South-West Face of Everest climb." I had to strain to hear the words above the clattering typewriters and rhythmic pumping of the duplicating machine. Beyond the plate glass windows, the red brick of the office block, the unkempt, lumpy car park, and the Home for the Destitute, I could glimpse the blue of the sky.

I stared dumbly at the trays of letters in front of me—access problems, committee meetings, equipment enquiries. Amongst them were invitations to receptions and dinners and requests to give lectures about the Everest climb—all demands to accelerate the headlong pace of my life. Their number diluted the quality of my work. 'Everest is a bloody bore,' screamed a voice inside my head. The previous evening I had given a slide show about Everest. It was as if I was standing aside and listening to myself. As time distances you from a climb, it seems you are talking about someone else. All the usual questions had rolled out at the end: What does it feel like on top? What do you have to eat? How do you go to the toilet when you're up there? Is it more difficult coming down? How long did it take you? Don't you think you've done it all now you've been to the top of Everest? What marvellous courage you must have!

Courage. Endurance. Those words drifted across the office and mocked my bitter mood of discontent. Meaningless. Courage is doing only what you are scared of doing. The blatant drama of mountaineering blinds the judgement of these people who are so loud in praise. Life has many cruel subtleties that require far more courage to deal with than the obvious dangers of climbing. Endurance. But it takes more endurance to work in a city than it does to climb a high mountain. It takes more endurance to crush the hopes and ambitions that were in your childhood dreams and to submit to a daily routine of work that fits into a tiny cog in the wheel of western civilisation. 'Really great mountaineers.' But what are mountaineers? Professional heroes of the west? Escapist parasites who play at adventures? Obsessive dropouts who do something different? Malcontents and egomaniacs who have not the discipline to conform?

"Will you answer this, Pete?"

"Oh yes, sorry."

Rita, one of the secretaries, was holding a 'phone out towards me. "Someone's ropes snapped, and the manufacturer says it isn't his fault."

"O.K. I'll deal with it." In the city, as on the mountain, there has to be a breaking point.

I had nearly died on Everest that September. With Sherpa Pertemba, I had been the last person to see Mick Burke, who had disappeared in the storm that swept over us during our descent from the summit. We had lost him on the summit ridge and it had been my decision to descend without him. But I had returned to the world isolated by a decision and experience I could not share. My internal resources had grown. At first, during the desperate struggle of the descent, I had a surge of panic. We nearly lost our way twice, and were constantly swept by avalanches in the blizzard, but then I felt myself go hard inside, go strong. My muscles and my will tightened like iron. I was indestructible and utterly alone. The simplicity of that feeling did not last beyond our arrival at Camp Six and the thirty-six hours of storm that followed. But I was to remember it in the months that followed.

Now back in Manchester, I was tired and depressed. My life had become dominated by one event. On Everest, the summit day had been presented to me by a large systematised expedition of over a hundred people. During the rest of the time on the mountain, I had been just part of the vertically integrated crowd control, waiting for the leader's call to slot me into my next allocated position. And yet, when I returned to Britain, as far as the general public were concerned I was one of the four heroes of the expedition, the surviving summiters. The applause rang hollow in my loneliness and the pressures of instant fame, although short-lived, made me ill. I yearned hopelessly for privacy so that I could digest the Everest experience. I longed for time to allow the thoughts which came to me in the early morning to take on form and meaning again.

I was now public property and, after eleven weeks away from the office, was left under no doubt that I had been allowed on my last expedition for a couple of years. I had sixteen committees to serve. Yet I felt in need of some new, great plan—some new project. I wanted to see how far I could push myself and find out what limits I could reach on a mountain. At the age of twenty-four there seemed so many mountain areas and adventures just within my grasp.

I was envious of Joe Tasker and Dick Renshaw's climb, not only because of the difficulty and beauty of the ridge they had climbed on Dunagiri, but also because I knew that two-man expeditions, in comparison with the Everest expedition, have a greater degree of flexibility and adventurous uncertainty and they generate a greater feeling of indispensability and self-containment.

Winter came; Joe Tasker walked into the office. He lived not far down the road, out of the city. I had not seen him since the early summer, when he had occasionally called in whilst organising his expedition.

"How's Dick getting on then, Joe?"

"He's got three black finger-tips—I don't know if he'll lose them or not. He'll be out of climbing action for quite a while. He flew home after three weeks in hospital at Delhi."

"Must have been an epic; how long have you been back?"

"Only a few days—the van died in Kabul and I had to hump all the gear home on buses."

A few weeks later it was Christmas time. I was at the end of days of travelling to meetings and lectures and was back amidst the telephones and typewriters, wilting under the headlong rush of urban life. Joe came in and sat down next to my desk.

Somehow, for Joe, the Shining Mountain had become more than just a backcloth to a hallucinatory ordeal.

"What do you think about having a go at the West Face of Changabang next year?"

I wished he had not asked so loud. Someone might hear him. "Yes, that would be good. Yes, I'd like to go; trouble is, I've just been off work for a long time on Everest—I don't think I'll ever get the time off for another trip next year."

Joe seemed surprised how readily I had shown my interest. I had agreed instinctively, flattered at his trust in me.

It was the Christmas party at the BMC and soon, upstairs in the pub, Joe was talking to Dennis. Then he came over.

"Dennis is really keen. He says, 'Leave it to me, lads'—thinks you might be able to get the time off, if the Committee of Management agree."

I didn't think they would, but kept quiet. I wasn't mentioning this to anyone. Joe's plans were sweeping me along.

There were now two fresh elements in my life. Joe Tasker and Changabang. I had never climbed with Joe, but was well aware of his reputation. We had met for the first time in the Alps in 1971, on the North Spur of the Droites. I was climbing with a friend, Martin Wragg, a fellow student at Nottingham University. We had started off on the route in darkness and had been intrigued to see two lights flickering a few hundred feet up the route. We passed them as dawn crept down the mountain—they were two English climbers who had been bivouacking—Joe Tasker and Dick Renshaw. 'Never heard of them,' I thought and climbed quickly on.

Martin and I were both too sure of ourselves, having climbed the North Face of the Matterhorn the week before. The Droites was badly out of condition, but we were young and inexperienced and kept on climbing as fast as we could. There was hard water ice everywhere, and I was forced to spend exhausting hours step cutting. But still these two climbers kept on close behind us. We couldn't shake clear of them. By late afternoon we had traversed onto the North Face, trying to find easier and less icy ground. It was snowing and I was exhausted. If the other two had not been behind us, or had turned back, we would have retreated many hours before. There were no ledges and Martin and I sat on each other's lap alternately through the night, while Joe and Dick bivouacked a little more comfortably a few hundred feet below. The following morning a storm broke and we teamed together to make twenty-two abseils back to the Argentière Glacier amidst streams of water, thunder and lightning. Once we reached the glacier, we split up.

I didn't see Joe for another four years.

During those four years Joe did a lot of climbing in the Alps, mainly with Dick, and steadily, in a matter-of-fact manner with complete disregard for the reputation of routes, achieved a staggering list of ascents, culminating in the East Face of the Grandes Jorasses in 1974 and the North Face of the Eiger in the winter of 1975.

After Christmas I went to North Wales to the hut of my local climbing club, the Mynydd, and confided to a friend about the Changabang plans—a blundering, stupid thing to do, for my girlfriend overheard me, and it was the first time she had heard the news. Before, it had been Everest that had obsessed me. By an almost mechanical transfer it was now Changabang.

I was living at home with my parents in early 1975. I asked Joe and Dick round to my parents' home for a meal. My mother, a keen reader of mountaineering magazines, laid on the full dining-room treatment. It was the first time my parents had met Joe or Dick. It was as if they were appraising Joe, examining the person who was taking their son away. Dick's fingers were still being treated and looked alarming. The unspoken question in the air was 'Joe's come out of the ordeal on Dunagiri without any scars—will he do this to Pete?' Throughout the meal, Dick was his usual quiet, polite self. Joe, however, was making digs

and gibes about the size of the Everest expedition and the publicity it
had received.

"I don't think the Everest climb was impressive as a climbing feat,
but as an organisational one," he said.

I wondered if Joe must have resented the fact that I had been on
Everest and not him. His achievement on Dunagiri had been formidable and far more futuristic in terms of the development of Alpine-
style climbing in the Himalayas but, despite Dennis Gray's efforts, had
received nothing like the recognition of the Everest climb. It was a
naïve thought—I was being over-sensitive about Everest, and the
sources of Joe's ambitions were a closed book to me. However it was
obvious that rather than feeling satisfied with his Dunagiri climb, it was
as if he still had an itch that needed to be satisfied.

After the meal Joe showed me the slides he had taken of the West
Wall of Changabang, which he had taken from the summit of Dunagiri and from the Rhamani Glacier just above their base camp, as he had
found melted water after the Dunagiri climb. Joe and Dick had been
so exhausted and unbalanced by their descent that they had split up and
descended the last 1,000 feet down different sides of the ridge. Joe had
staggered beneath the wall alone. He had been beyond thoughts of
climbing then. Vague plans only began to formulate in his head during
the long journey home. Examining the slides carefully, I was impressed
and daunted. The Face looked very steep and there were no continuous
lines of weakness on it, only occasional patches of snow and ice between
great blank areas of granite slabs and overhangs. This was Changabang.

Joe was not of the older mountaineering generation—on Everest I had
felt in awe of the media images of climbers like Bonington, Scott and
Haston—but here was someone with whom I could discuss the problems on equal terms.

"Where's this line then?" I asked.

Joe was taken aback. "Well, it just looks like an interesting Face—I
mean it can't all be vertical—there's snow and ice on parts of it. Anyway, when you get close to a seemingly blank wall, there are usually
some features on it." He mentioned ice slopes and pointed to shadowy
lines which could indicate grooves and cracks. Our fingers hovered
on the screen. Joe felt it was a crucial moment:

"Until I had a second opinion, I was not yet sure whether to
regard it as a fanciful daydream or a feasible proposition. If Pete
was sceptical about the feasibility of the project, the impetus

would be lost and my belief in the venture would begin to wane. I wanted to draw from him some appraisal of the idea, but he was non-committal. I only realised slowly that his question arose not from doubt, but from interest – he was intrigued by the idea."

I knew I must go there. I began to wonder if I would come back from such a wild enterprise – to succeed seemed impossible.

"What do you think, Dick?" I asked.

"It looks as if it might go," said Dick. But then he did not have to try and prove it. My mind took a great leap and accepted the whole project.

This climb would be all that I wanted. Something that would be totally committing, that would bring my self-respect into line with the public recognition I had received for Everest. My experience on Everest had left an emotional gap that needed to be filled. The BMC had agreed that I could take another two weeks' holiday on top of my four-week allowance to go and attempt it. I longed for the summer to arrive, and saw the long, intervening months as time to be endured.

Meanwhile, Joe was doing most of the work for the expedition. The first problem was to obtain permission from the Indian Government to make an attempt. Some Lakeland climbers were planning a route for the South Face and already had permission. Joe set about trying to persuade them and the Indians to allow us to go. Neither was happy at first. Joe, however, had powerful friends in India and, despite an early discouraging letter from the Indian Mountaineering Foundation that said, "We do feel that a team of two climbers attempting a peak like Changabang will be unsafe", friendly persuasion was applied and the permission eventually arrived not long before we left. The Mount Everest Foundation gave us a modest grant, after several members of the committee had expressed the sentiment "that a team of four might be more advisable". All this was fuel to Joe, encouragement to his awkwardness when faced with obstructions. An iconoclast by nature, he had no respect for the cults and legends that surround personalities and preconceptions in the mountaineering world.

I met Ted Rogers, one of the Lakeland team, whilst out climbing on Stanage Edge in Derbyshire one weekend. I asked him if they minded us going to the other side of the mountain. After all, they had been planning their expedition for nearly two years. Our organisation, in contrast, was at the last minute. His reply was rather guarded.

"Joe usually seems to get his way," he said.

Chris Bonington was the patron of their expedition and he had told Ted that he considered Joe's and my plans as 'preposterous'. "Still," he added to us at a later date, "if you do get up, it'll be the hardest route in the Himalayas."

On occasion through the spring, Joe and I met to discuss our plans for the expedition. Joe had acquired a temporary job working nights in a frozen food distribution centre in Salford. Every night he was in a huge cold store for several hours, where the temperature was between −15°C and −20°C. Much to the amazement of his workmates, who were always well wrapped up, he worked without his gloves on for most of the time, loading small electric trucks from the corridors of racking laden with frozen vegetables, meat, fish, ice-cream, cream cakes, chocolate éclairs—everything to cater for today's pre-packed way of life. It was not an enthralling occupation, but it meant that he was at home in the daytime and could attend to the work needed to organise the expedition during the day. He dashed about in a dilapidated car, stereo blaring wildly, his thoughts full of Changabang and his talk full of lurid stories about the complicated love lives of his fellow shift workers.

During snatched moments of spare time, I read books about the exploration of the area of the Garhwal, in which Changabang stands. I started by reading *The Ascent of Nanda Devi* by Bill Tilman, about the successful expedition to the highest mountain in India in 1936. I had the strange feeling that I had read it before. Then I realised that the book I had read before was Eric Shipton's *Nanda Devi*, in which he described the adventures that he and Tilman had met the year before, when they first penetrated the high ring of peaks that guard Nanda Devi and reached the Sanctuary at its foot.

They were the first human beings to reach there, and the story had a Shangri La quality to it, touching far back into the promised land of my subconscious. I had read the book when I was thirteen. Tilman's book jerked my memory and I re-read the book, in particular the passages where Shipton makes his first steps into the inner Sanctuary of the Nanda Devi Basin:

At each step I experienced that subtle thrill which anyone of imagination must feel when treading hitherto unexplored country. Each corner held some thrilling secret to be revealed for the trouble of looking. My most blissful dream as a child was to be in some such valley, free to wander where I liked, and discover for myself some hitherto unrevealed glory of Nature. Now, the reality was no less wonderful than that half-forgotten dream.

The words bumped around inside my head like a bell which had only just stopped ringing. Here was a subtle relationship between real place and mental landscape. I was becoming a willing victim of the spell of the Garhwal.

The mountaineer of today cannot hope to capture that feeling. To-day's frontiers are not of promised lands, of uncrossed passes and mysterious valleys beyond. Numbers of ascents of many mountains in the Himalayas are now into their teens. Today, the exploring mountaineer must look at the unclimbed faces and ridges and bring the equipment, techniques and attitudes developed over the past forty years, rather than the long axe and the plane table. There are so many ways, so much documentation, that only the mountaineer's inner self remains the uncharted.

Changabang had been climbed for the first time in 1974, by a joint British-Indian Expedition led by Chris Bonington. Like all wise first ascensionists of Himalayan peaks, they chose the easiest, most accessible line – the South-East Ridge. In June, Joe and I heard the news that a six-man Japanese expedition had climbed the South-West Ridge. They had used traditional siege tactics – six climbers had used 8,000 feet of fixed rope, three hundred pitons, one hundred and twenty expansion bolts in the thirty-three days it had taken them to climb the South-West Ridge. This news was, for us, surprisingly encouraging. We were beginning to think – from the comments of other British climbers – that Changabang was unclimbable by any other route except the original. Chris Bonington had announced our plans to the mountaineering public at the National Mountaineering Conference, and this had provoked a lot of comment.

"You'll never get up that wall, you know," said Nick Estcourt.

"I don't think so either," said Dave Pearce, "but I think it's great that two of you are going to have a go."

"It doesn't look like a married man's route," said Ken Wilson, editor of *Mountain Magazine*.

We consulted all the British members of the first Changabang climb.

"You'll have your time cut out," said Dougal Haston.

Joe asked Doug Scott for his opinion of the chances of climbing the Face, looking for some sort of reassurance.

"Beyond the bounds of possibility, youth."

"Well, you've got to go and have a look."

"Yes, youth, you're right. I'd take an extra jumper with you though," then—two days later—'phoned Joe up to ask if he might come. We were bent on a two-man attempt and to have more would increase opinions and divide the purpose of the unit. Just two of us would make the dangers and decisions deliciously uncomplicated.

On one, well-oiled night in the Padarn Lake Hotel in Llanberis, Brian Hall staggered across: "I think it's great that just two people have got permission for a route like that—it shows that the Indian Mountaineering Foundation are at last beginning to move with the times. But if something happens to you it will mess things up for people who want to go on small expeditions in the future."

Meanwhile, Joe Tasker was asking Joe Brown about the difficult rock climbing he had just done at 20,000 feet on Trango Tower in the Karakoram. When he told Joe about our plans, the veteran Brown wrinkled his oriental eyes with a calm born of experience and said, "Just the two of you? Sounds like cruelty to me." The consensus of opinion was that we stood no chance at all of succeeding; only close friends thought that we would do more than make a noble effort before retreating.

Don Whillans, however, was encouraging. He himself had planned to go to Changabang in 1968, with a team including Ian Clough and Geoff Birtles, and Don lent Joe and me a number of pictures of the West Face he had acquired from various sources. He looked at one of them and, planting a stubby finger on the icefield in the middle said, "Well, you'll be able to climb that all right—you'll just have to get to the bottom of it, and then from the top of it up that rock wall above it." He ended by summarising the situation neatly:

"Well," he said, "there's three things that could happen: you could fail, you could get up it, or you could not come back. You'll just have to make sure you come back, won't you?"

It was obviously something special we were going to try and climb. Neither of us felt particularly immortal, or that our gifts transcended those of all around us. We would just need a lot of determination and steadiness of nerve. Also, it was clear, looking at the pictures, that if we were to be able to keep on performing, committed, high up on that wall for days on end, we would have to select our equipment with absolute care. High on the Wall, we would not be able to afford to carry anything superfluous. We had no detailed logistical plan, but were preparing for various eventualities.

One of the main problems would be bivouacking. There did not appear to be many ledges on the Face—certainly none more than a couple of feet wide. So we persuaded Troll Mountain Products, in Oldham, to develop some hammocks for us. Single point suspension hammocks have been in use for some years, on the sun-drenched high rock walls of California, but they had not been used at high altitude in the Himalayas before. Troll made us two pilot models with a canopy and Joe and I tried them out one night on Scout Crag in Langdale, in the Lake District. We waited till it was dark—the pub had thrown us out and everyone had gone to bed—before creeping up the field and fighting our way inside the folds of material. It was a bad night, particularly after it started to rain. When dawn came we packed up quickly, feeling rather self-conscious dressed in high-altitude suits and wearing double boots in early May. I met some friends walking up the path.

"You're up early, Pete," they said.

"Mmmmm."

Joe and I decided that Langdale was not the best place to test our gear. It was too wet, warm and crowded.

The thought came with a rush. We needed to try the hammocks out somewhere really cold. Already we had ideas for modifications, but the real test had to be in sub-zero temperatures to find out how effective sleeping bags were squashed within the nylon walls of the hammocks. What about the cold store where Joe worked? Since the lads on the shift already regarded Joe as slightly eccentric, the approach to the manager was made very secretly. He was bewildered but agreed, although he had worries in case there was an accident—yes, we could try out our hammocks by spending a night there.

By this time my girlfriend had given me up in disgust in the face of all this fanatical dedication. Joe took me under his bachelor wing, promising me an introduction to the Manchester social scene. We went to the pictures and then to the pub, where we sank a few pints of ale before picking up the gear from the house where two tolerant friends were harbouring Joe in between his travels. Before leaving we rang up the security guard at the cold store, to check that the manager had left the key for us to get in. He had not, and had not even told the security guard anything about our plans. It was 11.30 p.m. and the beer had not helped Joe's clarity of speech and, at first, the guard was disbelieving.

"What, two of you sleeping here, hanging from a million pounds' worth of frozen food?" Gradually, however, he was convinced, and the absence of the key would be sorted out. "Leave it to me," he said.

At the cold store it was the night off for the shift and the security guard was the only person there. We bribed him to keep quiet with a bottle of beer and he opened up the great fridge doors after we had donned all our equipment.

"I'll open it up at six in the morning," he said. "You can sleep in that corner if you want, above the ice-cream."

At first the cold was stunning. We stumbled and thrashed around, getting inside the hammocks, standing on crates of cheesecakes and holding onto pallets of ice-lollies. Soon we were lashed to the girders that held up tons of ice-cream, our feet swinging wildly above our heads as we tried to remove our boots. After about an hour we were settled in. Then Joe started moaning. He wanted to go to the toilet, having drunk too much beer. I told him gleefully that he'd have to wait until 6.00 a.m. I was Everest-trained, and had got my plastic pee bottle for emergencies.

It was a surreal night. The lights inside were turned on and the freezer hummed monotonously. Halfway through the night there was a great rumbling noise and I woke, convinced that the hammock was toppling to the ground with all the crates avalanching onto me. In a panic, I slid out of the hammock and dropped six feet, on to the ground, still inside my sleeping bag—to realise that the noise had just been the freezer generating.

At 6.00 a.m. Joe slipped outside to relieve himself and sat chatting to the security guard. The first member of the day shift arrived and went inside to start cleaning up. He walked up and down each aisle, sweeping the place clean. I was still inert in my bright red hammock—and the workman noticed its enormous sausage shape above his head and passed on; he went outside to Joe and the guard:

"Hey, what sort of new food's that, hung in the ice-cream aisle?"

Coming out from the icy confines of the store, into the grey summer's morning was like stepping into a hot bath.

After that session Joe took the hammocks to Troll and had them fully insulated. He even persuaded one of the young seamstresses there to join him inside one to see if they would hold the weight of two. Meanwhile, a friend of mine who works in an engineering factory, devoted some of his research time to turning out some aluminium spacer bars so that the hammocks wouldn't crush us and the sleeping bags. Pete Hutchinson of Mountain Equipment, another local Manchester firm, designed special lightweight down jackets and sleeping bags. He made them longer than usual, so that we could, in an emergency, get into them with our boots on. We told them weight could be a matter of life and death so, under our instructions, they used such thin material that the down found little difficulty in getting out. We were to be accompanied on our climb by floating fluff! As an outer sleeping bag for the hammocks, we took artificial fibre bags. These would retain their insulating properties after many days of condensation—we would not have any drying facilities on the route!

We spent another two nights in the fridge before we were satisfied. If anyone—climbers—asked us, "What's this rumour—that you're training in a cold store?" we would reply, "You must be joking!"

Joe and I also selected our climbing equipment with care. Ian Stewart, who had been one of the cameramen on the Everest climb, provided a one-piece suit and double boots for Joe. We decided to take full body harnesses, because we would be carrying heavy loads up very steep rock and would risk turning upside down without their support.

The possibility of an accident was one that worried us intensely. "I know it sounds horrifying, the idea of just two of you, out there alone," said Joe, "but once you're actually climbing it doesn't feel any more committing than when you're doing a big route in the Alps. Still, we ought to be prepared for emergencies."

I was worried in case I let Joe down, and he was probably worried about the same thing. I had been on a two-man expedition in 1974, to the Central Alaskan Range with Roger O'Donovan. At first, this had been very successful and Roger and I had made the first ascent of the South Face of Mount Dan Beard. After that we had attempted Mount McKinley, but had been forced to turn back when Roger had become ill. I was intensely disappointed. On a two-man expedition, if one of you becomes ill, or is injured, you have to give up and come home. There is no alternative. Alaska and the Himalayas are long distances to travel for that sort of disappointment to occur. Joe and I were determined to be prepared for any medical emergencies.

Joe knew a doctor, Andy Hill, from his student climbing days, and Andy helped arrange all our medical supplies. On the various medicines he supplied for us he labelled clear, idiot-proof instructions such as "For sore bum, three up daily". He had us practising stitching and injecting oranges, instead of each other. We also made a visit to a local casualty ward and, under the watchful guidance of nurses, plastered up each other's arms. We were taking our training seriously.

Joe couldn't understand why I wasn't becoming flustered about the

organisation for the expedition. I would just shake my head and pro-
nounce, with irritating condescension, "It's nothing like organising for
Everest." Not that I had much to do with the organisation for Everest.
But now I was so wound up with my work for the BMC, dealing with
access problems, answering 'phone calls and letters, that I could only
provide Joe with occasional consultancy and encouragement. Also, it
was turning into one of the hottest summers in living memory in
Britain, and I was keen on doing some rock climbing. Joe's temporary
job in the cold store gave him a bleak, twilight existence and none of
his social hours coincided with anybody else's. He lived a half-life of
permanent semi-awakedness. At weekends he tried to adjust to being
awake all day, and then rush back to be at work for 10.00 p.m. on
Sunday night. We tried climbing together a few times, in North Wales
and the Peak District, but I tended to take the rock-climbing less
casually than Joe and kept out-climbing him and, at one point, we
decided on a 'trial separation' for a few weekends! I knew full well
that as soon as we were in the big hills Joe would click into action. Joe
was also confident that we could get on well together:

> "We often engaged in articulate gibing sessions with each other
> which often caused people to wonder that we should be going on
> an expedition together. On the other hand, it was useful to
> establish a good-humoured openness as a safety valve for when
> pressures should build up. If we could voice our thoughts it was
> likely that any tensions could be defined before they became
> destructive.
> "There were revealing moments, such as one weekend in
> Glencoe, when we were still warmly ensconced in our sleeping
> bags at 1.00 p.m. on a rainy afternoon, wondering which of us
> was going to have the drive to carry us up Changabang if we
> couldn't even get out of our tent on a wet, Scottish weekend.
> We must have shamed ourselves into action because we did reach
> the East Face of Aonach Dubh, to find that the rock was not too
> wet to climb on and completed three routes before the mad dash
> down to fit in a drink at the Clachaig before closing time."

I started doing some training runs. I had, by this time, moved into
my own home in New Mills in Derbyshire. This was right on the edge
of the Peak District, and there was only one row of houses between my
house and open moorland. Often, in the long northern light of the

evenings, I would go running up there, or I would go out with local climbing friends on the gritstone edges of the area. Gritstone always gave my favourite climbing, and I would turn to it for reassurance as to an old friend. Such evening exercise, after a long hot day in the office, helped to clear my mind; but only for a while. I needed to get away, to rediscover the clarity of focusing all my effort, concentration and skill on one big obstacle.

The thousands of tiny little pressures of urban life were closing in on me. Occasionally I had to make trips down to meetings in London. On one occasion, my train times dictated that I was early, and I strolled through Green Park and sat down under a horse-chestnut tree and wrote: "Life at the moment seems claustrophobic and narrowing, like Kafka's short story about the mouse being chased down a tunnel. It brings an increasing mixture of motives and complications. It's become an increasing struggle to rediscover a single-minded purpose and drive, and the freedom to move. Time races, absolutely races by, when you're in a job like mine. So many 'phone calls, little problems, papers to read, papers to write. Having a house, I suppose, multiplies the snags of life. Yet if I'm restlessly worrying about them, doing little jobs, continually concerning myself with all these problems, surely the spirit, the soul of life, will glide by unseen, as a deep current."

We booked a cheap flight to Delhi for the 22nd August. As the departure date grew nearer, the full consequences of going on a big trip to the Himalaya made their impact. I seriously doubted if I was going to come back. Joe and I threw a wild party at my house in New Mills, and invited all those who had helped us prepare for our expedition — and anyone else we could think of. An anxious curiosity not to miss anything kept us up drinking and dancing until daylight. After clearing the debris, we drove down to Charlie and Ruth Clarke's in London.

Charlie had been one of the doctors on the Everest expedition. His house exuded a relaxed calm. We had sent some food with the Lakeland team overland, some hardware with another overland trekker, and most of the gear by air. Now, we only had a few odds and ends to stuff into our rucksacks. Charlie, and Ruth, heavily pregnant, and Sheridan, their dog, reclined amusedly as we packed in their back garden under the hot sun. Four of my friends had come from New Mills to see me off. A young lady appeared at London Heathrow Airport to say goodbye to Joe. Once in the airport, the atmosphere changed and became tense and expectant. I couldn't think of anything to say to my friends. We had arrived at the last minute and the airline had overbooked on places. Jostling with many Asians in the queue, we were feeling hot and incongruous in our down jackets and double boots, which we were wearing to take precious weight out of our luggage. At last we got our places sorted out for the 'plane and stumbled through the barrier, with the inadequate sense that our last goodbyes had been awkward and self-conscious, and quite unrepresentative of our feelings.

I thought of these last vivid days in Britain many times during the weeks that followed. The memories circled around my mind as I walked up the glacier and lay down in the cold, during the long nights.

CHAPTER TWO

The Rim of the Sanctuary

22nd August–7th September

The humidity and crowds of monsoon August in Delhi sap your will to think and move. Joe and I were lying sweltering on grubby bunk beds in a doss house down Janpath Lane. Above us, a large fan hung from the cracked ceiling, swinging limply like a wounded bird. The manager of the place was unctuous and creepy — he didn't seem to trust us, so we didn't feel we could trust him. We wanted to move out as soon as possible.

Joe had stayed in a similar place on his way to and from Dunagiri the year before. The previous time I had been in Delhi had been with the Everest expedition, when we had stopped there for two days on the way back from Nepal. Joe and I were trying to climb Changabang on a budget of about £1,400, whereas the Everest Expedition had been sponsored by Barclays Bank International to a sum of £113,000. Then we had stayed in a five-star hotel, which cost 150 rupees each person per night. This time our accommodation was costing us seven rupees a night.

A girl came in wearing Indian clothes, talking in a London accent and scratching her backside. She had been living in a leaf hut in Malari with her boyfriend, surviving by rolling marihuana and selling it to westerners. She had come to Delhi for a gamma globulin injection against hepatitis.

"I've brought my own needle," she said. She had a slight figure and coughed heavily. Occasionally, during conversation, she would pause and rush to the toilet. "It's O.K.," she said, "I'm just being sick. I took too much opium in Old Delhi last night." She must have been about eighteen years old.

We walked through the streets. It was hot and muggy and sweat poured off us. A deep breath gave no ventilation. Everywhere were great placards and slogans, for India was at the height of the Emergency.

Their English language tricked us into half-familiarity and emphasised our remoteness from the problems of the sub-continent. 'Plant a tree', 'Only two children', 'Root out corruption', 'There is no substitute for hard work', 'Savings will help you'. Across the back of one crowded bus was written 'Talk less, work more'. Yes, I longed for action. For weeks now, in the preparation of our expedition, we'd had to tell people what we were planning to do and explain how we were going to do it. But deep inside, this had all felt hollow. I did not really believe that we were going to do the route at all. I wanted to stop talking and start some action.

Joe had some friends, Tony and Rosemary Beaumont, who lived near London. Tony Beaumont was one of the directors of an international company, Guest Keen & Nettlefolds, which had a sister company, Guest Keen Williams, with an office in New Delhi. This branch had helped Joe the previous year, and it had been friends of the Beaumonts in India who had presented our request for permission to climb Changabang to the Indian Mountaineering Foundation in person. Having raced in the Monte Carlo Rally, and taken part in ocean races themselves, the Beaumonts were in sympathy with the spirit of our project and we were indebted to them. So we went in to the office in Parliament Street, to renew acquaintances. J. D. Kapoor was there, beaming a welcome. Walking off the teeming monsoon streets into an air-conditioned office was like walking back into western reality, from the foreign into the familiar. J. D. accepted us immediately. He pressed a buzzer and refreshing drinks appeared.

"How can I help you?" he said.

It was a happy, friendly office and they helped us a lot, since there was a great deal of expertise there to assist us short circuit the bureaucratic networks of the Indian customs and excise. However, it still took us two days of trailing around long, impotent corridors of Kafkaesque bureaucracy to obtain the final papers that would release our airfreighted equipment from the airport. Everyone was always very polite and friendly, and presented us with cups of tea, but everywhere they would patiently explain away delays by saying that they were 'just adhering to the system'. If we complained they would just turn their eyes upwards helplessly and explain, "But it was you British who taught us these procedures." Perhaps my long hair and Joe's curly mop, and our denim jeans and plimsolls, did not give us the best appearance for obtaining co-operation from officialdom. One day we waited for two hours in the Customs office for a document to receive interminable counter-signatures. Above our heads hung a framed quote by Jawaharlal Nehru: "I am not interested in excuses for delay, I am interested only in a thing done."

Modern India has many faces. It has its ghettoes for the rich as well as for the poor. One of the attractions for me about going on an expedition is that it brings a sense of purpose to travel and tourism. It is the experiences below the snow line, with the people of the country as much as the climbing, that one remembers on returning to the west. You see all the sides of a country if you are trying to get something done, or if you are actually trying to organise something complicated in it. You learn a lot if you have to try to arrange insurance, buy enormous quantities of food, move large amounts of gear by local transport and hire porters who speak only a Himalayan dialect. All this brings you into close contact with the country — a contact that is often closer than that of some of the people who live there.

We collected some gear that a friend had left with an upper-class Indian family. The woman of the house talked with the airs of a Kensington lady Tory, with the blinkered aloofness of aristocracy. I felt uncomfortable talking to her, because Joe was in one of his off-hand moods. He had switched off, and it looked rude. I murmured a few platitudes and eventually we escaped past the servants and guard dogs, out of the colony of rich houses, into a taxi and back to the streets.

We also borrowed some equipment that was mouldering away in a cupboard in the flat of an Englishman employed by a bank. When we went to collect it, we talked to this lone Englishman — he was about our age. He was losing interest in life in the heat and sweat, and was full of complaints about his flat. It seemed palatial to us. Servants were cheap and his salary was just spending money. His social life was confined to the insular English community in the capital. Occasionally, Indians asked him around for a meal, he said, but sooner or later they brought the conversation around to the possibility of a loan. He seemed to live an antiseptic life, away from the living warmth, smells and hospitality of village India.

It was always back on the pavements that the culture shock, the abruptness with which the aeroplane had transported us from the west, hit us. This was the real India — muggy, smelly, with small children pulling at my clothes, and pointing pathetically at their small baby brothers and sisters. Many impressions, memories, smells, sights and feelings of my previous trips to Nepal and Afghanistan returned; as if they had lain dormant, forgotten, during the rush of life in England.

Now everything flooded back and started to feel real—as though I had never been away or had been living two lives.

We went to a tea room and ordered a meal. It was the cheapest place in Connaght Circus and we had peered at the kitchen behind the curtain. "We'd better stay off meat here," said Joe. Glasses of water came in. "Cholera cocktails," said Joe. We reeled off all the stock jokes of Europeans on the loose in Asia.

We seemed to be at a stopping place of the Hippy trail across India. Or, perhaps, the end of the trail for some. There were a few Australians and New Zealanders here—sporting stronger currency, but mainly Europeans and Indians sat at the tables. On the floor crouched an Indian, dressed in brown, sweeping a large wet rag across the floor. He moved it quickly around tables and people's legs. I watched him, fascinated. He seemed completely oblivious to life in the tea room above him. His vision went no further than the rag in front of him. I wondered what he was thinking about. Then a European approached us and started chatting. I talked to him. Joe looked suspicious. He was an Austrian and spoke very good English. Slowly, he spun out a long sob story about how he had ended up in New Delhi. His Embassy would not help him—they were besieged by such cases. All he needed was the train fare to Benares—he was pleading with us, as fellow Europeans, to help him. I was taken in, and was about to offer him some money, which we could not really afford to do. I have a fear of confronting people—a cowardice, perhaps. But Joe said to the Austrian:

"No, I've got absolutely no sympathy for you. There are millions of people in India who need help and money more than you, and I think it's pathetic for a European to come out here and end up in a state like you. What do you think the Indians think of us, when we come begging towards them. If I had any money, I'd rather give it to an Indian who really was in need."

The next problem, after the equipment had been extricated from Customs, was to find our liaison officer. The Garhwal Himalaya, the area in which Changabang lies, had been closed to foreigners for fifteen years owing to border troubles with China, and a dispute over grazing grounds on the Niti Pass, to the north of the Garhwal, had been one of the many issues that had started the cold war in 1954. Since the area was re-opened in March, 1974, expeditions other than those involving Indian mountaineers have only been allowed into the area if accompanied by a liaison officer—usually a member of the armed forces with some mountaineering experience. One of his duties, presumably, is to make sure the expedition does not stray over the 'Inner Line' (the area close to the Chinese/Tibetan border, inside which all travel is restricted), and to make sure that expeditions aren't working undercover, masquerading as mountaineering whilst photographing military installations or even, as is rumoured to have happened some years ago (although the device was avalanched), installing listening devices to monitor the Chinese over the border.

Our Customs papers, peak booking, and liaison officer had to be negotiated through the Indian Mountaineering Foundation. Mountaineering in India is still mostly done by the armed forces, and the IMF has its offices in the Military Defence block. To reach them you had to sign for a pass. They were situated in the corner of one overgrown block. There, Mr. Munshi Ram, the small, bald-headed, fussy secretary of the IMF, would beam a welcome and greet us in his high-pitched whine whenever we went around with some new problems. He found it difficult to accept the fact that neither of us wanted to call himself the leader. It did not seem necessary to us, since there were only two of us. He suggested that we took on a trekking and travel agent to organise the Customs entry and the transport and final porterage of our gear. The travel agents are parasites who profit from the slow wheels of the Indian systems and make a lot of money out of the most straightforward arrangements. They hover in the wings until their unfortunate victim is at his wits' end, trying to deal with the seemingly endless stream of problems, and then offer their help — at a price. But Joe had managed without them before and would manage without them again!

At last, at 5.00 p.m. on the 26th August, we met our liaison officer, Flight Lieutenant D. N. Palta, a pilot of the Indian Air Force. He had hoped to be returning to his wife and family in Chandigarh, 150 miles away, but had been diverted at the last minute to taking charge of us. In his early thirties, with a trim moustache, he was polite, well-spoken and serious, and from another world to Joe and me. He had a profound sense of duty to life and to the people of India that made me feel frivolous, anarchic and self-indulgent in comparison.

One of the obligations in having a liaison officer is that you feed and clothe him and pay for his transport. That evening Palta came around to our 'guest house'. He was visibly taken aback by the squalor we were living in, but said nothing. The boots we had brought for him were much too big and I felt embarrassed at the tatty clothing we gave him. It was functional, but was old gear that Joe and I had used in the past.

I felt uneasy that Joe and I were not living up to Palta's idea of 'an expedition'. As Palta left with his bundle of equipment, the manager of the 'guest house' tried to arrest him—he thought some illicit trading had been going on.

That night a rat ran over my stomach, quickly followed by another one in hot pursuit. Across the corridor, two emaciated Americans were talking. They were frightening sights of deteriorating humanity, all nerves and inarticulate, scattered intensity. A Canadian in the bed next to me was ill with a high fever.

The following day we went to the Superbazaar to buy most of our food supplies. There we trooped round in a trio, selecting rice, sugar and other basic commodities. It was useful to have three people there to carry things, but each acquisition became an abnormally complicated ritual of suggestion, agreement, reaffirmation, recalculation and further discussion. Joe and I were more used to dividing up tasks to be done and going about our separate ways to do them. With Palta there, eager to help, we felt we had to take note of his suggestions, otherwise he would feel shunned and dissatisfied.

The days when it was thought necessary to equip an expedition totally with food and equipment in Britain before it set out have now passed. Delhi has large shops, and few foods are unobtainable there. By the evening, we had everything packed into strong, cardboard boxes, rucksacks and kit-bags. We piled all the stuff into two taxis and careered towards Old Delhi railway station, surrounded by heaving carts, ancient buses and wandering scooters. One of the taxis brushed a man off a bicycle. There was a lot of shouting but no one was hurt. Soon we were back into the swirling chaos of hooting, shouting and screeching, where it was a matter of principle not to give way.

If we had been a big expedition we would just have hired one large truck, piled it with all the gear, and driven it three hundred miles to the mountains. Instead, we were to have the fun and excitement of moving sixteen items of luggage for that distance on various styles of local transport. It was a big money-saver, too, for now we were fairly money-conscious, calculating carefully so that we could get to the mountains and back.

All railway stations in India seem to have three times as many people in the booking halls and on the platforms than can possibly hope to squeeze onto a train. Among the crowds were whole families, just sitting or lying down, seemingly with nowhere to go. The poor lighting, dirt, the steam, the hooting trains and the crowds gave an atmosphere of turmoil. Some red-shirted porters rolled our gear onto a huge trolley and wheeled it onto our platform via two lifts and a tunnel under the lines. The tunnel was just on the water level, and there was water streaming down the walls to mingle with the heaving, sweating bodies of the porters.

"If Hell's like this, it must be quite exciting," said Joe.

I never ceased to be amazed by the number of people in the east. Thousands on the stations, on the roads, crowds and crowds melting away into the streets and darkness, sleeping on pavements and against walls.

The great steam train pulled us northwards through the night. The excitement, noise and dramatic strength, I remembered from childhood. When dawn came the plains of India were behind us. The early morning slanting light outlined shrub-covered foothills and ridges, and the air was cool. Despite the trials and tribulations of the journey, I was enjoying myself and feeling cheerful and relaxed. Now we were actually moving towards the mountains, all we could do was to meet each problem as it arose, as one of the early explorers of the Garhwal Range, Tom Longstaff, had advised: "The traveller must learn to live every moment in the present." This fiery, red-bearded explorer of the early 1900s had been the guru of the young mountaineers of the 1930s. Joe and I talked about him a lot.

From Hardwar railway station we went across to the bus terminus. There were large crowds of people around. As in most crowds, we felt that there would inevitably be people among them that we couldn't trust. When there are only three of you, it is very difficult to move equipment and guard it at the same time, so you start off with all the gear in one pile. Then someone carries part of it to where you're trying to get to, starts a second pile and guards it. That morning I was out-manœuvred. Joe and Palta appointed themselves guards and I found myself rushing between the two of them, carrying all the gear.

In 1905 and 1907, when Tom Longstaff had led his expeditions towards the Nanda Devi Sanctuary, he had started his long walk to the mountain from the plains. In the 1930s, Bill Tilman and Eric Shipton had started only a couple of weeks away from the mountains at Ranikhot. Joe and I were travelling by bus to within a few days' walk of the area.

From Hardwar we caught the bus to Rishikesh. There we moved to the next bus station on a pony and trap. The trap was so heavily weighed down it threatened to lift the pony into the air. Now we were on the main Hindu pilgrim trail, moving north towards the three sacred shrines of Gangotri, Kedarnath and Badrinath. From Rishikesh we took the bus to Srinagar. Here we had missed the last bus to Joshimath and so checked in at a Government-run pilgrim shed. The man in charge of the shed insisted that we filled in forms, giving many details about ourselves. This was probably quite a reasonable request, but forms and papers and regulations make me feel uneasy, particularly when I am on a climbing trip. They seem so futile and obstructive.

"Some control of movement is necessary," explained Palta, "and every town has a Government health service clinic and supplies inspector."

Although there were only boards to sleep on in the shed, it was clean and had washrooms. India demands adjustment – slowly I was becoming used to being perpetually surrounded by crowds, gawping at us and following our every movement. It was taking me many days to adapt to this shift of continents and to start thinking clearly and feeling normal.

By afternoon the monsoon sun was hot and heavy. After a rest, and feeling lethargic in the heat, we went shopping. It took a long time. In Britain I avoid shopping whenever possible. I just dash into the nearest shop and buy the closest equivalent they provide to what I want. Palta, however, refusing to be hurried, insisted that we did a comparative survey of all the prices and quality of merchandise that the various shops had to offer first. In the bazaar, there were shops, stalls and areas created for every trade, skill and need. We walked past a barber, grain merchant, shoemaker and tea maker. We were in a time machine, moving back to Dickens and beyond, back to Hogarth.

The pace of life in Srinagar was slow. It took a long time to select and buy our graded grains of sugar – we hadn't any ration cards.

"Look, you chaps," said Palta, "I think you should sort all your food into man rations, otherwise you won't know how much to buy." The simplest calculations easily confuse me and I winced at this.

"We'll buy a big sackful," said Joe.

One shopkeeper, sitting cross-legged behind his wares, refused to sell us a can of paraffin. Palta translated the reason. "He says he is a god-fearing man and cannot sell us so much." Palta persuaded him by writing an official letter.

Joe and I had a matter-of-fact relationship. Joe's phenomenal memory for telephone numbers and names made me feel dreamy by comparison. We talked always about the next problem. We didn't

often discuss any central issues of mankind. I was never quite sure if Joe was above or below that sort of intense discussion. He had studied to be a priest between the ages of thirteen and twenty-one—a restricted, cloistered existence against which he had eventually rebelled. But some motivation and belief must have been there once. One of Palta's first reactions, on seeing Joe's gentle face, curly hair and beard and blue eyes, was that he should apply for an audition for *Jesus Christ Superstar*! When Palta joined the two of us, it brought a shift in the topics of conversation. That evening, after tea, we discussed books, films and the value of mountaineering. Palta just couldn't understand why we were devoting all our time and energy towards climbing a superfluous rock in the middle of the Himalayas. To him, intelligent, highly trained and living in India, his country's problems presented all the challenges that an educated man could want. He had his country to defend against very real enemies, and a wife and family to support. Listening to him I felt very young. Perhaps Joe, I thought, three years older than me, would come up with something interesting to reply with. He didn't. A restless, confident individualist, he didn't offer any justifications. Perhaps he hadn't had to answer such questions before, or didn't feel any need to. But I had practice. Having climbed Everest and working for the British Mountaineering Council, I was used to explaining about mountaineering to people who knew little about it, to answering questions that sounded naïve to a mountaineer's ear. Also, attendance at numerous committee meetings had taught me to be a social chameleon—to smile and nod. I felt in the middle of this discussion. I knew we would soon be so interdependent that we couldn't afford to disagree too violently. Perhaps Palta was beginning to sense the seriousness of our objective, from the discussions that Joe and I were having together. I flinched as Joe explained to him that this climb would be, for us two, a culmination of many years of application and experience and that there was not the slightest possibility of him joining the actual climb. Palta was beginning to realise that he would be joining us in total isolation.

"It's a pity we haven't radios so that we can contact each other and civilisation," he said.

As I lay in my sleeping bag that night I, too, was beginning to realise. There would be no more ranks to throw at the mountain. Play it close to the wicket, a friend had said before we left home. Next door, many pilgrims were snoring.

It rained heavily during the night and became quite cold. In the

morning, as we waited for the bus to Joshimath, there were thousands of flies crawling and buzzing everywhere, reminding me of the obscene imagery of *Othello*. Mist and cloud curled around the forested hills about us. Flowers and leaves dripped heavy with rain. I couldn't name any of them. Flora and fauna are so varied, immeasurable in India. There was a dappled variation of light and shade in the clouds, with horizontal breaks of watery light.

Palta wanted to talk about logistics. Dogs skulked, circling us. Gradually, more and more people and eager coolies gathered around. Their predatory manner was quite threatening—it felt like the last scene of Hitchcock's film *The Birds*. "Where have you come from?" "Where are you going?" "What is in these bags?" The same ritual questions rolled out monotonously and I answered them painstakingly. I remembered the story told by Bill Murray, leader of the 1950 Scottish Himalayan Expedition, which was the last British Expedition to travel beyond the Inner Line in the Garhwal. He tired of answering all these questions one day and snapped back, "Why do you want to know?" "So that I can help you," came the calm reply.

Soon the bus left to start its eight-hour, one-hundred-mile journey up the valley of the River Alaknanda to Joshimath, 6,000 feet higher. The journey was long and winding, up towards one of the sources of the Ganges. With gentle irony, the locals call the road 'the gift of China', since it was built to enable the Indian army to gain easy access to defend the frontier. The many people in Srinagar with a Tibetan look reminded us that we were nearing the crest of the Himalayas. Half of the Indian army is now guarding the northern frontier, and the road had only been open to westerners for three years.

"Hey, Joe," I said, "look at that bridge. I could take a photo of it and sell it to the Chinese Embassy—it might pay for the expedition." Palta did not know how to take the joke and firmly told us not to photograph it.

It was difficult for Joe and me, coming from an island which has not been invaded for a thousand years, to understand the sensitive political tensions of the Himalayas. Whenever we laughed we had to explain the reason. Palta's puzzled uncertainty made us think he was wondering if the joke was at his expense.

We were in the first-class seats, just behind the driver, which meant that our knees were just tucked under our chins rather than rubbing against our noses. As we set off, the bus driver—a very little man—informed us that the steering wasn't power-assisted and, with a grin on

his face, pointed at the bends in the road as it twisted up the valley-side 2,000 feet above the river bed. "We lose about eight or nine buses down there every year," he said. Then he lit some incense at the front of the bus and waved his hand with a flourish. At that the entire bus started chanting prayers in unison. The most hair-raising of bends was heralded usually by encouraging reminders painted on the rocks at the side of the road, such as 'Life is short. Do not make it shorter.' Occasionally monsoon floods had washed mud and boulders across the road and these were being cleared frantically by road workers. As soon as there was a space cleared wide enough to drive through, on we would go. Joe and I would glance nervously at the door as the bus tottered on over such sections. There was a priest, a hen, and an old lady between us and the door. The driver glanced round and said, "Relax, nobody ever gets out when the buses go over."

The population inside the bus changed regularly, and we stopped occasionally for cups of tea. Up the valley ran the old pilgrim trail from Rishikesh—sometimes we could see it from the road. Many pilgrims, of varying prosperity and degrees of commitment, were in the area. Most of them today seem to catch the bus and make the trip in their holidays. We even met a Sikh from Cambridge. But there are many who walk. They seemed strangely detached. Some were dressed in red garments, others wore only a loincloth and were covered in white ash. The walkers had red-rimmed, far-away eyes and smiled and talked little. I tried to imagine where these pilgrims came from, and what significance the pilgrimage would have for them in their lives. The change of scenery alone must have been dramatic—to travel in the mountains after a life on the plains. The importance of their pilgrimage was in its physical act—in the effort they had to make.

In Joshimath the air was cool. For the first time in a week, I felt I could think clearly. We got off the bus next to the pilgrim shed and checked in there, before wandering up the main street. Joshimath is a pilgrim tourist town, perched high on the hillside above the Alaknanda. It consists of one main street of shops with corrugated iron roofs. Nearly every other shop is a sweetmeat and teashop. The mountains around were hidden from us by the monsoon clouds but, occasionally, long slanting rays of sunshine would break through. Above the town is a large military encampment that is self-contained, but down in the town we could see little of it. Joe had friends here—Mr. F. Bhupal Singh of the Neilkanth Hotel, and Yasu, a young local. We went to see them. Bhupal Singh welcomed us with a quick, kind smile and I felt an immediate sense of trust in him. Such openness is unusual in the plains of India, where politeness and formality, one feels, might be obscuring many motives.

In the evening we sat and discussed with Palta his role in the expedition. Palta had come with many maps and with a detailed brief for his role as liaison officer. These he was guarding carefully. Joe was, I felt, embarrassingly antagonistic towards the need for a liaison officer – he hadn't much respect for them. His liaison officer of the previous year had not lasted much longer than the first day's walk. We knew that one of Palta's instructions was to make sure that we didn't climb any peaks other than the one we had permission for. Joe and I spent a long time trying to tell Palta about the development of the world mountaineering scene, and how the trend was towards smaller parties tackling bigger and bigger mountains in a less formal style than hitherto. "Mountaineering is individualistic," we would say, "it can't be like an army exercise, it requires too much voluntary motivation." But Palta had only had a month's training in mountaineering, about five years previously, so it was heavy going. The same questions cropped up again: "I still don't understand how you chaps justify this climbing. What about your careers, the furtherance of humanity, your role in society and your duty to your country?" I muttered many reasons in reply – most of them rationalisations of ones I had heard other people give.

"It can develop your character," I said, "and make you more independent and hold things in realistic perspectives. The travel to the mountain as well as the mastery of mountaineering technique enlarge your experience so that you are more effective and interesting if you ever teach others, or even when you just meet people. Also, mountaineering has a pure exploratory strain in it – exploring human potential, doing things that nobody thought could be done before, finding things out about areas that are hardly known. It provides contrasts to help balance out the lives of people like us, who come from urban backgrounds. Anyway, I think any enthusiasm or interest is better than none at all. I find it so much easier to sympathise with people who are really interested and enthused about something – whatever it is – rather than without much interest in life, monotonously drifting. It was Eric Shipton's belief that a man is very fortunate and very rare, if he can truly say that he has found something profoundly satisfying in life which he enjoys utterly. And," I added defensively, "I enjoy mountains!"

Joe said little, and I was sure he was thinking, 'What a load of bullshit!' Perhaps I was trying to justify all this to myself. 'This sort of talk means more after a climb, not before one,' I thought, 'and we haven't done anything yet!'

We planned to spend two whole days in Joshimath, but we ended up spending three.

I awoke the following morning with my dreamland among the soft green hills of Derbyshire. The hooting of the pilgrims' buses brought me abruptly back to India. It had been a noisy night, with pilgrims coming and going and playing their transistor radios into the early hours. "What the hell can they find to jabber about all the time?" said Joe.

We spent two days sorting out the gear into porter loads of fifty pounds each, and buying rice, dhal, dried peas, pickles, curry powder and onions from the bazaar. Joe did most of the load-sorting — once he was involved in doing something, he tended to take over completely. Palta and I tended to stand in the corner of the room.

"You're a good worker, Joe," said Palta.

Also, a large spider had dropped from the ceiling to land somewhere amongst the equipment and neither of us wanted to be the one that disturbed it!

Joe was becoming irritated with Palta — though not openly. He felt that Palta always insisted that we did everything together, that every little decision — such as going for a cup of tea in the bazaar — demanded prior consultation and agreement. He could not bring himself to pretend that the liaison officer was not an imposition and that climbing Changabang was more important than Palta's feelings. Because of Joe's forthrightness, Palta regarded him as the Leader.

Joe and I were having some worries about finance, since Palta was — not unreasonably — insisting that we hired a porter to keep him company at Base Camp. This meant that we would have to clothe and feed another person.

Meanwhile, three of the South Face team had arrived, and we went out with them for a meal at our favourite café haunt, The Delight. It wasn't exactly five-star, and we amused each other by relating morbid anecdotes about stomach complaints, quietly keeping our fingers crossed and nervously glancing at the water and glasses for disruptive microbes. A bad gut could mean no climb. Joe and I were waiting along with them for their South Face truck to arrive, since two boxes of food and Gaz canisters for us were aboard it. The truck, and with it the rest of their team, was being delayed by a landslide further down the road.

This advance party trio had an air of solemnity which Joe liked to dispel. Being part of a larger group, their sense of purpose was more formal and they seemed slightly dazed by India. Joe knew them better than I, and often used to slip away for the relief their change of company gave him.

On the 2nd September we were all set to catch the 3.00 p.m. bus to the village of Lata, from where we would start our walk to Changabang. The South Face team had arrived and Palta hired a porter to carry our boxes on his head to the bus station. Then we discovered we had just done a dress rehearsal. Apparently the 3.00 p.m. bus had gone at 2.00 p.m., but had only gone five kilometres up the road on a private mission. It wouldn't be going to Lata until late tomorrow now. "Don't worry," said Joe, misquoting Kipling. "Here lies a man deceased, who tried to hurry the East." With that he escaped and sank into a chair in the back of a tea shop and drowned his sorrows with a sweet milky brew. Joe was always ready to relax if there was nothing else to do.

Later in the afternoon we went for a walk up through and above the military encampment. There, wearing our double boots, and much to the amazement of some local children, we climbed on some enormous boulders until we fell off among vicious stinging nettles. We were hoping to be able to see Nanda Devi, but the skies were cloudy and beginning to spit with rain. Eventually we found ourselves high on the hills in a sloping field full of apple trees and there a toothless old lady, with many rings in her ears, approached us. She held out some enormous red apples to us. They were delicious. She refused payment for them, smiled and stepped back to watch us move on. The gift of the apples was a simple, direct gesture which had been born of the hillside and not of the town and road we had left below us.

In the evening Palta took us to the Joshimath cinema. An earlier attempt to see the Hindu movie on at the time had failed because of an erratic electricity supply. The film lasted three hours and was called *Zameer*, meaning 'conscience'. It was about a millionaire who loses his son and finds him again. The film had song, dance, horses, a chase, some shooting and romantic love, all in an escapist, fantasy world. It was quite unlike the India we had seen in the previous week—there were no beggars and nobody was sweating. The hero and heroine seemed, to our western eyes, to be overweight—but being slim is not an attribute of beauty in India. "No wonder our small expedition is being judged poor and worthless because it's small," said Joe.

The theme tune had the little boy next to me singing his heart out, completely absorbed. It was to echo around my mind all the way to the glacier beneath Changabang. At the interval we bought some nuts from a stall outside, and ate them through the second half, in the dark. We only saw the grubs sheltering inside the shells when the lights went on. It was our last brush with the civilised fantasies of outside. Now we were moving inside, towards the Sanctuary.

At 7.00 a.m. the following morning, Joe was bustling about, assembling fifteen porter loads. By walking across the roof of someone's house from the pilgrim shed, we managed to place the loads directly onto the top of the bus. Now we had been joined by a Swiss trekker called Hans, who was intending to walk into the area at the same time as ourselves.

As we moved off I felt thrilled with the sensation of travel – always to move and never to arrive avoids many confrontations. I gazed at the view, thinking about other places I wanted to travel to, other trips I wanted to make to other areas of the world. The bus wound down towards Tapoban, a sprawling settlement of tea shops, a post office and a lot of mud. Here the high path which the pre-1970 explorers to the Garhwal had followed, joined ours after crossing the Kuari Pass. We could see another road winding up the Alaknanda valley, towards Badrinath, but now we had turned right up the valley of the River Dhauli.

History draws a false distinction between trade and exploration. It is facile to consider that the exploration of a Himalayan area started only when Europeans began to record their movements and discoveries there. We were now following a valley that had been brushed by the feet of the earliest tribes as a trading route between Tibet and India. At the head of the Dhauli lies the Niti Pass and at the head of the Alaknanda lies the 18,400-foot Mana Pass. The Mana Pass was the more extensively used. The first Europeans to cross the Mana Pass were Portuguese Jesuits in the seventeenth century, who were establishing a mission in Tibet. These priests were not geographers but, obsessed with their mission, travelled boldly, disregarding the time of year or the state of snow on the passes, putting their trust in God to guide them safely.

Soon after Tapoban we crossed the Rishi as it poured out of the Rishi Ganga. In 1950, Bill Murray had found there a square-slated shrine of Tibetan character, rigged by a score of tall poles from which flew strips of tattered cloth – offered in honour of the Seven Rishis who dwell in sanctuaries of the Rishi Ganga. These Seven Rishis, so the legend has it, are spirits who guard the sanctuaries of Nanda Devi, the bliss-giving goddess. I peered up the mouth of the dark and gloomy chasm, trying to glimpse some mountains and thought of the attempts made by W. W. Graham in 1883, and Bill Tilman in 1934, to enter the gorge by this place. It was only in the spring of 1976 that an expedition – the Japanese S. W. Ridge of Changabang Expedition, managed to force a way through this forbidding gash. They had to; the normal path was covered in deep snow and was, anyway, already crowded by the marches of the Indo-Japanese expedition and the Indian Trisul expedition. Today, at the mouth of the Rishi Ganga, is a military bridge and guard, and no sign of a shrine.

The bus dropped us and our loads by the roadside and very soon the headman of the village of Lata, Jagat Singh, appeared. He was very co-operative and wore a red flower in his fawn jersey. Soon Palta had arranged for fifteen porters to start carrying our loads the next day. Negotiations for porters is much easier in India than in Nepal and Afghanistan, as there is a fixed rate. It didn't take Palta long to settle with them. The men from Lata came down to have a look at their loads. Joe was pleased to recognise one of them, one of the 'untouchables' of the village, from the previous year. On the way back from Dunagiri, the winter snows had come early and nearly trapped Joe at Dibrugheta, on the Rishi Ganga. This porter, carrying an enormous load, had shown amazing navigational skill in a white-out. "He just stared into the mist and kept on going," said Joe, "and was right every time. I'd have had a hard time getting back over the top without him. I had to stop him rooting through the bags later on, though – he's still a rogue. I don't know his name – he only grunted to me."

One of the villagers, a large man called Tait Singh, was acting as shop steward. Many of them had bands of fleece twisted around their forearms and, with an air of dedication, were teasing one end of the fleece out into yarn onto the spindle, which they kept spinning by flicking it with their fingers. Joe and I had hidden our spring gauge (we both wanted to avoid the hours of load-haggling we had encountered on previous expeditions) and presented the loads as a *fait accompli*.

Fortunately, we managed to hire our porters whilst the South Face Expedition were still sorting themselves out. They had arrived at the same layby in their white truck – 'the ice-cream van', as one of their number, Jim Duff, called it. They were not a big expedition – by comparison, the Japanese had hired fifty porters in the spring, and the American Nanda Devi expedition had used over eighty porters and one hundred and twenty goats. The South Face team hired half their forty porters in Joshimath. Still, I could not help feeling pleased at our small, compact pile of gear compared to their long lines of labelled boxes, and I think some of the South Face team looked back at us in envy. Joe, however, was thinking that he would like to go on a larger trip some-time, with plenty of time and money to sort things out.

The next morning, the 4th September, we started moving in the pouring rain, up a narrow path that wound among wheat fields. After half an hour we passed through the village of Lata, which Bill Murray called the most wonderfully sited village he had ever seen in the Hima-layas. But we could see little of the height and space around it. We could only see the village itself, its houses set back on stone terraces. Each house had its own courtyard and was half wood, half stone, with the families living on the wooden upper storey, reached by a ladder descending from a balcony. Their habit of salted tea-drinking, liking of ornaments and trinkets and often mongoloid faces, showed we had reached the fringe of Tibetan influence. Lata is fairly prosperous, since it is low enough to produce crops and hence it was comparatively un-disturbed by the closing of the border, in contrast with the villages further up the Dhauli Ganga that lie within the Inner Line. The build-ing of the road brought employment and, since 1974, the influx of expeditions has meant that many able-bodied men in the village have been employed as porters. These changes have brought some pros-perity, but not stability. Much of the money from expeditions has been diverted to middle-men in Joshimath and elsewhere and, although the pay is good, the work is seasonal.

As we passed Lata, we met two students from Cambridge Univer-sity, Rosemary Scott and Anthony Cohen. Rosemary had just finished a survey of the nutritional value of the diets of five of the sixty-five families in Lata.

Lata was the last habitation on our way to the mountains, and soon we were high above the village, following the ancient shepherd route into the Rishi. W. W. Graham, the enigmatic cowboy of nineteenth-century Himalayan exploration, had been the first European to find it. We were climbing around the back of one of the spurs that formed the mouth of the Rishi Ganga, and the day's walk involved about 5,000 feet of ascent up to Lata Kharak, a meadow high above the Dhauli at about 12,000 feet. We wandered up the path and, as the skies began to clear and the sun came out, we crossed a stream. "This is the last water till we get to the top," said Joe. By the stream there was an old lady washing, with such an enormous ring through her nose that it had to be supported by a clip in her hat. I asked her if she minded my taking a photograph. She did, and looked angry. Always, the westerner feels he has to possess everything, even if it's only a picture on celluloid!

I felt satisfied that morning, and relaxed. Adventures lose their mystery and worry once you are embarked upon them. Everything seemed to be taking shape. I was feeling happier than I had been at any time on the previous year's Everest expedition. The whole trip was purely ours; there was nothing superfluous. There didn't seem to be the built-in redundancy factor, as there had been on Everest. Also, I felt far fitter than I had the previous year — the running must have done some good. It was good to be walking into the Himalaya again. It felt as if I had always been there, and the year in between had been a dream.

From Lata Kharak, briefly, we had tantalising glimpses of the white snows of Bethartoli Himal and Nanda Ghunti across the Rishi Ganga. In the woods below there was a hidden spring. Nearby, living in a shelter, was a yogi. He was isolating himself from humanity for the summer, and hid from us in his sanctuary. Our porters crowded under a tarpaulin and lit a fire as the rain came in. Some of them had terrible coughs and were probably doomed to die within the next few years of T.B. I went for a wash — determined to be careful about personal hygiene and not to risk jeopardising the trip by illness.

In the morning, in the mist we moved up the ridge, over a pass and scrambled around the steep, twisting spurs on the other side until at last we reached Dharansi, the open ridge. Here there was a tent, and two shepherds, whom the porters greeted. They obtained a sheep from them and led the luckless animal all the way down the steep slope into the Rishi Ganga — it would provide their supper that night.

Below us we could see the 'stone and meadow' of Dibrugheta, which Longstaff had called 'a fragment of Arcady dropped amid chaos' where 'amid the vertical confusion of the landscape the horizontal instantly invited relaxation and repose'. We raced down in the drizzle. Flanking us towered great diagonal sheets of mica, sparkling through the mist.

At the bottom we found Hans, sheltering with his two porters in a cave blackened by bivouac fires. "That chap's having a ball," said Palta. Palta couldn't understand why two people wanted to go and climb a dangerous mountain, but he could see the sense and fun in wandering around an area, looking at the scenery. However, he was nonplussed that Hans had turned up without any permit, and simply walked into the area.

Whilst we were with Hans, a mail runner from the American Nanda Devi expedition arrived and announced that three members had reached the summit on the 1st September. We moved over the flower-strewn meadow to our camp site amidst tall pines and boulders of old camp fires. Unfortunately, the porters with our tents were hours behind and we had a long wait under our umbrellas. It was dark by the time we put up our tents. We asked Palta to light a primus stove, but he couldn't. 'No wonder he wanted a porter to help him at Base Camp,' I thought.

"When do you chaps usually do your toilet?" asked Palta. "In the morning or in the evening?"

Later, Joe muttered, "He's doing all right on the walking, but why do things seem so bloody complicated whilst he's around? Even the simplest tasks such as cooking and lighting a stove get confusing."

I was trying to be friendly, and to put him at ease, but it was hard work.

The next day we climbed steeply behind Dibrugheta. Joe reached the crest first. "Come up here," called Joe. "It's Big Nanda."

He knew how much I wanted to see that mountain. I arrived in time to see the summit of Nanda Devi through a hole in the clouds, rising above the sacred ground of her Sanctuary, surrounded by legend of inaccessibility. Far below us, the slender thread of the Rishi led our eyes back towards the mountain. It was a fleeting glimpse, for soon the mists closed all mountains from us.

We spent the day traversing the slopes 2,000 feet above the gorge. I was feeling quite tired, but was soon entranced by the thousands of flowers that littered the slopes. The sky was grey and it was the earth that drew my eyes to it. No wonder the Garhwal is called the Garden of the Himalayas. No wonder that F. S. Smythe wrote a book in 1938 called *The Valley of Flowers* about Bhiundar Valley, near Joshimath. The droplets of water that hung from the petals brought a freshness and immediacy. They were of all colours, and gave a gentler beauty to the fierce landscape on which they were scattered.

"What are you photographing those lupins for, Joe? They grow in everyone's garden back home."

The monsoon had swelled the streams that poured down the side of the gorge and which we had to cross. When we reached one very strong torrent, Tait Singh dramatically took immediate charge, stood

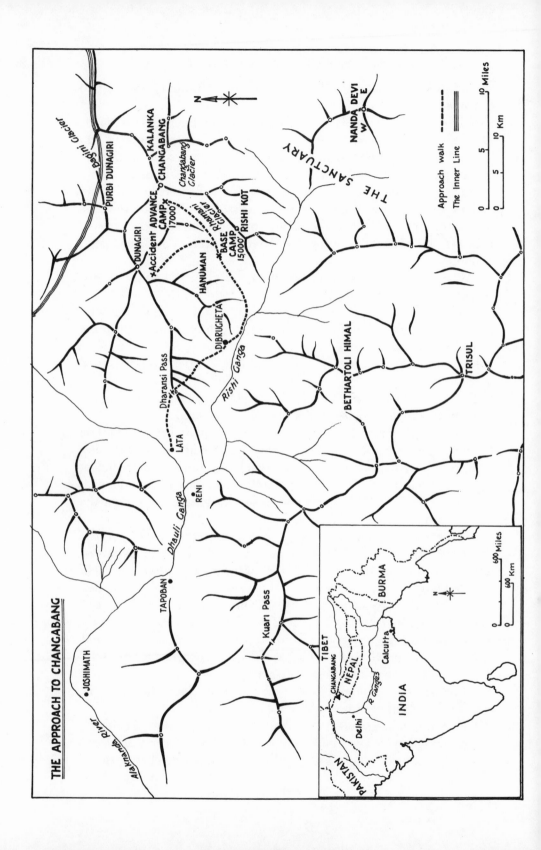

THE APPROACH TO CHANGABANG

Approach walk ------
The Inner Line ═══

10 Miles
10 Km

NANDA DEVI
E
W

THE SANCTUARY

Shoini Glacier
Dhauli Glacier

KALANKA
PURBI DUNAGIRI
CHANGABANG
Changabang Glacier

Accident ADVANCE
CAMP 17000'
DUNAGIRI
Rhamani Glacier
Rhamani River
BASE CAMP
15000' RISHI KOT

HANUMAN

DIBRUGHETA

Rishi Ganga

BETHARTOLI HIMAL

TRISUL

Dharansi Pass

LATA

RENI

Dhauli Ganga

TAPOBAN

Kuari Pass

JOSHIMATH

Alaknanda River

PAKISTAN

TIBET

CHANGABANG
NEPAL
BURMA

Delhi
R. Ganges
Calcutta

INDIA

600 Miles
600 Km

in the middle of the current and helped the loads and people across. "The shop steward's proving a good lad," said Joe.

Below us, we could see the Rishi through the clouds. Occasionally we had to use our hands to scramble up the steeper areas—it was a long way to fall if you were careless.

It was a cramped camp site on a slope, and I was feeling irritated with Palta, who seemed particularly helpless, whilst Joe and I pitched the tents, slipped the polythene sheets together over them, and lit the stove. Our tents were still soaking from the previous evening. It rained again. Tomorrow we would reach Base Camp—the porters were making the six-day stage walk in four days.

Joe and I woke early. "Since liaison officers are sent to watch us," said Joe, "they ought to pay their way. This assistance/guide bit is rubbish!"

It was a lovely morning. The mist had gone and I was startled to see the exposed position of our camp site and the sense of space around us, as the Rishi Gorge was opening out to the Sanctuary of its head waters and glaciers. Now we were to turn up towards the Rhamani Glacier and Changabang. Palta had gone, as usual, for his toilet as Joe and I collapsed the tents and cooked the breakfast.

Palta returned with a startling ultimatum. Either we sent back for more fresh vegetables or he returned to civilisation with the porters. He said, "Look, you chaps, I will make sure you and your loads get to your Base Camp. But if I am not going to be any use to your expedition, I prefer to go back. Never in my life have I eaten such appalling food. I don't know if you have gained your ideas about Indian cooking from watching these people," he added, waving a hand at the porters, "but even my servant eats better food than you two do."

He was trying to force us to make the decision, but it was obvious he was unhappy and wanted to go home. I felt guilty about having brought so much beef with us. I had completely forgotten about the Hindu taboo about cattle. However, we had offered him all our lamb and fish. Also, I felt bad about Joe's earlier critical attitude. After all, Palta had only two days' notice that he was coming with us, and it had been two years previously when he had put his name down, volunteering his services as an expedition officer. But it was difficult for us to humour his fixed, class-conscious ideas and his proud intelligence—particularly for Joe, who was always quick to sense any form of pretension. In many ways, Joe had more regard for the tough resilience of the porters, cheerful in their poverty. From the start it had been clear that ours was not the sort of expedition Palta had wanted to be the liaison officer for. First he had bemoaned the lack of a radio transmitter; then he had insisted that we had a porter at Base Camp to keep him company. Now it was the food. He refused to be helped, and his stiff upper lip approach seemed to provoke unnecessary suffering. He just didn't understand the nature of the adventure. So we were to be alone.

Apart from my mind being preoccupied with Palta troubles, the morning walk was magnificent, with views of the wilderness in which we were to act out our adventure. Changabang was hiding until the last.

Unknown to us, that day, high on Nanda Devi, a tragedy stranger than fiction was occurring. At 24,000 feet, four American climbers had moved into a position to attempt a second ascent of the North-West Face/North Ridge. Up there, a blizzard was blowing and one of the climbers was slowly weakening from an abdominal illness. The following morning she died, and the three remaining climbers committed her body to the snows of the mountain. In 1948, Willi Unsoeld had announced that he would name his daughter after the most beautiful mountain he had ever seen. Willi was on this expedition with his daughter, and it was she who had died. Nanda Devi Unsoeld as a mortal, young and charming, had, so many Indians say, returned to her 'home' — she had been the goddess personified.

As our route twisted towards the Rhamani Glacier, we rounded a corner. Suddenly we saw it. In a slot formed by the ridges of Hanuman, the Monkey God, Kalanka, the Destroyer, and Rishi Kot, the fortress of the Rishis, soared the glistening milk white shark's-tooth of Changabang — 'The Shining Mountain'.

I rolled their names around in my mind. I pointed my camera at Changabang and took a progression of photographs — 28 mm, 50 mm, 75 mm, 150 mm, in a rush of lenses. As the mountain drew nearer it struck deeper, richer chords of awe within me. No wonder Tom Longstaff called Changabang "the most superbly beautiful mountain I have ever seen". F. S. Smythe's description lived — "a peak that falls from crest to glacier in a wall that might have been sliced in a single cut of a knife". The charisma given to it by its early sightings was fulfilled.

Joe was looking at me. "No anthems playing in my head," he said.

Slowly, the thought crept back — dared we presume to attempt to stand on its summit? Now I was seeing the West Wall live, after I had known it so well from photographs. Yes, the 'link pitch', the ramp of snow that we had first seen on the photographs taken by the Swiss mountaineer, André Roche, from the summit of Dunagiri in 1939, was still there, offering a possible line to the central icefield. Our attempt would be a bold enterprise, but I couldn't think of anyone I would rather make the attempt with than Joe. Soon we moved in amongst the moraines and Changabang lowered its head.

At 11.40 a.m. on 8th September, we arrived on the meadow where Joe had his Base Camp for Dunagiri the previous year, and all the loads thumped to the ground. It had been quite a gaspy walk — our altimeter read 15,250 feet. The mist swirled and hugged the ground, and the porters crowded eagerly around for the big pay-out. We handed out the notes and arranged vaguely that we would let them know when we wanted porters to help us ferry our equipment back to civilisation.

"I've nothing personal against you two," said Palta. And we hadn't against him. He left with the porters.

Joe and I sat amongst the boxes and kitbags and watched them disappear into the mist. "A bit of a lonely place to come for our summer holidays," I said to Joe.

"I was here for six days by myself, last year, after Dick had gone," said Joe. "I started imagining things towards the end."

We put the tents up. Then Hans arrived with his two porters. "I am here for two days," he said in his clipped Austrian accent. "Then I go to the Sanctuary."

Joe and I ate mashed potato and lamb slices for tea and shared our Christmas pudding, rum and custard with him. "This is the best dessert I have ever tasted," said Hans.

All other problems had stopped. Now we would contend with the universal elements — cold, height, rock, snow, all recognised and familiar. All mountains, all over the world, have something in common. I could feel at ease now we were among them . . . it no longer felt as if we were in India. I could understand it all.

CHAPTER THREE

The First Stone

8th–20th September

We took a rest day. It snowed heavily all night and then the snow turned to sleet. Our world was just our tents, some rough wiry grass, a tiny stream and then, through the thick drizzle, the boulders and dark earth of the moraine. I woke up eventually around 8.30 a.m., after twelve hours of much-needed sleep. I lay in the tent, stunned with altitude, looking at the blue nylon in front of my face. Joe and I were in separate lightweight tents and I was relieved to hear Joe move at last and put on the brew in the Base Camp tunnel tent. I didn't feel very hungry, but we managed to put down cold porridge and wheatgerm, followed by rice and pilchards. Joe prepared a jelly for teatime. I had a headache just behind my eyes and felt dizzy when I stood up. This, combined with worries about my stomach and a pain in the lower part of my back, made me feel a right old crock. Still, I knew that it was the general lassitude induced by the altitude that was giving me this hypochondria and, when I admitted anything to Joe, he said, "Well, you know what Shipton says — 'No illness ever stopped a man who really wanted to reach a summit.'"

"How's the altitude affecting you?" I asked him.

"Oh, it feels just like home."

"Oh yes, just like after a night at the boozer."

"If you think I'm stoical, you ought to climb with Dick — then you'd think I'm a real softy."

Joe had had his appendix out when he was a child, and mine was still in. There seemed such a low chance of it giving any trouble, that I shut myself from the idea. But Joe loved to tease me about it.

"How's your stomach today, Pete? Any little twinges? Don't worry, I've got all the instruments here and the book to follow. It's only a minor operation, after all."

We crept back to our tents, under our umbrellas. I looked at mine

with amusement. My Gran had given it to me for my twenty-first birthday. If she could see me now! I was reading, in between dozing in and out of consciousness, *Zen and the Art of Motorcycle Maintenance*. Joe was reading Gorky, *The Three*. We had a rather serious selection of books with us with which to pass the time. Also, apart in our tents, we were scribbling in our diaries little confessions about ourselves, and comments about the other. Joe was wondering if he was out of practice at high altitude exertion and suffering. Also he was commenting:

"Pete is more relaxing than Dick to be with, but his doziness
can be amazing at times. Not that he's lazy, he just doesn't think."

On the other side of the field Hans was crouching inside the shelter of his bivouac tent. He didn't emerge all day.

The sun was returning, the weather was clearing and so were our heads, and we determined to go up onto the glacier, look at the Wall and find a site for our Advance Camp. Hans was going to leave after taking some photographs of the area from a vantage point. After we had spent a couple of hours drying and sorting our gear in the sunshine, we said goodbye to him and left on our exploratory wander.

When we reached the top of the valley next to the moraine, about 1,500 feet higher up, we could see the whole of the cirque of mountains that ringed the Rhamani Glacier, with Changabang standing proudly at the end. A branch of this glacier turned towards Dunagiri, towards Bagini Pass between Changabang and Dunagiri, which Longstaff had crossed in 1907. We could see the route taken by Chris Bonington's team in 1974. They had arrived at the point where Joe and I now were. Martin Boysen, a member of that expedition, had written:

We had come in hope of climbing the Western Face, a rock route which looked inviting on our faded photographs. We were now confronted with a precipice, the like of which I had not seen outside Patagonia: an enormous sweep of vertical and overhanging rock, plated here and there by ludicrously steep ice. The route we had originally contemplated was obviously so difficult it was laughable.

Instead, they chose to cross the steep ridge separating the west and south sides of Changabang, and climb the mountain from the other side. The point where they eventually crossed the ridge was Shipton's Col. In September, 1936, Shipton had reached that point from the

other side, during his second expedition into the Sanctuary, and sat there for one hour, gazing at the white cliffs of the mountain.

Joe and I picked our way across the rough stone of the moraine at the side of the glacier, towards Changabang—two tiny figures in a vast amphitheatre of mindless snow and ice and granite. I was day-dreaming. 'Somehow, I don't feel alone in the mountains. Sights such as these make me flow with strength. All the time dormant mountaineering memories re-emerge, memories of a hundred situations and problems carefully solved. Experience helps me deal with the pain of altitude, with uncertainty, incredulity almost. Before a big climb I can rise above these things because I know them. I have felt them before. I don't feel at all confident that we'll get up that wall, but I know we're tackling this climb very thoughtfully and intelligently. Memories seem so logical, certain—events seem to have emerged so rationally and inevitably. Lines on photographs of mountains look so obvious and certain, and belie the agony that put them there. But here we are, at the foot of the Wall, with our climb before us, and there's absolutely no way we can predict how it will go. What does it say in that Zen book? "... You are never dedicated to something you have complete confidence in. No one is fanatically shouting that the sun is going to rise tomorrow. When people are fanatically dedicated to political or religious faiths or any other kinds of dogmas or goals, it always is because these dogmas or goals are in doubt ...."'

A distant thin tongue of moraine stretched along the glacier, towards the foot of the West Wall. It looked a good place to set up our Advance Camp. The ground was rough. Often we had to cross gullies filled with enormous blocks of granite and we could hop from one to another. The sun had melted the ice on the glacier into crazy patterns and we crunched over them, sending collapsing tiny sheets of ice into tinkling submission, into pools of water and air. Across the surface of the glacier poured three or four streams, gaining force as the sun moved to midday. All the time, new angles of the West Wall presented themselves, and we stopped frequently—partly to gasp at the thin air, but mainly to stand and stare at the West Wall. As we walked we passed underneath the dramatic granite cliffs of the ridge between the Rhamani Glacier and the subsidiary glacier that stretches up towards the south side of Dunagiri. On the other side of the Rhamani, we could see the icy slopes of Rishi Kot and the line of steep cliffs that stretch towards Changabang, under Shipton's Col.

Soon Joe's Dunagiri route of the previous year peeped around at us.

It looked formidable — but mild in contrast with the West Wall which persistently drew our eyes. We discussed the Wall little, except to make occasional remarks about possible lines of weakness, breaking down its apparent impossibility into a series of logical steps. All its buttresses, its walls, its slabs, its cracklines, its patches of ice were becoming imprinted on our minds. Joe was as subdued as I:

> "Monsoon ice and snow still coated most of the mountain. The photographs and colour slides, viewed in distant Britain, had held no hint of the massive, inhospitable atmosphere of this colossal wall. It confronted us like a petrified wave with ice dripping from its rim. My memory had faded in the intervening months since I had last seen it and I wondered what impression it was making on Pete. Neither of us expressed any anxiety to each other . . . I hoped we hadn't taken on too much."

At the end of the moraine we dropped our loads and looked up at the Wall through some binoculars a friend of mine had lent us for the trip. A great detached block that must have weighed about thirty tons seemed to guard one way through the overhangs to the icefield. The alternative route to the icefield, the link pitch, more towards the middle of the Wall, looked frightening. Perhaps it all was — as Bonington had said — 'preposterous'. For the previous eight months, whenever we came across quotations or anecdotes which seemed to give us some encouragement, we would relate them to each other as a reassurance. The most notable was a quotation from Longstaff: "You must go and rub your nose in a place before being certain that it won't go." As if to reinforce his dictum, we could see Trisul, the scene of Longstaff's greatest achievement, far across the other side of the Rishi Ganga. In 1907, with Henri and Alexis Brocherel, brothers of Courmayeur, and a Gurkha, Kharbir, he climbed nearly 6,000 feet, in one day, to reach the top and then descended the same evening, some 7,000 feet, before camping for the night. They had climbed higher than anyone else had ever been at that time.

As Joe and I turned back down the moraine 'valley' to Base Camp, the setting sun was colouring the snows of Trisul. Behind us the suspended stone of Changabang was also glowing, with clouds drifting around it, asserting its height, their movement emphasising its stability.

That first day's walk onto the glacier was the first of six days' load carrying from the 9th–14th September, during which that day's pattern was repeated. We would wake with the sun and load about forty to forty-five pounds weight of gear in our sacks and cross all the glacial streams whilst they were low, in the early morning. We marked our route and the site of the Advance Camp with cairns, but after a while we found that they weren't necessary, as we soon recognised individual boulders. That helped. As we were pounding about with our heavy sacks on, from boulder to boulder, I was usually in a semi-daze, and my lips were blistering in the bright light. My thoughts were always wandering, and it was a relief not to have to concentrate too hard on the route-finding. I could distance my mind far away from the beast of burden that was my body. My mind would usually drift back home, to the last things I said and did with my friends. I had worried thoughts and laughing thoughts.

Apart from the second day, when Joe stayed behind at Base Camp to sort the gear out because he had a headache and diarrhoea and I went on my own, we always seemed to stick together, stumbling about, living in our own thoughts. I felt an inexplicable need to stay within about a hundred yards of Joe. I could still taste the disappointment that had ended my Alaskan climb and was worried about slipping and twisting my knee. I was turning into a hypochondriac, waking with slight nose bleeds and feeling slight pains in my shoulders and over my heart. I was much more physically or hygienically aware than I had been on previous expeditions. I was carefully changing my underwear, washing and combing my hair and cleaning my teeth and keeping warm and comfortable. I was constantly checking my pulse rate, to gauge my fitness and state of acclimatisation. I knew that Joe would feel hopelessly let down if something simple, but damning, happened to me. I wondered if he felt the same.

We would sit by the pile of equipment we were accumulating at Advance Camp and eat some chocolate and stare at the Wall, before going back down. We kept on seeing new possibilities, we were obsessed with looking at the Wall. Soon we had resolved a line to attempt. After taking as straight a line as possible to a col in the head-wall ridge of the Rhamani that melted into the West Wall, we hoped to establish a camp and attempt it from there by its left-hand edge. By doing this we would gain about 1,000 feet in height. The alternative of trying to find an ice cave amongst the icicles that swept over the great sweep of slabs below the link pitch in the middle of the Face, was unattractive and we decided against it. Reaching the icefield looked as if it would be a major crux.

After each walk we felt a little better acclimatised, and our times improved. It was good fun racing back down the glacier. We were always trying to photograph each other in stupid, compromising situations, such as becoming soaked in the afternoon meltwater streams, trying to topple enormous boulders like mushrooms on the glacier, and gripping great phallic pinnacles of ice. It was a battle of quick-draw cameras. The way and the views were becoming familiar. Their familiarity helped us to adapt, and reassured us.

Base Camp was always shrouded in afternoon cloud when we returned to it and we called it 'Bleak House'. But still it felt like home. Once we were back we would make a big meal and doze around, reading and chatting, talking about climbing and life back home. Joe, without a settled job to return to, was wondering what he would do on his return. He was tiring of his years scratching a living to support his climbing. I, on the other hand, having nearly always had a steady job or a place in college, was envious of his resourceful independence. Then we would begin to think of the next day's prospect of going back up 2,000 feet onto the glacier. Joe didn't like getting up in the morning.

"This load-carrying's harder work than climbing," he said. We wished we had kept a couple of porters on to help us with the slog of load-carrying, or had a liaison officer to help us at this stage — after all, we had been promised "one of the best climbers in India".

We had a folder full of photographs of the Face, and these provided moments of doubt and hope. But these moments were always personal. Conversation was cool and factual. For days we had been wandering underneath the Wall, prevented from attempting it by our own logistic snarl-up — the very thing we had wanted to avoid. Then we would retire to our sleeping bags, to our own thoughts and dreams. For months I had been building myself up mentally for the route. We were both working hard and building up a mutual trust and respect. I thought of home, of all homes I had ever lived in. Joe was reading *Nana* by Zola, with its depressing view of women. He dreamt about lots of people arriving from many directions. Don Whillans turned up, and then the American expedition we had heard was going to attempt Dunagiri. In Joe's dream it was an expedition of blonde, surfing girls from California.

On the 14th September, we finally left Base Camp. We put a little note in a polythene bag with a stone on top of it, just inside our tent doorway: "To whom it may concern", with a meagre message saying we were away, trying to climb Changabang, but should be back in a couple of weeks. Then we shouldered enormous, top-heavy loads weighing about seventy pounds each, containing all the remaining gear we thought we would need.

"I wouldn't want to carry this much in Britain, never mind up to 17,000 feet," said Joe.

It was late afternoon when we left and we were overtaken by darkness on the glacier, after watching the sunset move up the West Wall.

We put the little nylon tent up haphazardly, cooked some corned beef and mash and shrank inside our sleeping bags, out of the cold night air. The glacier was behind us for a while, we hoped. Above us, the sky was white with stars. It was an uncomfortable night—rocks were sticking into us, stonefall was rumbling from the two ridge peaks opposite Changabang. The moraine on which we were camped was creaking and groaning. When we woke up in the morning, the temperature was −14°C.

Whilst we were sorting out our food and equipment we discovered that something had raided our cache of food and, ignoring many other edibles, had prised its way under some plastic sheeting and opened a box of thirty-six Mars Bars. There were no wrappings or debris left, except the ripped box. Thirty-six, individually wrapped, two-ounce bars had disappeared without trace. There were no tracks in the snow—whatever had taken the bars had probably approached on the moraine.

"It's probably a small, nibbling animal," said Joe, "like what happened last year at Base Camp after Dunagiri. Every night something raided my food supplies—it carried off chocolate, Christmas cake, Mintcake—even my toothbrush! I tried to trap it for five days, but I never even saw it."

Perhaps it, or others of its species, lived on the glacier also. But still we could not work out how it had managed to carry off the separate bars.

"Whatever it was," said Joe, "can't have been that clever. It forgot to take with it the free voucher for some more."

We spent the day fiddling with our equipment, nailing and glueing our gaiters to our double boots, choosing the correct ratio of clothing to wear, sharpening and adjusting our crampons ready for action, not wanting to be caught unprepared. Everything had to be just right, and it always felt reassuring to feel at home with equipment, to identify with it, to have handled and fitted the familiar objects on which we were to depend so much. The tools of the craft. As the afternoon shadows lengthened, I was satisfied that the food and equipment were all ready, things were as near perfection as they could be, and now it was up to the feet inside the boots, the head inside the helmet, to perform. The first objective was to establish a camp on the ridge.

On the 16th September we set off in the shadows of the morning. The feeling of tenseness in the stomach, forgotten for some months, that always grips me as I approach the uncertain and the unknown, returned. The harnesses and crampons were put on, the ice axe and hammers slotted into their quick draw holsters. Soon there was just the crunching of our crampons in the snow and the enclosed feeling of hard breathing and heart thumping with the altitude as we moved across the edge of the glacier where it curled upwards towards the foot of the ice slope. Above us, the ice slope stretched in twisting runnels and gullies, up through rock buttresses to the ridge. As we kicked into the snow, the sounds of ice particles danced down the slope.

We crossed the bergschrund, where some snow had slid from above and bridged the gap. The angle suddenly changed and we tip-toed up the ice, hammer and axe in our hands, tapping gently into the ice for support. We were stepping from one existence into another.

"It seems in good nick," said Joe.

"No point in getting the rope out," I said, and we started on up — occasionally taking pictures of each other. The viewfinder could frame the steepness and the position, but not the effort the altitude imposed upon us. I would count ten or fifteen kicks upwards and then have to stop to gasp for breath until my head cleared. Without the rope, each could take the slope at his own pace, which turned out to be similar. I am a couple of stone heavier than Joe, and felt awkward as I looked at the lightness of his movements. I was worried, because in places the ice on which we were climbing was only about six inches thick. We were climbing on great sheets of it which were lying over loose rock and stones. Then, as I moved my weight up, the ice groaned and creaked.

All my senses went tense and alert. There was a sharp crack that bit my ears like a gunshot. I stopped instantly, inert with fear, imagining that a whole sheet of ice was breaking off, with myself on it, and that I was within a split second of plunging hundreds of feet off the mountain. But nothing happened.

"Did you hear that?" I asked Joe.

"Yes," he said, "I felt it as well. It should be all right though, it's just readjusting under our load. Anyway, there's nothing we can do about it. It's just a risk we'll have to put up with."

Soloing doesn't feel as isolated if someone else is climbing a few feet away, but now we quickly decided to move at least fifty feet apart to lessen the load on particular sections of the ice.

Whenever I stopped for a rest, I fixed my eyes on a rock on the ridge but it never seemed to come any nearer. It was intricate work, finding the most stable part of the ice slope. It was a thousand feet high. The early sun was moving now, warming Dunagiri, but seemed an eternity from us, on the west side of the mountain. Changabang was a tall mountain for the sun to creep around. I couldn't feel my toes at all — they were numb with cold. I was experimenting, trying out an idea I had heard was practised by American climbers in Alaska — wearing Neoprene socks as an insulating barrier. It wasn't working. I knew that eventually, when the sun touched us, I would have to take my boots off and warm my feet up again — toes left numb for many hours can quickly become irrevocably damaged. A silly mistake could stop the expedition.

For the final four hundred feet we turned into a shallow gully. The last few feet, now at an altitude of 18,000 feet, seemed endless. But then, suddenly, it was over. We were greeted by a rush of cold air as we reached the ridge. The Bagini Glacier appeared down the other side — often imagined, but now seen for the first time.

On our right was the vertical sweep of granite of the North Face of Changabang. That cold, dark ice-streaked wall never felt the sun. Its height reinforced its Gothic gloom. I hoped our route did not stray onto it. At its top were the 'Horns' of Changabang, on the Summit Ridge which we had seen on photographs of the South Side of the mountain. The wind was evidently stronger up there — flurries of snow spiralled madly around them, over four thousand feet almost directly above our heads. Another circle of mountains had appeared before us. The North-West Face of Kalanka soared in an icy arête directly to its summit — a new angle on what had previously always appeared to be the gentler sister of Changabang. Beyond that mountain was Rishi Pahar, Hardeol and then Tirsuli, the mountain that avalanched André Roche's Swiss expedition when they attempted it after climbing Dunagiri in 1939. On our left, twisting like the ramparts of a great fortress, was Purbi Dunagiri. To the north lay the Latak peaks, visited by the Scots in 1950. But all this was forbidden land, for Joe and I were right on the Inner Line. The border lay just behind them.

Beyond these white peaks, through the gaps between them, we could glimpse the brown plateau of Tibet. At last I had seen Tibet — on the summit of Everest, a horizon that should have been two-hundred-and-fifty miles had been dragged down to one hundred feet by a storm.

The view beyond the crest zone of Asia heightened our feeling of isolation. The tension of the climb disappeared as I breathed in the view. My feet were now planted firmly and my hand steadying me on rock, whereas before my life had hung on four crampon points and aching calves. Looking back down the Rhamani Glacier, Base Camp was a puny blue smudge on the moraine. New mountains were springing from behind ridges. Rishi Kot seemed to have ducked and, once again, changed its mood. Joe was relieved at my happiness:

"I had not experienced any urgency for a change of scene, but Pete seemed to find it oppressive in the Rhamani where our field of vision was restricted. In a way, I felt responsible for having brought him to the area and apologetic about its shortcomings. But now Pete was, for the moment, placated like someone with claustrophobia given a glimpse of open air and freedom."

Not far to the west, along the same ridge on which we were standing, was the Bagini Pass, which Tom Longstaff had crossed on an exploratory trip prior to the Trisul ascent. Accompanied by Charlie Bruce, the Brocherel Brothers and four Gurkhas, he had seen virtually the same view that we were gazing over now. At 10.00 a.m. on 22nd May 1907, on the third day after leaving their Base Camp at the foot of the Bagini Glacier, they reached the Pass after some hours of step cutting. They were carrying enormous loads, including rifles and ammunition and food for ten days. They didn't know what lay on the far side, except that the glacier melt-water that probably stretched down on the far side would eventually join the Rishi. They didn't know if they would enter the Inner Sanctuary, or if they were only entering the Outer Horseshoe. They didn't know, once they got into the basin of the Rishi, whether they would be able to get out again. They took a chance. Using primitive pitons and all the six-hundred feet of rope they had with them, it took them five hours to descend the thousand feet into the Rhamani. They had not, of course, any of the sophisticated ice-climbing gear that Joe and I were using. Longstaff regarded their descent as the only piece of climbing he had done in the Himalayas that would have been regarded as 'stiff' in the Alps. Over the following days, with ever-dwindling supplies, they managed to find their way out over the route that Joe and I had used to walk in. For Longstaff, it was

"the happiest, most enchanting week I have ever spent in the mountains". They had reached about the limit of what was possible in the
way of cutting loose from one's base. As a contemporary had commented, "Longstaff is one of those people on whom Providence
smiles." Today, for Joe and me, it was an achievement sanctified by
time, and had none of the competitive aura of the rush after the last
great problems of modern Himalayan climbing.

I looked long and hard down the Bagini Glacier. The politics of the
seventies would prevent anyone from following Longstaff's journey
today. However, in 1907 Longstaff had wanted to go to Everest. Nepal
was closed to all foreigners and Tibet, owing to the big power politics
of that time, would not allow a big expedition in. So he had come to
the Garhwal.

Joe and I were too far down the ridge and too far away from the
Wall. We looked apprehensively at the cornices that hung over the
ridge and put a single rope on between us. I moved delicately along
the ridge, weaving over rock steps and around pinnacles. When the rope
went taut, Joe followed and we moved together. This was exhilarating
—the sculptured, windswept mushroom and rolling shapes of snow
along the ridge had never felt the feet of man. It was satisfying to leave
an intelligent line of footprints along them, threading the safest route.
It gave the same excitement that I had as a child when, on a cold clear
morning, after heavy snowfall, I had risen early and planted my tracks
across the previously undisturbed snow-carpeted fields. Perhaps it was
ego urging to dominate. I don't know, but it was enjoyable and made
me feel alone.

The morning sun was now moving quickly down Bagini peak, a
20,000-foot shapely cone on the ridge which undulated from us towards Dunagiri. Soon it would reach us. First it started to touch Joe,
then myself, forming a short twilight zone of about ten feet upon the
ridge. I looked upwards to see the sun nudging over the South-West
Ridge of Changabang, in a cascade of light over the West Wall, still
in shadow.

"Timing our climbing with the sun is going to be critical on the
route," said Joe. "It's going to be too bloody cold to do hard climbing
in the mornings."

I looked at my watch. 10.00 a.m. It would be nearly two hours before
the sun was properly established on the Face.

Suddenly the ridge started to rise steeply into the Wall. "We won't
be able to hack a ledge for the tent any higher up than this," I said. I

cleared some snow off a granite slab and started to take my boots off. My toes were white with cold and I warmed them with my hands till they were pink and tingling. The inner voice was ticking over — 'Look after yourself, don't exhaust yourself, eat well, keep warm, then you'll keep going.' A larger expedition would have given more comparison of fitness. I always expressed my worries and it seemed that I had more complaints, more physical ailments. I could never trick Joe into admitting a weakness. It was a game:

"Are *your* feet cold, Joe?"

"No, are yours?"

"Oh, no, it's just that my lace has come undone."

We were imposing ourselves on the ridge. We started to hack out a ledge, and the same feeling of reassurance that I had felt lower down on the ridge returned. What had been a bleak, hostile, windswept snow ridge we were turning into home. Even parts of our proposed route above our heads were beginning to look feasible, although a colossal banner of overhangs, 1,500 feet above us, cut across our view.

The descent was harrowing, but was brief, and we were carrying empty sacks, having dumped our loads on the ridge. We had taken three hours to climb up — it took us only one and a half hours to descend. As we walked back across the glacier towards our Advance Camp, it began to snow lightly. We had lost count by mid-afternoon of how often the West Wall had been in and out of its personal clouds. About ten times. The weather pattern seemed stable — but for how long would it hold?

We were exhilarated with our morning's climb. A detached part of me was becoming intrigued at how much I was enjoying myself. Once I could habitualise into climbing the Wall, perhaps it would seem no different from any climb I had done before. There didn't seem to be much objective danger on our proposed route, but we were going to have to give effort continually.

In the late afternoon I went for a walk by myself, to see if I could find the remnants of the Japanese Base Camp below the South-West Ridge. They had hidden the traces well, and it took some time to discover the blackened mound left after they had burnt their refuse. I rescued a polythene bottle full of paraffin from underneath a boulder, and picked up some sticks of bamboo that would be useful for anchoring the tent on the ridge. As I moved back around the shoulder, I could see our Advance Camp below and the stick-like figure of Joe next to the tent. He was cooking the evening meal. He looked bravely insignificant in the wilderness of peaks around.

I had an uncomfortable night and woke about three in the morning. I had been disturbed by the sound of distant rockfall. My stomach was rumbling and I couldn't get back to sleep. It was cramped inside the tent and I was huddled inside two sleeping bags. Outside the temperature had plummeted to −20°C. Then I heard a sound that made my flesh creep—a low growl outside. It lasted about thirty seconds. Then there was some sniffling, a scuttling noise, and I heard one of our pans knocked over. I did not dare move. After five minutes there were no more sounds and I felt it was safe enough to wake Joe. I nudged him.

"Hey, Joe, there's something outside the tent," I whispered hoarsely.

He didn't seem too concerned. "Don't open the door, you'll let the cold in." I agreed with him. If I opened the door, whatever it was was probably so timid that it would have run away at the sound of the zip. And if it didn't run away, and was not timid, we would probably regret having opened the door in the first place! However, after another ten minutes my curiosity took control and I peered outside. It was a brilliant moonlit night- the whole glacial cirque was bathed in colourless light. But there was no sign of anything living.

In the morning the fresh snow of the glacier from the previous afternoon was criss-crossed with tracks. They seemed to come from, and return eventually to, the northern corner of the glacier, beneath the Bagini Pass. One line of tracks paced backwards and forwards from the tent. The tracks seemed to have been made by a four-legged animal—it was difficult to gauge how big they were, or how many animals were involved, because of the loose powder snow. Bears? Leopards? Yeti? Mars Bar-eaters? We did not know the answer.

That day, the 17th September, we went back up to the ridge to ferry some equipment and to pitch the other lightweight tent up there. We would not have had the energy to carry anything heavier than lightweight, six-pound tents such as this. However, Bill Wilkins, of Ultimate Equipment (an American, whom we referred to as Ultimate Bill) was very worried when he gave us the tents. "Don't use them too high or in much wind," he warned, "they're just for backpackers." He had stitched a snow valance around them and this proved very useful as we perched the tent on the narrow platform. I became over-enthusiastic in enlarging the platform we had started the previous day.

"Look through this, Joe," I said. I had made a hole through the cornice and we could look down through the proposed tent floor at the Bagini Glacier, 1,000 feet below.

"We'd better move it a bit the other way," said Joe.

The wind rattled the tent but we tensioned it off on ice hammers, deadmen snow anchors and pieces of bamboo, and tip-toed gingerly back down the ice slope to Advance Camp. There, it snowed heavily for one and a half hours, and this stopped us getting on with all the little preparation jobs we had planned. When the snowfall stopped, Changabang looked plastered, as if it had just been creamed by a giant barber. But within half an hour it was clear again, having shaken the surplus layers off in a couple of enormous powder slides.

"Here in this endless and gleaming wilderness I was removed farther than ever from the world of man . . ." I closed the book of Hesse's poems and took a sleeping pill, hoping to avoid another disturbed night. As a result I overslept. Joe was always absolutely hopeless at getting up in the morning, and could never be relied on as an alarm clock. As a result it was late morning by the time we set off. The sun was on us, draining us. We both felt lethargic and were only managing about twenty paces at a time across the glacier. By the time we had reached the ice slope we had both decided, without any discussion at all, to leave the sacks on the snow till the morning, turn back and call it a rest day.

Joe and I discussed our proposed descent route from Changabang (on the assumption that we even got to the top of the mountain). Through binoculars we could see the fixed ropes that Bonington's team had used, still hanging from Shipton's Col. The idea of descending their North-East route and the popping back over Shipton's Col after having done the West Wall was appealing. With a bit of luck we might pass one of the camps of the South Face team on the glacier, and stop for a cup of tea. We had received various opinions from the first ascensionists about the feasibility of this plan. Martin Boysen thought "It should be all right". Chris Bonington changed his opinion from encouragement to dissuasion. "It's a very tricky ridge," he had finally said. "I'd go back the way you've come, if I were you. Better the devil you know than the one you don't."

It was a day of peace amidst days of effort, a lovely relaxing day. It was a jewel in my memory during the days that followed, the calm before the storm. There was little wind and just an occasional puff of a cloud in the sky. The only sounds were the creakings of the shifting rocks and ice of the glacier and surrounding peaks, and these sounds only accentuated the silence. The mountains were peeping through the mask of self-struggle that could so easily obscure them from my vision. I remembered a very similar day I had spent over four years previously with two friends in the Hindu Kush, during my first expedition to the Himalayas. It had been the day before we set out on the North Face of Kohi Khaaik. Three days later we had emerged on the summit, dehydrated and exhausted, above a very difficult and dangerous route, to face a long descent and a sixty-mile walk back to our Base Camp without food. Perhaps this, too, would be a calm day before our strength and will were tested.

Joe was relaxed on that day. "It doesn't seem as oppressive up here, as it could be with Dick," he wrote in his diary. "It's a bit more light-hearted." Sometimes I felt as if Dick was with us, Joe talked such a lot about their experiences together. He always talked of Dick's self-discipline, frugality and determination with a mixture of amusement and awe.

As the day wore on, Joe and I became immersed in our books. Joe was reading *Night Runners of Bengal*, and I became submerged in *The Odessa File*. They were easy books to read, and we escaped with them for a while.

After we had picked up the loads on the following day, the 19th September, and carried them up to the camp on the ridge, we were ready to move. On the 20th September we piled all the remaining food and equipment we would need into our sacks and climbed up to the tent on the ridge. Our food could stretch to about fourteen days and we hoped that would be long enough time to do the route. The loads were heavy, about fifty pounds each, and it was tricky work climbing the ice slope. It was our fourth carry there and, we hoped, the last time we would set foot on that slope.

We had a thousand feet of eight-millimetre terylene non-stretch rope with us, and a few old climbing ropes of our own. Our planned tactics were to run out all the fixed rope, returning to the camp every evening. We thought we probably had enough rope to reach the icefield. Then, after all the rope was fixed, we would set off with all our remaining food and the hammocks, pulling up the ropes behind us as we ascended. Working from our hammocks above the icefield, we would then run our ropes out again, up the upper rock tower, push on through to the summit and descend the other side. It all sounded deceptively simple.

Since it was only late morning we determined to start on the Wall that afternoon. We decided to lead four rope lengths at a time. In this way the one in front could get into the rhythm of leading, and the one following could switch his adrenalin off and rest his mind for a while. I had first go. I climbed without a sack, wearing my blue one-piece Everest suit and with all the hardware draped from my full body harness. Joe was to follow, carrying all the rope to be fixed in his sack.

"I've never used these things before," he said, fingering the jumar clamps that he was to use to climb up the rope after me.

"It's as good a place as any to learn," I said.

Keeping well to the right of the cornice, the climbing was straightforward until I reached a point a hundred feet above the tent. The ridge was disappearing, curving into an ice-coated slab. I tapped a piton in a crack and teetered up the ice on the front points of my crampons. Scraping with my axe, I managed to clear a handhold, pulled myself up to it and mantleshelved onto it. Above it the slope became uniform again. It was hot work, kicking up it in the sun. By the end of the afternoon I had run out four rope lengths and Joe had led one—seven hundred feet of climbing. We had reached the foot of the Wall that stretched upwards to the barrier overhangs that guarded the foot of the icefield. We felt elated.

"At this rate, we'll be on the icefield tomorrow," said Joe.

"Somehow, a certain tension had been broken—we had started; the old familiar preoccupation with the problem in hand; gone were the fears and anxieties of the time when all we could do was look at and think about the mountain, not knowing what it would involve, what it would do to us . . . we estimated we could reach the summit inside a week."

Quickly, we abseiled down the ropes, straight to the tent door, took off our crampons and flopped inside. I suddenly felt tired. It had been good to start the climbing so positively, but the altitude had a draining effect. We nestled in our sleeping bags and cooked a meal of American freeze-dried meat, to which we added potato powder. After that we had some honey pudding, a piece of the fruit cake which my mother had baked for us, and some tea. For the first time ever, I took a Ronicol Timespan, that we had been told couldn't do any harm and might clear the sludge in our capillaries, by dilating them for eight hours. This we followed with a vitamin pill and a Valium pill to help us sleep. "We're a couple of high-altitude junkies," I said.

Neither of us believed that these did any physical good, but it was a reassuring ritual and a nightly ceremony.

It was cosy inside, once I had turned my mind off to the drop on either side of the tent. We had laid out all the ropes and the two hammocks on the floor of the tent, to insulate us from the snow underneath the thin ground sheet. The wind was continually blowing across the tent, rattling and flapping the nylon. It was a disconcerting noise and I felt uneasy about the siting of the camp. But there was nothing I could do about it and I drifted off to sleep.

CHAPTER FOUR

The Barrier

21st–27th September

A thin empty buzzing, like a bee trapped in a can, scraped at the surface of my consciousness. It was Joe's alarm wrist watch which we had placed on an aluminium plate between us. It was pitch dark. The wind over the ridge was flapping the tent rhythmically, powerful and threatening. Joe still seemed to be sleeping. My mind retracted and the immediate world floated off again.

My eyes sprang open. I looked at the luminous fingers on Joe's watch. An hour must have passed; it was 6.30 a.m. Cold dawn, a long way over the mountains, gave a hint of grey light on the inside of the tent. Thoughts tumbled in. The route! The time! Breakfast! I twisted my arms outside my sleeping bag, shuffled forward to the zip on the inner tent and pulled it down. I put my head torch on and looked at the thermometer: −20°C. The weather was definitely becoming colder. Pulling my gloves on, I unzipped the outer door where the wind met my face, whipping the flap into the air. I pulled my axe from the side of the tent and hacked at the snow wall of the cornice. Using the adze, I was able to break off large chunks of snow that rolled into the tent entrance. The fine powder and disturbed ice crystals spun round, stinging my face and pouring down my sleeves. I grabbed the zip and shut the world out again, then lit the stove. It was a fresh Gaz cartridge and the propane-butane mixture quickly started melting the bulging mass of snow I had crammed in the pan. Joe stirred briefly and turned over. I tried to doze as well, but the melting snow needed constant attention. Breakfast was on its way—all to be served in our one-pint plastic mugs—first a mug of tea, then porridge, then a tin of fish, then a hot fruit drink. The melting and cooking took two and a half hours. Joe just took the courses, muttering "Ta", his eyes moving in and out of sleep, cocooned in his own thoughts, pretending that the daytime had still not arrived.

As soon as the stove was out Joe allowed the day to start. "Don't worry, I'll be cooking the evening meal," he said.

"Am I expected to cook breakfast all the way up the route?" I asked.

"Why, do you want me to cook that as well?"

We could start moving around inside the tent in our one-piece suits and boots. Before leaving, we stuffed our pockets with sweets and chocolate to sustain us during the day. Outside on the ridge there was only room for one person at a time to put his crampons and body harness on. We had decided never to jumar up on a rope attached from the same anchor point at the same time. Joe was ready first and, since it was his turn to lead, he set off from the start of the fixed rope where it curled away from the tent door. It was 9.45 a.m. After he was past the first anchor I followed him.

We were both carrying sacks full of gear and rope and it was hard work. The terylene seemed soft and vulnerable as the teeth of the jumar gritted into it and I sank my full weight back on it. Dressed in all the high-altitude equipment, carrying a heavy sack, I felt like the lead weight used for testing ropes. And sometimes they snapped — I ought to know, as part of my job was investigating mountaineering equipment failure. These ropes had no standard — they were made for yachting. What would the BMC Technical Committee think of me? And what if a peg came out? I knew that low-stretch ropes such as these were not designed to take much of a shock load. I never seemed to trust pegs that I had put in, it was as if I knew their weaknesses too well. I wished someone else had put them in, then I could rely on them blindly! My mind and body were now completely alert to all the dangers, refreshed after the night's sleep. Above me, Joe disturbed the snow and it bounced down in spray and chunks. The wind and cold in the flat morning light were hostile. But I was a prisoner of my own ambition, and persisted on up the ropes.

Joe was waiting for me, perched on a step in the ice. He racked some of the hardware onto the rings in his harness and started to uncoil a couple of ropes. I emptied the remaining gear out of his sack into mine, and tied onto the same piton. It was a wordless ritual. Joe set off up the ice, tapping his axe and hammer in, moving his feet up quickly and neatly.

"You should be able to go straight up from there," I shouted, when he was about twenty feet above my head.

"The ice is really thin on the slab here," he said.

He made another move up and I could hear the sound of metal

scraping on granite. Then he started fiddling with his rack of pitons, selected a thin knife blade, and tapped it into a crack on a rib of rock on his right. 'Come on,' I thought, 'we've got a lot of ground to cover.'

"I'm coming down," said Joe. "I'll try it further over on the right."

"But there's reasonable-looking ground about ten feet above you," I said.

"I don't think this peg's any good . . ." said Joe.

It looked too far off the route to go to the right to me. 'I wish he'd stop messing about,' I thought. 'I'm sure I could bomb up there, he just doesn't like to commit himself to a hard move.' But I said nothing. Each of us had to look after himself beyond a certain point. It would have been easy to comment, but unfair unless I had tried myself. Thoughts could be brutal, they had to be, but only when they mature into constructive opinions should I speak them. The success of the climb was all that mattered.

It would be psychologically bad, at this stage in the climb, for Joe to relinquish the lead to me.

"O.K.," I said, and paid the rope out carefully as Joe descended below the peg. 'I'll have to get that out,' I thought.

Joe disappeared around up to the peg, tied my rope through a sling on it and I lowered myself down on it until I could move around the corner and up to where Joe was sitting. I untied from the rope and pulled it through the sling and back to myself.

"You should be able to get back on line by traversing back up through those blocks," I told him. I was feeling impatient, on edge, the idea of climbing the whole Wall above was worrying me, but I had to wait my turn.

Joe moved off, edging along a huge, seemingly detached block the size of himself as if he were walking the plank. The sun had now wheeled fully onto us and the rock began to seem more friendly. Whilst Joe pegged over a bulge fifty feet above me I sat on a sloping ledge. More of Tibet was emerging but I had no inclination to gaze. I still wanted to lead but, at the same time, was suppressing my impatience, part of me recognising it as irrational. It seemed to take Joe an age to lead the pitch. When I came to follow, it was the first steep bit of ground I had to jumar on the route and spinning out from the rock unnerved me. It was impossible to tell how difficult the climbing had been for Joe—I was just the following climbing machine that jumared and took the running belays out. I found Joe directly above the spot which he had failed to lead.

"I'll go down and swing the ropes around," he said. He descended the rope I had fixed in place and, after detaching it lower down, swung precariously around the edge of the buttress on it, whilst I protected him with a rope from above. Then he jumared straight back up to me and we straightened the fixed rope out.

"We'll probably have to do a lot of this sort of tidying up of fixed ropes as we go along, if we're going to stretch it to the icefield," I said.

The icefield. It seemed further away now than it had seemed the previous day.

Joe began to turn on the pressure in his climbing. When he realised how late in the afternoon it was, he quickly climbed 150 feet up the broken ground of rock and ice above us. It was a fast piece of climbing and brought us to the point where the angle of the slabs tilted from 55° to 65°. We were still 250 feet below the barrier of overhangs. We were getting near them, if only slowly. We could only live in the present and think of the next obstacle. If we kept on tackling the Face as a series of obstacles, each with its own solution, then we would have to reach the top sometime.

We fastened all our superfluous equipment to the high point and slid back down the ropes to the camp. The abseiling was fast and straightforward and we were pleased to arrive at 5.30 p.m. — it was still light. There would be hard climbing the next day, but that could have been next year for all we cared. Soon we had some hot drinks in front of us inside the tent and the comforting thought of twelve hours' rest ahead of us.

All that night and the next day the bitterly cold wind blew. By this time the alarm had twinged us into action. We were back into position and ready to climb by 10.30 a.m., having woken at 5.00 a.m. and moved off by 8.30 a.m. After taking his crampons off, Joe started up a long groove line that stretched up in the general direction of the overhangs. It was magnificent, hard, steep, free climbing, mainly jamming and lay-backing up the crack which was rough and ragged — rather like the famous beautiful granite of the French Alps. But Changabang's granite, not marked on geology maps of the area, had an air of mystery. It was this intrusion of white, coarse-grained granite that gave Changabang its miraculous shape, unlike all the mountains around it. It was so white that when he first saw it, Longstaff had thought it was snow lying on cliffs at an impossible angle. To us, it was so sound and rough to clasp, it was as if it had been made to climb on.

Joe belayed to a large flake of rock, high in the groove and I took over the lead. Many clouds obscured the sun; it should have reached us by then. Occasionally, to do difficult moves or fiddle with equipment, I had to take off my mitts and climb with just my under-gloves and fingerless mitts. There was a lot of ice in the back of the groove and I managed to smash most of it off with my short ice hammer. As the distance of rock between myself and Joe increased, I began to enjoy myself. This was what I'd come for. I had come for the physical thrill of climbing, not for swinging around on perilously thin fixed ropes. For a hundred feet of climbing I felt confident and light and indestructible. I felt relaxed, rapturously free from a sense of effort, pain and danger, and in total control. Even the altitude almost ceased to complicate my breathing.

The feeling did not last long. The groove dwindled out into a holdless wall at the same steep angle. I had used nearly all my equipment up. Twenty feet above me, the Wall looked as if it relented, over at its right-hand edge, underneath the overhangs. If I could traverse diagonally up to that point, perhaps we could turn the overhangs through their right-hand side, where they looked as if they were at their narrowest point. I would be climbing right above the main Wall beneath the icefield — a near vertical drop of about 1,050 feet. My boots felt big and clumsy as I stepped away from the comforting security of the crack and balanced on two tiny footholds. Below me, Joe was waiting in the wind:

"That was my stint done. Pete took over the leading, up a groove towards the overhangs. Now we were on a real wall. There was no shelter from the wind. I shuffled about to find the most comfortable position on my footholds; Pete was out of sight in the cloud. I was cold.

"The cold had been driven right through my bones. The rope only moved out slowly; I shouted up to Pete that there was not much of it left, with no idea of what he was doing. Through a brief clearing in the cloud I saw him bridged across an ice-choked crack. There did not seem to be anywhere for him to rest. I was anxious. His calls to me were unintelligible, as mine probably were to him. Mist closed in again, more time passed. 'What the hell is he doing?'

"There was no rope left. I shouted to him, as well as a dry throat would let me. He must have realised what I meant. I undid the knots which tied me to the stance, in order to give him a little more rope; I hoped, that hope based on confidence, that he was safe and could not fall. With me untied, it would be very serious if he did.

"My whole physical being tensed with the cold, untensed and shook, trying to find some warmth. It was starting to snow. I interrogated myself with questions about our sanity — 'When will we stop this madness and get down to warmth?'

"'Come on, Pete,' I screamed in my mind."

I reached a thin crack with the tips of my fingers and tapped a soft steel piton into it. It seemed secure, so I used it to lever my feet and weight up until I could reach higher with my other hand. I scraped some snow away from the start of a depression in the Wall and curled my fingers around a hand hold. Trusting everything to this, I lurched up, my feet scraping against the rock and mantleshelfed on it. The effort had me gasping frantically for air. From there I hooked my ice hammer on an edge of rock and pulled up on that to teeter onto a sloping snow-covered shelf. I knocked in the only two pitons I had left. One of them seemed fairly sound so I yelled, "O.K., Joe, I'm there." Then I noticed it was snowing. I had no idea how long the pitch had taken me to lead, it was as if time had stopped, I had been so engrossed.

Within moments the clouds opened and deluged snow, then hail-stones. It was only mid-afternoon and we might have done a little more climbing, but the storm precluded anything except descent. I hammered in two more pitons and tightened and fastened the fixed rope I had trailed behind me. I had to knot two ropes together and then jerked back down them through the cloud to Joe.

"It's an impressive situation up there," I said. "We might be able to get around the overhangs to the right. There's quite a balcony to start from." And that's what we called it after that.

"I see you've fixed my two old climbing ropes," said Joe. "They should be all right, though I wouldn't jerk the yellow one too hard, I've fallen off on it a few times in the past."

We started abseiling quickly down, back towards the camp. The storm only lasted half an hour, and by the time we had reached the tent the evening sun was streaming through breaks in the cloud. Then suddenly, amazingly, the wind, which had been our constant companion all the time on the ridge, dropped completely. The tent stopped rattling and we no longer had to talk above its noise to each other.

We finished our evening meal with Christmas pudding and custard, to celebrate.

"I wish we had a cassette player up here," said Joe. "A bit of rock music wouldn't go amiss."

I was still scribbling diary notes onto bits of paper. I had left my diary on the moraine at Advance Camp, thinking that if anything happened to us on the Wall, then at least someone might find a record of what had happened to us up till that point. Also, I censored it — I didn't write about occasional disagreements Joe and I had, or worries I felt about the route. I thought, 'What if this is the last thing I ever write, and somebody reads it?' I find things said and done in the strange world of an expedition, once recorded, become inflated and can be easily misunderstood by the non-mountaineer or uninformed commentator, eager for 'the reasons behind the tragedy'. Joe was intrigued by my assiduous writings:

"I wondered why Pete wanted to preserve the situations, rather than use every conscious minute to savour them. He was usually full of apt literary quotations and when I told him that Graham Greene had said that a writer's greatest problem was not trying to remember, but trying to forget, he thought that I had made it up to excuse my laziness in keeping a diary."

My finger-ends had been chewed by the rough granite. We had to change our under-gloves many times because of this wear and tear. Fortunately, we had brought many pairs. I carefully put antiseptic cream on them, followed by plasters — I knew how easily infection can run amok when the flesh is weakened by exposure to the cold, having had a septic foot on the Hindu Kush expedition that had made my foot so swollen I could not put my boot on. I dusted my feet, massaged them and changed my socks before getting into my sleeping bag. Frostbite or infection could be our greatest enemy. It was only 7.30 p.m. by the time we settled down, and we were both asleep by 8.00 p.m.

The night closed my fitful dreams from the mountain, as if the climb on Changabang was just the surface of my life, irrelevant compared with my other life in the west. Only for a fraction of the time in my life was I climbing and my dreams were always about memories and situations and people at home.

The morning of the 23rd September was clear and still. We slept past the alarm, but still managed to move away by 8.00 a.m. I set off, jumaring first. The previous evening I had tied the two ropes knotted together below the Balcony on to the soft metal piton I had tapped behind the flake. This, I had hoped, would make it easy to ascend diagonally. As I was half way up Joe's frayed, old yellow rope, there was a little jerk and I somersaulted backwards. 'God, the rope's snapped,' I thought, 'I'm dead.' Rock was hurtling past and I glimpsed the glacier two thousand feet below. Then the rope began to tighten and stretch and spun me round into an upright position till I was yo-yoing up and down, hanging out from the Wall around the corner from the Balcony. At first I did not know what had happened. I gasped and then took brief breaths, looking wildly around me. The rope was still attached above me—the jumars had bitten deep into it, but the protective sheath was still uncut. 'I should be all right,' I thought. The knot on the rope above me had held, and so had Joe's old ropes. I looked up, along the line of the rope, trying to find the reason for the twenty-foot swinging fall. The peg behind the flake had come out. 'My fault,' I thought, 'I put it in.' Still, it had held my weight the previous day. 'Thank God I didn't fall on the eight-millimetre terylene,' I thought, 'even if it hadn't snapped, the jumars would have sliced straight through it.' At that moment Joe appeared around the corner, lower down the fixed ropes, about a hundred feet away.

"You're going slowly today. What are you doing over there?" he shouted.

"Oh, I just thought I'd go for a swing over this wall and see what it was like," I said. "The peg I put in half way up to the Balcony coming out, helped me."

"Christ," said Joe. "I thought I heard a little yelp and a clatter. Can you get back from there?"

"I can as long as the rope doesn't snap."

Fun is closely linked to fear. I began to slide the jumars slowly up the rope, trying to avoid any sudden sharp movement. After fifty feet I was on the Balcony. It had taken two and a half hours to reach it from the camp. The uncontrolled feeling of being flung about helplessly that the accident had brought, had shaken me—avalanches, falls, cars rolling, I had experienced them all in the past. Death could so easily follow that. The barrier of overhangs now stretched far out above our heads.

Over on our left, the overhang jutted out fifty feet from the Wall. The only line through it was an overhanging groove a hundred feet high. We couldn't see if there was a crack in the back of it all the way, and doubted if we had the equipment to climb it. It would be all artificial climbing and might take us an exhausting two days. The only hope was to the right.

I racked a lot of equipment to my harness and dumped my sack on the Balcony next to Joe. It was difficult to decide what, and how much, to take. If I took too much, I would exhaust myself carrying all the weight and would be unable to do any free climbing – if some were necessary. Suppressing a knot of fear in my stomach, I moved to the edge of the Balcony. The exit from the Balcony was guarded by a seemingly detached block about four feet square. I had to use it. I slid a long knife blade piton in a crack that lay at the top of it, attached a long sling to it, and leant tentatively on it. It held. I leant on it with more confidence and looked around the corner. Below, the white hard granite swept downwards without a break or a feature to halt the eye. It bowed beneath me and I could not see where it eventually merged with the lower icefields that swept across the wall in curving bands. From here I could look right across the entire West Wall, to the South-West ridge. Great bold sweeps of rock with hidden amphitheatres and great barriers of icicles, hundreds of feet long, confronted me. I squinted at them, for the sun was moving over the South-West ridge into a powder-blue sky. 'Good, it'll warm up soon,' I thought.

I peered up at the overhangs above me. There seemed to be a ramp line that stretched diagonally right and upwards intermittently through a series of stepped roofs. The whole structure consisted of suspended blocks of granite on top of each other. I looked back at Joe, "There's some sort of line up there, sort of solid but detached."

I tapped a one-inch knife blade into a crack just over the edge of the first roof and clipped an etrier into it. I put my foot into it and gently gave it my weight, looking downwards and hunching my shoulders under my helmet in case the peg came out and smashed into me. I hopped in the etriers, it still held. So I launched out up the rungs of the etriers and pulled over the edge of the roof feeling very vulnerable. The first peg is always the worst – if it had come out I would have smashed my back on the Balcony. That sort of injury would have brought complications, for we were without the helicopter safety network that exists in crowded mountain areas. From the peg I made two strenuous free moves and locked myself into a little niche in the overhangs by wedging my knees on one side of the niche, and my back against the other side. I was about fifteen feet above Joe, but could only see his feet from where I was, for his head was hidden by overhangs.

I was in the sunshine, but Joe was in icy shadows. Because of how he was tied onto the belay, he couldn't move into the sun. I saw one foot stretch out into the sunlight, then the other. He was trying to warm them up! He was painfully cold:

"Over and over again I asked myself what I was doing there, and made another promise that this would be the last time."

I was facing the wrong way though managed to twist painfully around and place another piton, just over the tip of the overhang above my head. At full stretch I patted it in, timidly. I had a morbid fear that the whole overhang would collapse with me if I shook it too hard. How did I know it would not? Nobody had been there before!

From there a sloping, uneven ramp, a foot wide, stretched upwards across the leaning Wall. It was plastered by white ice that was stacked along it, smoothing it flush against the Wall. Leaning out on the piton I started trying to smash the ice off with my axe. It was hard work. I hacked until my arms were exhausted and I could hardly open my fingers or lift the adze, panted until some strength returned, then started again. Eventually the hard ice at the back of the ramp came away and I managed to place a piton in it. This I pounded in as hard as I could, then used it to gain some height. Two more pitons higher up, the ramp stopped for a couple of feet and then bulged out again. Holding myself in balance with one foot on the ramp and one braced against the Wall, I reached across to where the ramp started again. The ice was too far away and seemed too hard to smash off. My mind was working quickly, absorbing all the tiny details around me, bringing movements into slow motion. In the white granite in front of my eyes were particles of clear quartz, silvery muscovite and jet black tourmaline. My attention floated to them; they emphasised my insignificance—emphasised the fact that I was fragile, warm-blooded and living, clinging to the side of this steep, inhospitable world.

My mind jerked back to the situation. There was only one thing to do. I leant across and hooked the pick of my ice hammer on the start of the ice, attached my etrier to it and began to ease my weight across into it. It was a long stretch, and I knew if I lost my balance the resulting sudden movements would pull the hammer off and probably some pitons as well. "Watch the rope, Joe," I shouted. He could have been a thousand miles away. 'If I fall now,' I thought, 'I'll swing right out into space and have quite a job getting back onto the rock—if I've the energy.' The hammer held. I put an ice screw in, above the hammer. It went in four inches. I tied it off before putting my weight onto it. I could see a foothold, the first one on the pitch; it was no bigger than the top of an egg cup. On my fingers, scrabbling for holds, I made two moves across and got my weight over it. If I was careful, I could rest and assess the situation.

What a place! I looked at my watch—I had been climbing for two hours and was bathed in sweat, although the rock and the air were cold. It had been some of the hardest climbing I had ever done. The air was soundless, emphasising the loneliness of my situation. Where would I go from here? Fifty feet above me I could see the massive detached block we had seen hanging below the icefield when we had examined the Face through binoculars from Advance Camp. We had called it 'the Guillotine'. No, not up there. The angle of the Wall had eased just off the vertical, and I carefully traversed for fifteen feet to the right, pain in my worn finger-ends forgotten, submerged in action. The rock became crumbly, and I had great difficulty in placing the only pegs I had left. I hammered in a nut, after excavating a little crack for it with my hammer, tied the rope off and shouted down, "O.K., Joe, come on. I'm there. Or somewhere. Gently does it." I was standing on one tiny foothold and my leg muscles were exhausted and quivery. I tied a couple of long slings to the pegs and stood in them.

Drained, but deeply satisfied, I hung there. It had been a struggle but I had made some progress—and was it not a struggle that I was seeking? Here, there were no spectators, none of that inflated, blown-up feeling of having everything filmed and recorded that there had been on Everest. The mountain was challenging our tenacity—but we would not give in.

Joe swung around the corner alarmingly. He was carrying an enormous sackful of gear that must have weighed fifty pounds. 'I hope those pegs hold,' I thought. Part of me wanted recognition for the piece of climbing I had done.

"Sorry it took me such a long time," I said, as he came across to the peg where I was hanging. Half of me meant that—the other half was fishing for a compliment.

"It must have been quite hard," he said.

No, we couldn't share out fears or achievements on this climb, we had to have a business relationship. If we opened up our relationship whilst on the climb, the mountain might exploit our weaknesses. We must present a united front against the mountain and swallow the subtleties of interaction. Self-preservation had to come first, even if this made us cruelly unsympathetic. Looking after my own life was evolving as a full-time occupation. I was tired, but did not offer Joe the lead. The icefield was in the top of my mind and I wanted to reach it.

It was a complicated manœuvre, changing over the belay with Joe, making sure, checking and counter-checking that each of us was still clipped on, and none of our equipment was in danger of falling off. The struggle, the sun, the situation and the altitude had dazed us into a dream. But the discipline within me recognised that this was the time a mistake could be made.

There was a groove above the belay, and I started up that. It seemed to dwindle out in the overhanging wall in the direction of the Guillotine. After twenty feet of straightforward artificial climbing, I thought I could see a line of weakness high on the right, where the foot of the icefield plunged over the wall in an enormous Icicle. I was climbing on a rib parallel with it. If I could reach the Icicle, climb the rock next to it, and then climb back onto the ice where it swept over the edge, then there might be a possibility of reaching the icefield. But to reach the Icicle I would have to tension down and commit myself to a long pitch. There was no time for that, the rock was already reddening with the sinking sun and we had to sort out the fixed rope through the overhangs. I clipped my rope through a karabiner to my high point and lowered myself down to Joe.

"You're missing some good atmospheric effects," said Joe.

I looked around and saw the mist billowing around the Wall.

"We'd better get down," I said.

We tied the rope off in six places on the pitch. "It'll be a grip going up and down through that lot, with all those pegs, knots and krabs in the way," I said.

"Yeah, a real Toni Kurz pitch," said Joe.

Toni Kurz was the Austrian climber who died on the North Face of the Eiger in 1936. Following the successive deaths of his three companions, he managed to rope down almost into the arms of a rescue party which, due to the bad conditions, was unable to ascend a small overhang to reach him. A knot in his rope jammed in a karabiner and he died of exhaustion whilst still just out of reach. A nightmare name for a nightmare pitch.

Back in the tent, after our meal, we scribbled our daily notes. "Someday, I'm goin' to get there," hummed Joe. A Carole King song. It was the only line either of us could ever remember. "I think it will be the key pitch," I wrote, "it feels a sort of psychological breakthrough for me; if that doesn't stop me, nothing will. But things are going very slowly."

Joe wrote: "It must be the hardest climbing in the Himalayas. Little niggling things seem to get on our nerves. I wish Pete was more considerate." Above us, the light faded off Changabang like sound receding.

Back the next morning, it was as if we had never left the arena. Refreshed after a night's sleep, I approached the Icicle in a different mood. Leaning down on tension from the rope, I cut steps across it, hoping that the ice was glued firmly to the rock. I kicked across some snow, onto the rock on the other side. It was a spectacular situation. One of my ropes hung over to Joe like the Golden Gate. A perfect crack split the wall above. I climbed it for twenty feet and suspended myself from some slings. It was a pitch that had been mainly diagonal and a tricky one for Joe to have to follow. Where I had tensioned down onto the ice, Joe had to lower himself and climb down, facing the possibility of an awesome pendulum swing across the void towards me.

"How am I expected to do this?" he muttered, then saw that he had no option except to have a go. A few neat movements and he was across.

Twenty feet above our heads, the Icicle appeared to change angle into a tiny little gully that crept down from the icefield.

"I'll climb up as high as I can above our heads, place a peg and tension across on the rope," I said. I put my crampons on, ready for the manoeuvre, knowing that as soon as I swung down onto the ice I would be committed and would have to climb—there would not be any room to change footwear, once started! The crack we were hanging from petered out fifteen feet above us. I hammered a peg as near to the top of it as I could reach, then tapped another peg in upside down behind a fragile flake of rock on the wall. Then I started leaning leftwards out on the rope. It was a hot, cloudless day—the best yet—and conditions were as perfect as they would ever be at this altitude for attempting this sort of hard technical climbing.

Watching my footwork very carefully, crampons grating on the rock and flashing in the sunlight, I eventually reached a point where I could just touch the Icicle if I stretched across with my ice hammer. I was arched across on tiny footholds and faced a big pendulum from the tensioned rope. Below me I could hear Joe's camera clicking. 'I mustn't mention it,' I thought, 'must call his bluff. But I hope he's holding the rope all right.' Then I spoke. "Watch the rope, Joe, I'm moving onto the ice." I swung down onto the ice hammer, hoping that it would not prise a lump of ice off and catapult me off as well. It did not. I smashed the pick of my axe in and kicked the front points of my crampons. They held also, but all my weight was on my arms. The cold discipline of ice-climbing technique moved into the front of my mind, not allowing hasty movements. First the axe, then the hammer, I tapped in above me, then the 'bunny hop' of bringing my crampons up until the adze of the axe and the hammer were level with my eyes. Then repeat. Thoughts of falling were now thrust to the bottom of my mind. I was committed and lost in movement. Then the angle eased. A rock jutted out of the ice and I smashed the ice from off the top of it and planted my foot sideways. I was nearly fainting from the effort. The oxygen debt that the previous few minutes had built up was blurring and fading my eyesight. The ice around me momentarily grew dark.

It gave a surge of relief to start moving up the shallow gully of ice, with my weight now over my legs rather than on my arms. I stopped at the first place I could make a ledge for both feet and brought Joe up. Once more we were trying to straighten out the line of the fixed rope and Joe managed to save a whole rope length by detaching himself and the rope behind him from all runners and belays since the stance at the end of the Toni Kurz pitch. This meant we could abseil straight down the overhanging rock next to the Guillotine, avoiding any detours. My four leads were now over and it had taken me nearly three days to do them. For me, the Barrier had been crossed, now the iron was returning to my soul; I was rediscovering that feeling of inner invincibility that I had felt on the descent from Everest. Had the climbing not been so utterly demanding, I could not have felt this way. Above us, the prospects seemed rosy, with the icefield stretching upwards for five hundred feet to the Upper Tower.

"I might as well get a pitch in," said Joe, and he swiftly moved up the icefield, crossing a few bulges where the rock broke through. Then, after 150 feet, he tapped some pitons in and abseiled back down to me. He seemed happy.

"Without stopping to talk about it, by some imperceptible transition of thought, it was clear that we could climb the West Wall, provided we could stick it out. The icefield had a symbolic aura about it, and entering it was like entering other secret places — there was the same air of privilege and mystery about it. I had the same feeling about the Spider on the North Face of the Eiger."

Soon, we were winging down the ropes back to the camp. Whilst we were on the first few abseils, the sun began to set. Cloud was pluming off the entire length of the South-East Ridge of the pyramid of Dunagiri. The sun had reddened this windswept cloud and it looked as if the entire ridge were aflame, like a burning beam of wood. I saw Joe below me, never slow on the draw with his camera, taking photographs rapidly. 'Typical,' I thought, 'he'll get all the best pictures.' Seizing my camera, I tried to take a picture but the film was finished. In fumbling to change films, I watched with dismay as the exposed film slid between my fingers and bounced, at ever-increasing speed, over the Inner Line and fifteen hundred feet towards the Bagini Glacier. I lost film of two days' climbing that could never be replaced.

"I got a good cover photo there," grinned Joe, when I reached the tent. I just grunted. It had been a hard day.

"I think about the soft things in life a lot" [noted Joe in his diary that evening. About the beauties of the sunset he wrote:] "They're phenomena only partially observed, and hardly appreciated, from a corner of my mind which makes me photograph them to look at some time when I can enjoy them."

So many things can happen in two days. Back home, I would have been to a few meetings, travelled to many places, read the newspapers, received and sent a stack of letters, used the telephone continuously, perhaps watched television and been to the pub, played some records. But here, all such communication, company and movement was locked in the past. For two days on Changabang the only motivating, all-consuming purpose had been to climb the Barrier.

We now had three ropes left between us — once we had used those up, we would have run out 1,700 feet, including all our climbing ropes. It was a long way to jumar back up on the morning of the 24th September.

"It's a good thing we haven't much more rope," said Joe as we left. "We've got to stop soon or we'll use all our time and energy up jumaring. Also, if we keep on going backwards and forwards through the Toni Kurz pitch and past the Guillotine, sooner or later one of us is bound to make a mistake going past all those knots and pegs and unclip the wrong thing."

"We'll move up with the hammocks and pull the ropes up tomorrow," I said. "There aren't many camp sites up here."

Three hours later we reached our high point of the previous day. We were carrying very heavy loads, since we were taking food and equipment to leave at the high point in preparation for the big move the next day. The rope length next to the Guillotine which we had straightened out the previous day was exhausting, since we were hanging free. Here, we had tied off our climbing ropes and these, being nylon, stretched and bounced us up and down in the air like helpless puppets as we jerked our jumars up. I switched my mind off to the possibility of rope abrasion or anchor failure and kept toiling upwards.

To lead brings excitement and draws hidden strength; to follow relaxes, then enervates. The situations were spectacular and I was taking photographs furiously, to try and recapture the scenes of the previous day's dropped film. Joe moved quickly and dynamically up the ice and I envied him the liberation of movement that the change in angle of reaching the icefield brought. For the first time I felt closely involved with his leading, because there was much action to watch and, because of the scanty protection, the consequences of a fall would have been disastrous.

"The icefield was a bottle-green, repulsive colour, several hundred feet to the top. Rather than climb directly up the ice, I climbed to the left, where rock showed through. It was less fatiguing than tip-toeing up hard ice. The rock was poor and shattered if I tried to hammer in a peg. Frequently, as I teetered precariously up, I had to make wild moves to escape from a crumbling hold and grab something else, which might be only marginally more sound. All the time a prohibition on falling drummed inside my head. I was more exhausted from the nervous tension involved than from the physical exertion. From the top of a slab of rock I hooked my axe into the ice above, stretching as far as possible to reach beyond where the ice was just a veneer over hidden rock. By an awkward manœuvre, I put on my crampons and was now equipped to perform in the medium of ice for the last hundred feet up to the top rim of the icefield and the base of the huge upper tower of rock up which we next had to find a way."

Jumaring after Joe was a nightmarish struggle. I had to jumar up the nylon ropes for fifteen feet to take in the stretch before I could start gaining height. Joe was leading without a sack, so I was carrying all the equipment in mine, and it pulled me back continually. With the sack on my back, like a crippling symbolic burden of sin, every step demanded a conscious effort of will power. The settled weather was beginning to break up and clouds were swirling up onto the icefield from lower down on the Face. It was snowing lightly. But the weather was irrelevant to my enclosed world. I kept on collapsing for a rest on my forearm, hand gripping the jumar. The altitude was affecting me far more than it had done up until that point in the climb.

Joe was waiting for me at the top of the rope, looking around, watching my struggle. To my inner world he seemed remote, complete, disgustingly refreshed, seemingly unaffected by human weaknesses. Every time I collapsed I could hear his camera clicking as he took photographs of me. A great wave of emotion engulfed me. I remembered hearing some friends in Manchester commenting about Joe's lecture on Dunagiri. He had shown slides of Dick collapsed, flat on his back, on the summit ridge. They had thought it in bad taste. The camera does not lie—it is cold and factual, and unmoved. And yet the person behind the camera, clicking the shutter, seems to take on some of its qualities. Joe seemed to be obsessed with recording everything that happened, everything that I did. What was he going to do with the pictures? Give a lecture on 'How I took Boardman up Changabang'? In the heat of suspicion I gasped as loudly as I could, "If you take another picture like that, I'll thump you."

As soon as I had said it, the balloon of my ego deflated. When I reached Joe, I tried to explain. He was cold, perhaps shocked. I wished I hadn't bothered explaining, I lost respect. So I hardened—we had to stay within our shells to do this climb. Joe was astounded and appalled by the incident:

"It is true that we were on edge, but it amazed me that his anger should be so close to the surface. Under stress there are always a thousand assumed reasons for losing one's temper, but in one's mind it is clear that they are only the product of the circumstances and one holds back. Peter, for reasons which I did not understand, displayed his anger and I was alarmed that he should be so childish. I wondered if he was worried about his image after Everest, and whether he believed in all the bullshit which goes with being in the public eye.

"The incident was a minor one, and this was not the place for an argument."

By mid-afternoon, Joe had run out the three rope lengths. We put all the food, Gaz canisters and hardware we had brought with us into a green bivouac sack and attached it to the anchor. I set off down first. The clouds were boiling up beneath our feet and through them we could see the Rhamani Glacier in the shadow of encroaching darkness. Rishi Kot was shifting moods and colours with the moving clouds and setting sun. The lighting around us had a hypnotic effect. The relaxed feeling of sliding down the ropes without a burden, untrammelled and free, brought a sense of release to my mind, already dazed with altitude and fatigued after the day's effort. Nothing worried me, I felt that if the anchors came away or the ropes snapped I would just float down onto a cushion of clouds.

The big swing from the foot of the icefield, past the Guillotine, down a rope with an awkward knot half way, brought my senses back. *Tous les grandes chefs sont tues en rappels*. All the greatest climbers are killed abseiling! The phrase had been in the very first book on mountaineering techniques I had read when I was fourteen years old. The phrase echoed around my head as I lurched down through the Toni Kurz pitch. The discipline had returned, once more the knot and rope systems were being checked with constant care. The sun had disappeared and I descended through a cold and clinical world to the camp. It had been a long day, and we had been a long way up the mountain.

That night the wind started again.

At dawn, on the morning of the 26th September, I woke feeling tired and stale. The tent and the mountain were in cloud and it was windy. It did not take much discussion to decide to call it a rest day. But having made that decision, I felt uneasy. We were eating valuable food and, even more important psychologically, we were losing the upwards momentum we had sustained so far. Joe, however, once the decision had been made, resigned himself to it, closed his eyes and drifted off into a somnolent haze. At first I was surprised at his firmness, then I envied him. I decided I could only follow suit and engrossed myself in the gripping, escapist world of *Night Runners of Bengal*. An afternoon snowfall reinforced our decision and by dusk there was no change in the weather. After our evening meal, we set the alarm for 5.00 a.m., hoping that the big move would get under way then.

Breakfast postponed the decision. We were rationalising, trying to be realistic—and we were weakening. The weather was still uncertain and so were we. The mist had cleared from around the mountain but the sky was white with high clouds.

"It's almost impossible to read the weather here," I said. "I mean, if you saw cirrus like that in the Alps you'd think there was a monster front coming in, but here it's impossible to tell."

"It'll be a bit committing to be stuck up on the icefield, having taken all the ropes away, if really bad weather comes in," said Joe.

The problem was being thrashed out, openly and directly. We were both saying exactly what we thought.

"We could stay here as long as we liked if we had a string of porters bringing us food all the time," I said, "but I'm not sure we've got enough food up here to do the route anyway."

"There's bugger-all at Advance Camp," said Joe.

"Well, we're certainly low on sugar and bog paper," I said.

"That sounds critical," Joe replied. "Somebody might have arrived as Base Camp by now," he added.

"We've made steady progress every day—it'd do us good to have a change of scene. We could bomb down to Base Camp this morning if we set off now, pick some things up and then come back up to Advance Camp this afternoon. Then tomorrow we could quickly move back up to here and start the big move. We'd have only lost a day!" I had voiced the suggestion, but it had not been mine. It had evolved, naturally, from discussion as our decision.

Climbing down the creaking icefield was a new sensation of climbing concentration, after all the roped technicalities of the previous days. Once we were walking along the moraine, we were astonished to find ourselves feeling weak and beginning to tire. Perhaps our limbs were not used to horizontal walking—we were staggering clumsily from rock to rock. The mountain began to look remote and hostile. Through the binoculars, at Advance Camp we could pick out the line we had taken through the Barrier and up the icefield. The cache of the bivouac sack was the only sign of our visit we could see. It was a mere speck at 20,000 feet—3,000 feet above us, 2,500 feet below the summit. Our progress, our high point of which we had previously been so proud, began to look pathetically lower down the mountain the further we moved away from it. All the earlier doubts flooded back. The sun began to shine mockingly down on our retreat. We became hot and dumped some of our clothing under a rock before carrying on. Turning down the moraine valley, towards Base Camp, was like turning down one's home street. I could recognise every boulder. The Base Camp tent was tucked around a corner and it was impossible to see it until you were only a hundred yards away. Hungry for company, we lurched round the corner. No one was there. Even our note was undisturbed. Nobody had passed that way during the previous ten days.

We cooked an enormous meal, drained some of a bottle of Indian Lion Rum, and lay about on the grass. Nothing had changed, everything was as we had left it — except the little stream next to the tent had dried up. We agreed it was over-optimistic to think we could go back to Advance Camp that afternoon. Joe flopped back on the grass under the tent awning, leaning against a rucksack, his sun-hat tilted over his eyes, like someone on the sidewalk of some sleepy Wild West town at high noon.

"Just think," he said, "it was a year ago yesterday when you climbed Everest." I had not realised until then. Everest had dropped from my mind.

CHAPTER FIVE

Survival

28th September–2nd October

"I'd better have a wash and put on some clean underpants for the summit," said Joe. "You never know what might happen."

"You might get knocked over by a bus," I suggested.

We were trying to sort ourselves out for the walk back up to Advance Camp but the task was, as usual, expanding to fit the time available and it was three in the afternoon by the time we gained the impetus to leave Base Camp.

What day of the week was it? Ah, Tuesday. Tuesday, 28th September. That made it three weeks since we had arrived at Base Camp and nineteen days since Hans had left. Before leaving I unearthed my 'fixtures' diary. I glanced down at all the committee meetings I had missed in Britain and tried to link them with events on the mountain, hoping that the process would grind my fixation on our climb into some sort of framework of reality. It was as much use as reading an old newspaper.

As we reached the head of the moraine valley, snow started flying about in the air in showers and a cold wind blew up from the direction of the Rishi Gorge. We sheltered by an enormous boulder, about twenty feet high, perched on the moraine. Joe said he thought we ought to go back to Base Camp, arguing that the weather-pattern was completely unsettled and that Changabang had a lot more snow on it than before. I said that he was being influenced by the fact that we were in an isolated snow shower and we had a lot of them in the afternoons — that Changabang looked unchanged and, anyway, always shook off fresh snow quickly. We would never get up the climb if we lost our upwards momentum and kept on turning back at every opportunity. I was trying to argue the case rationally, but I felt guilty that we had wasted two days and, at the same time, felt an unreasoning impulse to get back into the mountain to see if the conditions could force us back down. It was a difficult situation and, although on the surface very calm, was the first tactical disagreement we had had. Neither of us knew if we were arguing from a balanced evaluation or an irrational urge. I had the morally stronger position because I was arguing for the more positive move. Yet I knew Joe well enough to respect his judgement, and quickly suppressed a momentary worry that his motivation was weakening. Perhaps it was I who was choosing the easy way out? Eventually, we decided to carry on to Advance Camp and to assess the situation from there. The decision had been made and neither of us referred to it again.

Once on the glacier, we were slowly overtaken by darkness as we searched for the clothing we had left under a rock on the way down the mountain. We had marked the rock with a cairn, but had forgotten which of the three parallel glacial moraines we had left them on. It took us an hour of wandering up and down before we eventually found them in the moonlight. It was bitterly cold.

"Bloody sweep searches," said Joe. "It's like being on a mountain rescue training course."

I was obsessed with the plot of *Night Runners of Bengal*. Thinking that we were coming back up straight away, I had left the book at Advance Camp. On arriving there I picked it up immediately. I didn't want to risk taking it up to Camp One and failing to finish it. It was too heavy to take on the route and I thought I might never see it again, since it was unlikely that we would be going back up the creaking slope to collect gear after we had climbed the route and descended the other side of the mountain. Joe was irritated at the waste of torch-battery power, for whilst he was preparing the evening meal, I was reading the end of the book to find out what happened. If the battery had faded, I would have been desperately concerned—I was so involved with the book that it would have been a mishap on a par with a small boy losing a bag of sweets. Changabang had made me vulnerable to roads of escapism.

The icefields on the slope up to the ridge camp were shrinking. Large areas of rock and rubble were uncovered. Where the ice managed to cover the rock, it was thin and unstable. It was a taxing climb, trying to select the safest-looking route up this increasingly dangerous ground. The relief on reaching the Ridge and wandering along it to Camp One was greater than usual.

We reached the Ridge Camp early and started the lengthy packing of all our equipment. We planned food for at least six days. Once we were bivouacking in hammocks, our organisation would have to be faultless. We sorted all the different meals into independent stuff bags, then marked them heavily in Biro—'Breakfast', 'Supper', 'Brews', 'Day food'. One of the stuff bags we marked with a big cross and after much discussion, compiled a first aid kit for the climb, including Ronicol for frostbite, Dalmane sleeping pills and Valium tranquillisers, and some ampoules of Omnipon as a painkiller in case something disastrous happened.

Once we had packed all the food, two sleeping bags each, hammocks, fuel and the remaining hardware, our sacks were stacked so high they reached chest height when stood on the ground. They weighed about sixty pounds each.

Afternoon was well established when we eventually started. It was windy but no snow was falling. Innocently, we were encouraging each other forward on a wave of optimism, thinking it would take us only three hours to reach the top of the fixed ropes, including pulling the ropes in after us.

Joe set off first and I followed. It was soon apparent that the sacks were too heavy and that we were not well rested. After I had coiled three ropes from behind us and pulled another one up, I was very tired. With my enormous sack, and ropes draped all over my shoulders, I could hardly move my jumars. I was clipping them past a peg when a jerk wrenched me backwards and sideways. I grabbed the rope to steady myself. The stitching on one of the shoulder-straps of my ruck-sack had ripped undone—the sack had toppled over and was now hanging from one shoulder and my waist strap. It took a long, awkward time to improvise a new attachment. Snow was now starting to fall, wind whipped. Above me, five rope lengths up from the Ridge Camp, Joe was hunched against the wind, waiting for me.

I had done this before, in the Alps, in the Hindu Kush—stubbornly pushed myself into a situation and then watched myself trying to get out of it, fighting it out. I stopped, gasping with the load, and looked up at Joe, wondering what he was thinking, what motivated him. Perhaps I was just being over-dramatic, too subjective, and Joe was feeling calm, objective and factual.

We were both thinking upwards; to retreat for the night whilst only five pitches up, might have been an easy physical move to make then. But that would have been an impossible decision to make, for we had not yet hit the mountain with everything we had.

How else could we learn?

"We might as well stop here for the night," said Joe. "We'll never get up to the Balcony before it gets dark."

"We'd better try and get some food and drink down us before getting into our hammocks," I said, "and you have got the stove."

I was convinced that Joe, the master of Alpine winter and Himalayan bivouacking, would be able to sort out a meal and a comfortable night. I was sitting in slings; Joe was standing on the top of a rock spike. Calmly, and methodically, he unpacked the tower stove and pan and the brew materials, clipping everything on as he progressed. I watched, fascinated, as he clipped his blue polythene one-pint mug onto his harness. Blue harness, blue oversuit, blue mug – they all matched! I got my mug out and did the same. The mugs looked strangely incongruous, spattered occasionally with gusts of spindrift, hanging below our frozen beards. They looked pathetically expectant, like Oliver Twists in a queue. Joe hacked a little shelf out of the ice and balanced the stove on it. The Gaz was reluctant to light and spluttered ineffectively. Joe had a struggle melting the ice and snow, keeping the flame sheltered from the wind and balancing the pan over it. I noticed him burn a gaping hole in his mitt, but he did not mention it. 'If you've got a job to do, you just get on and do it.' I remembered he had said that sometime in the meaningless past. After two hours he served two lukewarm mugs of Oxo. We gulped them down within a few seconds. We could not stand the wind and cold much longer and decided to munch chocolate and marzipan for our meal, and to get into the hammocks as soon as possible. It was growing dark and the Salford fridge of our dress rehearsals seemed far away.

"I'll hang off the fixed rope and be the first floor," said Joe.

"The necky bugger," I thought. "He's going to hang all night off that eight-millimetre terylene. What if it gets chopped by a falling rock from above? He won't even have a back-up system."

The spike below looked much the safer alternative for me to hang from, although it would hardly feel like the ground floor. It wasn't my role to voice my worries to Joe – perhaps I was just thinking soft thoughts that didn't dare creep into his mind! Once I was fighting to sort out my hammock and its cowl, I was back in the world by myself. Joe was isolated four feet of vertical space away by his identical, but individual, struggle:

"Snow was everywhere. This was real – no simple exit through a cold store for a warm cup of tea, a chat with a security guard

and a drive home for some 'proper sleep'. . . In the cold confusion
I found that I was lying in my hammock with my crampons still
on; they were tearing at the fabric. It was essential to fasten the
straps of the canopy beneath the hammock, to keep the wind
out—one of my straps snapped."

Everywhere there were bits of hammock, ropes and slings. It took a
long time to get inside. The movements were exhausting and the altitude made me gasp for air—and there was not much of that available,
once I had pulled the cowl down. I had only two karabiners and it was
difficult to decide how to use them—to clip gear or myself on? Taking
my boots off was absurdly acrobatic. I had to raise my legs vertically
upwards inside the roof of the cowl to reach them whilst lying flat on
my back. The thrashing movements that this entailed gave me the
shuddering thought that if the stitching came apart, I would burst
through the bottom and plunge two thousand feet. My life was hanging
on the threads of an Oldham seamstress. Once the boots were fastened
by their laces from a sling in the ceiling, I started worrying that one of
the laces would snap. Without boots I would be helpless. I could not
continue the adventure in stocking-feet!

The next problem was to unpack and shuffle inside the duvet and
the two sleeping bags. In taking the terylene sleeping bag out, its stuff
bag slipped between my fingers and fell out of the hammock. I yelped
out loud, my nerves on edge. I was loud enough to reach Joe above the
roar of the wind.

"What's up?" he shouted.

"Oh, I've just dropped my stuff bag," I called back, cursing myself
for a typical, over-dramatic reaction.

After much wriggling and squirming, I got the sleeping bags pulled
up round my shoulders. It had taken one and a half hours to get
established. I nibbled some chocolate, trying to close off my mind to
the situation. Unfortunately, we had taken our spacer bars up to the
high point and left them there; with nothing to hold the sides of the
hammocks apart, they held us in a vice-like grip, inhibiting breathing
and movement. I took a sleeping pill, which helped me drift in and out
of consciousness through the following twelve hours of darkness.
Each time I woke, it was with a shock to realise where I was. On one
occasion I had to poke my head out from beneath the cowl to breathe
some more oxygenated air. I was greeted with a faceful of spindrift.
Ten feet above me, I could see the hanging black sausage shape of Joe,

and beyond that the dark outline of the Wall and Summit Ridges of Changabang. There was no problem of perspective on this mountain—it just towered over us. Beyond the ridges, clouds paced across the moon, hiding me from its light. Through gaps in the clouds I could see occasional pinpoints of stars. 'If you can see a single star, then set out!' went the saying. I hunched back inside the hammock, trying to conserve heat. A wry undercurrent of self-parody appeared in my mind and suddenly helped me realise that, against all reason, I was in control.

Dawn came to us independently:

"The night was endless, uneasy and cold; the hours to movement and warmth seemed infinitely long. Any change seemed desirable, our situation could not have been worse.

"Showers of spindrift poured down, squirting through the gaps between the cowl and the hammock, my feet were protruding and were numb and I was very uncomfortable. But one can adjust to almost anything.

"Morning was a subtle shift in the darkness to a greyness, then light. There was no incentive to move. I was relieved that the long journey through the night was over, but the world outside was unattractive."

There was no relief from the powerful gusts of wind, which were playing with a myriad of ice crystals—throwing them up and down the Wall at random. It had stopped snowing but it felt as if it still was. The sun, if the clouds stayed out of the way, would not be on us until 11.30 a.m. The clouds were ominously dark over the Garhwal. I wondered if Joe would move. My mind was shirking from any decision, but felt concerned at the same time because, going on the previous day's pace, we had an energetic day ahead of us.

"Hey, Joe," I shouted above the wind. "Shall we get up?"

There was no response. I shouted the same thing again—louder.

"What?"

"Shall we get up?"

"Yeah."

He sounded strange when he shouted, it was a side of his voice I rarely heard. I could not imagine him shouting except when compelled to because of communication difficulties.

I had imagined that Joe, being organised on bivouacs, would soon be ready. He had not much respect for my bivouacking ability. I always used to reply to his taunts at my disorganisation by saying that the only reason he was so experienced at bivouacking was because he always climbed so slowly and had to spend a lot of nights out on the mountains. That morning, I thought, I would dress and pack quickly. I slipped out of the sleeping bags and pulled on my boots above my head, after extricating them from the tangle of equipment that hung from the various loops inside the hammock. I left the duvet jacket on, it was so cold. I decided to pack my sleeping bags and tighten my boot-laces once I was standing up outside. Gently, I eased myself out of the end of the hammock and put my feet into the slings I had left there the previous day.

The wind was gusting up to about fifty miles per hour. I removed my outer mitts and, with my fingered gloves and fingerless mitts on, quickly stuffed the sleeping bags away, bundled the hammock into my sack and started doing up the laces of my inner and outer boots. I had had my overmitts off for about five minutes by the time I had finished. Then I realised—some of my finger-ends had gone hard and I couldn't feel them. I cursed myself—normally I was more careful than that. I tried blowing warm breath onto my fingers, but it was no use. Then I unzipped my oversuit and pile jacket and thrust my arms across my chest and my fingers deep into my armpits. Slowly, some circulation returned, but I knew some damage had been done. I had done something similar to my fingers on the South Summit of Everest whilst mending some oxygen equipment, but there the wind had taken one and a half hours to injure me; this time it had happened at more brutal speed.

Above me there was energetic pushing and bulging inside Joe's red hammock. It reminded me of the picture of Winnie the Pooh in the story where Wol's house falls down and Piglet is struggling, com-pletely disorientated, underneath the carpet. After an hour, Joe emerged. He was completely dressed and packed, except for his hammock, and looked obscenely warm.

"I've got frost nip," I announced.

"What's that?"

"It's like what Dick got, except not as bad—I hope. Don't worry, it won't stop me."

Joe was winning at bivouacking.

I was embarrassed about my fingers. Joe was concerned:

"It could have been that the Expedition was finished. By all
appearances the hardest half of the mountain was yet to come and
a lot more damage could happen to Pete's fingers in the next few
days . . . But his determination was an indication that in spite of
any petty, irrelevant antagonisms and animosity, we had not lost
sight of the fact that we were here to climb the mountain."

Our attempts to cook breakfast were a fiasco and soon had to be
abandoned. We could not even light the stove. Hoping that it might be
warm and sheltered in the afternoon, on the icefield, we decided to
press on. We both knew about the debilitating effect that going for
long at this sort of altitude, without food or drink, would have. Without six pints of fluid a day, we would become dehydrated and, without
necessarily realising it, become weaker and start making irrational,
potentially dangerous decisions. It's easy, when climbing at high altitude, to become blinkered, to hold one fixed purpose in your mind,
but to be unable to allow any changes in weather or your fitness
to influence you.

I jumared a rope length ahead of Joe. By the time I had reached the
Balcony my hands were numb again. I knew that my only hope in
retaining some use in them lay in painstakingly doing my best to warm
them. For three-quarters of an hour on the Balcony, I blew on them,
put them under my armpits, under my crutch. By the time Joe had
arrived I knew that three fingers were virtually useless.

The sun had broken through the cloud and was shining down at me
from the South-West Ridge as I started up the Toni Kurz pitch. Spindrift was cascading down the icefield and bursting over its edge. By
the time it reached the beams of sunlight touching the edge of the
Balcony, it was dispersed by cushions and up-draughts of air. It hovered
all around me, in a million sparkling points of light, dazzling me as I
looked over my shoulder across the sweep of the Wall. At first its
beauty mocked me, like the forced gaiety of the tinsel finale of a
television spectacular. Then it allured and drew me out of myself—this
beauty was inhuman, but it was not petty, grasping or transitory. I
could appreciate it, despite the hardship I was enduring.

Soon it was the sack that started to develop a personality. As I
lurched up the Tony Kurz pitch it would swing about and catch on the
overhangs, and then try to topple me backwards as I was stretching
upwards to clip past a peg. I began to hate it for its obstinacy, its un-
wieldiness. I was sure that the weight of the sack, combined with mine,

would pull a peg out or even snap the rope. As I moved around the last roof to join the ramp, I swung out uncontrollably and struggled with my feet to keep my balance.

"This is desperate," I yelled to Joe. "I'm going to dump some of the gear on this stance."

In a brief, shouted conversation, we agreed to take a couple of days' food to the high point, run out the three hundred feet of terylene rope we had retrieved, and then come back down and pick up the dumped gear and remaining ropes sometime later. Joe must have been feeling the strain too. By the time I had finished re-sorting the stuff sacks and had clipped some onto the stance to leave, Joe swung around the corner onto the rampline—he had left his cache on the Balcony.

The overhanging jumar by the side of the Guillotine seemed appallingly steep. The rope lengths up the side of the icefield seemed to last forever. I was moving up them so slowly that the stretch of the rope seemed to be absorbing all my efforts. The top of the ropes never came nearer, the ice never moved past my side and the ridges of the mountains around me did not become any lower. I was in a semi-daze and my movements were as jerky as a clockwork toy. The afternoon was slipping past. Clouds filled the trough of the Rhamani Glacier whilst we were touched with sunlight above them. But, scoured by the icy wind, we felt no warmth.

Late in the afternoon I arrived at the high point. The gear was still intact in the green bag. When Joe arrived he went straight into the lead. It was now nearly a week since we had gained any new ground and this had some thin taste of progress. The icefield was now petering out into the slabs that lined the foot of the Upper Tower. Joe reached the top of the ice and started climbing a crack that tilted diagonally across the slab. Since there were no holds on either side of the crack, he either leant along the crack, jamming his feet, or swung off onto the holdless slab below and, bracing with his feet against the slab, slid his hands up the crack. When he was fifty feet up it started to hail. Soon everywhere was white and I could hardly see him. Hailstones were bouncing and rushing down the slabs in torrents. I heard the sound of a peg going in. My eyes screwed up with the effort of peering up through the splintering hail at the dark shape of Joe, and I gripped the rope tightly. But he could look after himself. He lowered himself down and swung in next to me.

"It's just a shower," he said. "I'll get back up there tomorrow."

We pulled the hoods of our oversuits over our heads and leant in against the rock, looking down at our feet. Ten minutes later the hail had stopped falling from the sky, but on the mountain it was still moving. Changabang was shaking itself clear. Soon the shower was brushed away, just a memory for us, an irrelevance for the mountain.

There was nothing to discuss. A small rock buttress was sticking out of the ice. We moved ten feet apart and hacked ourselves steps in the ice and slammed in three pegs each, from which we proceeded to suspend our hammocks. We could now retrieve the spacer bars, so the hammocks would not restrict our breathing as much as the night before. As it was too windy to cook, we just struggled into our wobbling shelters.

We knew we were steadily deteriorating, but could not realise to what extent. There was no objective standard from which to judge. Vaguely, we assumed that if we kept on going upwards, things would right themselves eventually, and that the wind would drop soon. I was exhausted, but did not tell Joe and he did not tell me how he felt. That was the unspoken part of the game. If he did not give up, I would not. That night I dreamt of a warm, toasting, tropical beach with a hot sun high in the sky and not a breath of wind.

I do not know if it snowed or if it hailed that night, but the wind seemed alive, tearing and lashing us with spindrift. Avalanches rumbled past us, like distant trains in the night. Fortunately, we were on the left-hand edge of the icefield and missed their full force, being protected from the funnel above the icefield by the Upper Tower. At dawn they were still roaring past us. They were not killers though; Changabang was too steep a mountain to accumulate enough snow to crush us and sweep us off its sides.

The cold was seeping into my bones. It was not the cold of contrast that you feel in urban life, that makes you shiver when you move from inside to outside a building. This cold was gnawing at me from all directions.

"Shall we wait for the sun before we move?" I shouted.

Joe agreed. I knew I could not afford to lose the body heat that getting out of the sleeping bags into the morning wind would entail. Was I being decisive, I wondered, or was he just waiting for me to make the weak decision?

It was a long morning and the awaited sun brought no comfort. It was a false reprieve. Once we were out of the hammocks, I helped Joe shelter the flame whilst he melted snow over the stove to make a fruit drink. It took such a long time to melt that we did not wait for it to warm up, but drank it straight away. I levered open a tin of fish. Inside, the fish were frozen to their sauce and tasteless, but we forced them down our throats, knowing that if we did not at least try to eat, our efforts were doomed.

The day was moving into the afternoon and Joe finished the pitch which he had begun the day before, running out 150 feet of rope.

"Right," shouted Joe. It was the nearest word he ever used to the rigorous ritual of five climbing calls taught in the mountaineering centres back in Britain. When I left the stance, I realised I had been on the same few square feet of mountain for twenty-four hours. On reaching Joe I was disappointed to discover that he had found no ledges.

"Look," he said, "we're level with where the Japanese Ridge starts levelling out."

Our altimeter had stopped working many days before on the ridge, and we could only assess our progress by looking across at the mountains around us. With the scholastic documentation typical of Japanese climbers, the leader of the South-West Ridge Expedition had sent us a detailed 'topo' of their route, and we used this to assess our altitude. It was exciting how much just one new rope length opened out the view.

We had decided that I should run out the next and only rope length we had with us, but it was too late. "I'll lead it in the morning before we go back down to pick the gear up," I said.

"It's your turn to cook," said Joe firmly. "I've done all the messing about with the stove for the last two days."

I took the orders and he handed the stove over to me. We had some footholds large enough to stand on comfortably, and I tried to cut a sheltered perch for the stove in some ice on the rock at waist level. By the time I had the stove firmly upon this, it was dark. It took half an hour and a whole box of matches to light the stove in the wind. I managed to melt a panful of water but it would not get hot enough to dissolve the Oxo cubes to make a meat drink. So I chewed up two Oxo cubes in my mouth and spat them into the pan. Joe was trying to shield the stove with one of his bivouac bags, but the air kept on blowing around or underneath it. The freeze-dried meal — our favourite, Chilli with Beans — refused to boil and was quickly swallowed half cooked. It had taken two hours in the darkness to prepare a few mouthfuls.

An hour later we were lying in our hammocks. What was it I had been told as a child? If you cannot get to sleep, then just think pleasant thoughts, think about nice things. Dreams were a pleasant escape.

Soon I was back in a day during my school summer holidays. Outside it was pouring torrentially, with rain lashing the window and making me feel snug and warm and protected. There was no one on the streets outside. The world was indoors. I was lying on my bed, reading a book. Then the window smashed open with supernatural force; curtains flew and papers scattered everywhere. I woke up. The hammock cowl was inflated like a balloon, clear of the spacer bars and I was swinging out from the rock. The wind had veered and was now gusting from below. I fought my arms clear from the sleeping bags and grabbed the fabric which was billowing and crackling hysterically. With some spare bootlace, I reinforced the clips that were supposed to be keeping the cowl down. In doing so I lost so much heat I had to move quickly back inside the bags and resign myself to the wind blowing the cowl off my feet. I concentrated on wriggling my toes, hoping to fight off the cold. The spindrift seemed to have stopped finding us, perhaps because we were above the icefield, but the wind was veering and accelerating, snapping around us angrily, finding the chinks in our defences. It was an exhausting night and I could not sleep.

Three days and nights we had passed with virtually nothing to eat or drink. Surely we could not last much longer. At dawn something snapped inside me.

Descent was the obvious decision. I never thought otherwise. What would we prove by staying just to squeeze out another rope length? After it had taken me an hour to get out of my hammock, I stuffed it and one of the sleeping bags into the green bivouac bag to leave behind, and started to prepare to set off abseiling down. I knew if I stayed any longer above the icefield, even though the weather looked as if it might be settling, I would suffer from the exposure and frostbite that had already set in. Joe looked across at me.

"What are you doing?" he asked.

"I'm going down of course," I answered.

It seemed so obvious, all my instincts were telling me to get down fast.

"That's the bloody trouble with you," Joe exclaimed. "You're always changing your mind."

"You're joking, aren't you?" I asked, incredulous. "You don't think I'm going to do any leading after a night like that? I think we should bomb straight down to Base Camp, leaving as much gear as possible up here. We'll just burn ourselves out if we stay on the Wall any longer. We'll just need a bit of rope to abseil the section we've cleaned lower down."

"Just keep me informed," said Joe, and offered to go down first, so that he could sort out the ropes. My frostnip was making fiddly finger work difficult. We did not even discuss where we were going down to, but Joe had not argued:

> "Retreat was so welcoming. We were living from moment to moment. There was no promise of coming back, the way to live the next few moments was to descend, thaw out, eat and relax."

The icefield drifted past in the soft shapes of a dream; my mind was as numb as my finger-ends. I felt on the brink of fainting. Soon I was moving past the knot next to the Guillotine. It was a complex man-œuvre involving clipping the jumars above the knot, taking off the descendeur and placing it below, then replacing the jumars below the knot. I gathered all my concentration and started reaching into a grim recess of my mind. Yes, the iron was there if I needed it. The Toni Kurz pitch went slowly, but without any problems.

Quickly, Joe refixed the ropes down to Camp One, and I followed. Three rope lengths above the camp, I was changing over my descendeur past a piton anchor when it slipped out of my fingers. It bounced off, down the Wall. We had not any spares. I fumbled for some karabiners and clipped six of them together and across each other on the rope to form a friction brake.

The sun was warm on the tent when I arrived and Joe's feet were sticking out of the entrance. He was asleep.

"Where's the brew then?"

"There's no pan."

"What about the dried milk tin, that should do?"

I crawled into the still air of the tent. The sun had warmed the inside. It was the first time I had been in a warm atmosphere since we had packed the stuff bags there, three days before—it seemed a lifetime. We packed some snow into the tin on the stove. It melted effortlessly over the flame. Civilisation at last. I lay back drowsily. Then I started up. My fingers were shooting with agonising pain—the circulation was beginning to return. They throbbed, bringing tears to my eyes.

"Does it hurt?" asked Joe.

"Only when I larf," I said through gritted teeth, inwardly rationalising that the injury was not serious.

Joe was very sympathetic and dug out some Fortral painkilling tablets from the first aid kit.

"You're supposed to be able to crunch these like Smarties without much effect, aren't you?" I asked.

"Dick used them for his fingers and thought they helped," he replied. "You don't want morphine, do you?"

"No, it's not that bad. It's only like a bad dose of aches. It'll wear off in a minute!" And so it did; but my finger-ends felt very tender and I still could not feel the ends of three of them.

The blackcurrant drink, when it was ready, was the best drink I had ever tasted. I rolled it around in my mouth like a refugee from the desert.

As I stood up and moved along the ridge towards the ice slope, I tottered slightly.

"You all right?" asked Joe.

I was beginning to see a new side to his personality. 'He can be kind and considerate,' I thought. "I'm feeling a bit dizzy," I admitted.

Joe had a pill ready for every ill. "Here, try one of these Vertigon," he said. "I used them coming down off Dunagiri and they seemed to help."

The ice slope went past mechanically and I was past caring about its creaks and groans. Advance Camp was a haven when we eventually staggered into it. We polished off the only food that was left there—some rice and a tin of corned beef—and stayed for the night. Base Camp could wait. *Night Runners of Bengal* was lying on the groundsheet, where I had left it. I remembered that I had thought I would have returned to it over Shipton's Col. I opened it and read through the parts I had skipped past before. I lost myself by candlelight in the Indian Mutiny until my eyes closed to sleep. Changabang was far away.

CHAPTER SIX

Recovery

3rd–8th October

There was no breakfast on the 3rd October. All day stretched ahead, offering plenty of time to move down to Base Camp. Joe decided he would photograph the Upper Tower of Changabang as the morning sun moved onto it. The left-hand edge of the West Wall, the line we wanted to follow, was usually picked out in the morning if the clouds behaved themselves. He collected all his camera equipment together, and moved across the fresh snow of the glacier. 'The last time he was over there,' I thought, 'was when he was coming down from Dunagiri.' That was when he took the photographs of the West Wall that were to fascinate him so much later. He had taken them automatically, whilst hallucinating through lack of food, just as some sort of a record. To him and Dick on Dunagiri, Changabang had been simply the mountain that prevented the early morning sun from reaching them. Now it was the mountain that nothing would stop him from climbing. He was so confident that we would climb the Upper Tower, he was recording the scene before the adventure occurred. 'That's professionalism,' I thought, and admired him for it. I was impressed that he was already thinking about climbing, after our recent epic, when all I wanted was a rest. As he moved further away into the distance, the tracks behind him wavered around haphazardly in the snow. 'He's not completely fit then,' I thought with relief.

It was half past eleven before I moved off along the familiar route back to Base Camp. 'Perhaps the Americans will be down there,' I thought, as I turned down 'our valley'. There was a strange feeling about the ground as I walked down by the side of the moraine, but I couldn't decide whether or not all the scuff marks had been made by Joe and me previously. Perhaps some animal had made them. Small stones had been disturbed in places; every few feet I noticed something subtly different. I felt rather apprehensive as I turned around the corner to Base Camp. As usual, the mist was down and Bleak House looked eerie as I approached it. Nothing was disturbed. Not even our message to passers-by had been moved. I rummaged through the boxes and eventually rooted out a much-missed Mars Bar, and gobbled it down. I had been longing for it!

The brew I had put on the stove was just beginning to come to the boil when Joe arrived.

"Did you notice anything different about the valley on your way down?" I asked.

No, he had not. We cracked open the bottle of whisky and lounged about, both feeling chatty and relaxed but 'spaced out' after the effort of the previous days. I washed and bathed my fingers in antiseptic solution and bandaged them up, whilst Joe cooked a meal. I started on a course of Septrin to ward off infection. Unlimited food, unlimited brews—this was Heaven. We had brought the smallest and most effective primus down, and this purred continuously, producing a succession of drinks, steamed puddings and large meals.

The relaxation and 'restoring' of our stomachs continued all the next day at Base Camp. Without discussing the future, we savoured the security, warmth and ease of life on level ground.

Joe was a master of the anecdote. He would deliver one in a relaxed, comfortable way, and it nearly always had a subtle little twist or point at the end. They were never particularly self-revealing, although he always emerged in them as the normal person who gets involved in weird and wonderful places and events, or in dangerous situations. On the 4th October at Base Camp he prattled on amusingly between bouts of eating and reading. He always refused to philosophise, to try and draw any hard kernel of moral or ethical point from his stories. It was as if he always fought shy of intensity in conversation. I did the same. His stories stood alone. The rest was up to me. Often he would repeat a story I had heard once, or even twice before, or had read in one of his mountaineering articles. I did not mention it to him—I was probably doing the same! We rarely probed each other about details of our private lives—if either wanted to mention anything, it was up to him. I envied Joe the number of contacts he had gained in the mountaineering world, that he had acquired on the sheer strength of his achievements and personality. He was truly 'one of the lads'. I had come to know people, I sometimes felt, more through my position as National Officer of the British Mountaineering Council. I could never seem to get involved in the close-knit mateyness of the climbing social world, which always seemed to be designed to repress as much as it expressed.

Joe was a strange mixture of ruthlessness and consideration. Occasionally he would make extraordinary gestures of thoughtfulness. However, there were just two of us; we had to share tasks, and often by confrontation, he would manipulate me into doing something — small things, like fetching the water or cooking the next meal — that I would otherwise have sat back and hoped he would do. He used to tease me as a hot-house climber, somebody who had all the lucky breaks and never really had to suffer, saying that I had acquired a knack of getting people to do things for me. Well, he was not going to have any sympathy with that, and I knew it. I used to dread giving him justification for complaint. The problem was, I tended to sit lost in thought and, if there seemed to be little to do, not to think or act dynamically until the last minute. Joe seemed much more competent and organised around the camp.

There was always an 'edge' to the relationship between Joe and myself. With brittle over-familiarity, we joked at each other's expense, always on the verge of direct damning comment. Joe managed to take this less seriously than I:

"There was a non-co-operative hostility towards each other in things which did not matter. If an argument became too heated we grew accustomed to using the catch-phrase, 'Don't worry, it will be all right when we get back.' It was a code which meant that we both acknowledged that any tensions were due to our unusual circumstances."

It seemed that neither of us ever opened up completely. There was always a tension that held us apart and this helped us retain our individuality. We had enormous respect for each other's climbing ability. This, for me, was a marked contrast to the most demanding climb of my youth, in the Hindu Kush, when I had felt utterly alone. Then I was the only one in the party with the combination of skill and drive to pull us out of the situations we ignorantly got ourselves into. With Joe, I knew I could relax when he went into the lead, for he was so motivated that he would get up the piece of rock ahead.

On that day, however, the climb was hardly mentioned. Joe talked, as he rarely did, about his childhood and his home. He came from a strong Catholic family, and his father was a caretaker at a local school in Middlesbrough. He was the eldest son, with four brothers and five sisters. Before leaving for the climb he had spent a brief weekend at home. He had not, of course, made the point to his family that it might have been a last farewell. They had been glad to see him. They would have preferred him not to go off on such risky undertakings, but had long since ceased trying to dissuade him, except by the occasional subtle suggestion that he might occupy his time more fruitfully. When he had started climbing it had been their strong disapproval he had found worrying—it had shaken his confidence. As time went on they became used to the fact that he kept coming back in one piece from climbs in the Alps. They started to see that there was more to climbing mountains than running risks for risk's sake and they took more interest in the climbs he was doing. For earlier climbs, Joe's mother had given Joe medals of different saints to take with him; for Changabang she did not. For the first time she said as he was leaving, "Enjoy yourself", rather than, "Be careful."

Between the ages of thirteen and twenty-one, Joe had trained at Ushaw College to be a priest. He related strange, wryly amusing stories of the cloistered isolation of the place; the tensions and anomalies that exist in all residential institutions were even more emphasised there. For eight years he had been deprived of contact with the outside world, deprived of newspapers, television, alcohol, the company of women. Religious services had been held seven times a day, starting at six in the morning. As Joe had grown through his teens, he had started having more and more confrontations with the authorities at Ushaw, rebelling strongly against the restrictions that, to him, came to seem meaningless. He became entangled in a major row one Christmas when he and a fellow pupil sneaked off to a nearby plantation and returned and erected a Christmas tree. Institutional life was not for Joe, he felt that if he let go and sank into the flood of the organisation he would lose his identity and become slowly and irrevocably changed. Then he discovered climbing, in a quarry near the college. His early climbing was done without any instruction. He did not have many friends to go climbing with and often went soloing. His friends had always regarded him as physically lazy, and he could never be enthusiastic about conventional sports with formalised competition. But in climbing he found something different. He was frightened, yet fascinated by it. It was so irrational and pointless that his rebellious awkwardness found an outlet in it.

Joe left Ushaw and went to University to study Sociology. Seven years later we were trying to climb Changabang, and it seemed to me that Joe was still reacting against his days at Ushaw. His moods varied, even during that day at Base Camp. He would drift out of a chatty mood and start looking serious and intense. His intensity frightened me and I wondered if I had the same quality—if it was necessary to have that quality to climb Changabang. Was he prepared to accept a greater level of risk than I? Joe did not seem to be as happy all the time as I felt when I was in the mountains. I wondered if he was worrying about the fact that he did not have a job to go back to when we returned to England. He was still the rebel. Perhaps this mountain was purging something inside for both of us? I thought of the shores of the coasts of Scandinavia that are still rising a few inches every year as the earth's crust readjusts from the weights of the ice age, although that was many thousands of years ago. Joe seemed like this, continuing to readjust. Would he always be like that?

In the late afternoon we settled down to reading. Joe was now reading *Zen and the Art of Motorcycle Maintenance*. I had found it a radical, disturbing book, but one which needed far more academic discipline to absorb than I could muster on an expedition. Joe just dismissed it completely. It was as if he felt he had wasted enough years discussing the finer philosophical points of life. He wanted action, the total involvement of climbing. It was one of the few things that brought him satisfaction.

Joe saw himself as very practical and down to earth. I was more romantic and idealistic. Joe saw in me many aspects of what he was trying to put behind him, to escape from. As a result, some issues and feelings that were of greatest importance to me, I could not discuss without embarrassing us both.

I was reading Zola's *Germinal*. Reading a book helps me, particularly as it had absolutely nothing to do with mountains, but can transport me into a different world. Obsession is always a danger for the mountaineer—I found that reading for long hours during that afternoon restored some sort of normal balance to my thinking and values. It was because I was involved in the bleak world of strong contrasts, between fear and exultation, danger and security, between life and death, that the finer balances of hopes and fears of people living hard-working lives began to take on new meaning. The grim struggle of the miners in northern France against appalling working and social conditions involved me deeply, and threw a question mark over our adventure.

Unlike the miners in France and, almost in the same way, unlike the people in the Garhwal struggling for daily survival against harsh physical conditions, Joe and I were here seeking a survival situation. We had been struggling for survival not because of force of circumstance, but because of a deliberate choice we had made. Our adventure was a pampered luxury that we could afford to enjoy, it was pure self-indulgence. As the mountain writer, Geoffrey Winthrop Young, once wrote, "Our poignant adventure, our self-sought perils on a line of unreason to the summit of a superfluous rock, have no rational or moral justification." This was an honest thought I do not think Joe would have accepted. As I read, the crowd scenes in *Germinal* scattered and thundered around my mind, and self-questioning and Winthrop Young faded into the background. My headtorch was broken. Joe mended it and I read on. Zola was reaching out over a hundred years to hold me in thrall in the dark days of northern France. Meanwhile, outside the tent the weather seemed to be settling. The moon rose strongly over Rishi Kot. At 10.30 p.m. I finished the last page. Thoughts of the Shining Mountain had waited for a day.

On the morning of the 5th October, our minds slowly returned to the problem. Joe and I had booked our return flights to London for the 18th October. We knew now that if we went back up the mountain we would miss the flight. If we missed the flight, we might have difficulty in obtaining seats on another one. We would not be able to tell our parents of our change in plan, they would be expecting us and would immediately start worrying. Even if I caught the 18th October flight, I would be two weeks late for work. If I arrived back even later, it seemed probable I would be out of a job. But there was no thought of abandoning the route. We were committed to getting up the climb, even while we were down at Base Camp. The decision had been made without question, and it had been an easy choice, to risk our lives 6,000 miles from home. The two of us had developed into a powerful, intense unit, a compound being with a single motivation—to climb Changabang's West Wall. If we had been on a bigger expedition the whole situation would have been much more complicated. It would most likely have been more lighthearted, too. There could have been more scope for the good-natured gibes that always accompany a group of easy-going climbers. That we should climb the West Wall was now becoming the most important thing in the world. Nothing would stop us. The steady pressure of risk, that had forced us into being alert for weeks, had generated an intensity that, during moments of reflection, was frightening. The whole venture had become bigger than our lives. Yet, at the same time, our combined abilities seemed to have made a third, invisible quality outside ourselves, in which we had implicit faith.

Joe sensed the menace of the unfinished task ahead:

"We both wanted to go and finish it. I was surprised at my own persistence. There was no joy left in it—just hard work remaining; an ordeal in whose value we had to believe during this period of darkness and discouragement, believe without any glimpse of the satisfaction there would be in having completed the climb."

The autopsy was thorough. We discussed over and over the mistakes we had made during the three nightmare hammock nights on the Wall in the storm. We went back over the equipment used and tactical weaknesses. We had been defeated because the hammocks had not been satisfactory in the bad weather we had encountered. We had not been able to cook and, hence, eat or drink properly for four days. We would never be able to climb the Wall if we could not cook. Also, getting in and out of the hammocks had been a debilitating struggle at altitude and it would have been only a matter of time before we dropped some vital piece of equipment. Perhaps the main disadvantage was our being almost completely isolated from each other the whole time. There had been none of the relaxed, easy discussion that could occur in the evening when we were in a tent together. We had been many feet apart, unable to communicate, locked in our own thoughts, buffeted by the wind in isolation. It had been impossible to use any light-hearted banter about the situation, to bring it into perspective. We discussed the possibility of taking the inner from the tent at Advance Camp with us, and trying to hack out a ledge at the top of the platform to pitch it on. To reinforce this tiny tent, we could take with us some of the thin bamboo poles left by the Japanese at their camp at the foot of the South-West Ridge. We would just have to keep our fingers crossed that we could make a ledge wide enough, and that the fabric would withstand the wind and snow.

It had been becoming steadily more windy at high altitude all the time we had been in the area and we revised our thoughts about the clothing we would wear for our return to the Wall. Even at Base Camp, it was much colder than it had been a month earlier. Joe unearthed an extra duvet we had brought with us for the porter who had been going to stay at Base Camp with Palta. I decided to take my Everest one-piece down suit.

We knew that this attempt on the Wall would be our last and that it would be a race against time. The previous year the winter storms hit Joe while he was walking out of the area on October 15th. Clearly, it could be suicidal to risk being caught out on the mountain too late into the month. As we had only enough lightweight freeze-dried food to last a week, we decided to take our primus stove and pressure cooker up to the ridge camp, so that we could cook our local food of rice and dhal up to the last possible moment.

As we sorted through our equipment, we found our folder full of photographs of the Face. We studied these for an hour, and tried to convince each other that all that separated us from success was just over a thousand feet of difficult climbing. Joe packed a few of the photographs in the medical box. The route finding on the Upper Tower looked as if it would be tricky, so we would need these on the route to refer to at night, to gauge our progress and direction.

The biggest decision which we had to make that morning was whether we were still going to stick to our plan of going down the other side of the mountain, if and when we had climbed it. The idea of descending the ridge on the other side whilst in the sort of state we had been after the hammock epic worried me. Also, I thought that the South Face expedition had probably left the Changabang Glacier on the other side by now and would not be able to help us if we tried to descend in a bad state. However, the alternative of coming down the West Wall was not much more attractive, apart from the fact that we should be able to retrieve our equipment. We would have to abseil all the way down the Wall — most of it without fixed ropes to guide us.

It was a difficult decision to have to make and we decided to put it off until the following day, when we would go across from Advance Camp towards the foot of the ropes leading up to Shipton's Col. There, we hoped to examine the state of the piton anchors, in case we had to come down that way, and also try to retrieve some rope to string along the lower part of our route, in case we returned via the West Wall.

We had done so much climbing in the previous few weeks that much of our equipment had been badly damaged. Joe spent all morning mending his gaiters, stitching, glueing and tacking the tattered bits back together. Our woollen mitts needed darning, our oversuits patch-ing, our crampons sharpening; buttons needed sewing back on. It was enjoyable therapy. As usual, our departure time dragged on into afternoon, and we decided to have lunch before we left. We rewrote the message to leave outside the door and destroyed the optimistic one we had left there on 28th September.

The pressure cooker was hissing vigorously away and Joe and I were lying around on our ready-packed sacks when, simultaneously, we saw a figure coming down the moraine valley. We were astonished. My pulse raced. This was a situation I had forgotten how to deal with — other people! I put the zoom lens on my camera and took a few pictures of him discreetly as he reached the level of Bleak House meadow. Joe, also, had his camera out, but kept on coolly clicking away openly as the man approached.

"Hallo," we said eagerly.

"Hi there." He was American. He did not seem at all surprised to see us.

We soaked up his news avidly. He was called Neko Colevins, a member of the South-West Ridge of Dunagiri expedition. There were nine Americans, one Mexican and an Indian liaison officer on the expedition. He was rather vague about their progress on the mountain. Apparently they had arrived at their Base Camp about a week previously.

"Where is your Base Camp?" I said.

"About a couple of hundred yards down there around the corner," he replied.

"Effin' hell," said Joe, "that's typical of the porters. Lazy lot. They conned you to have your camp down there so they would not have to carry the gear up here."

Neko seemed very self-assured about their expedition and talked in round terms about it. I offered him some of our lunch, which was now ready — he seemed surprised and quickly declined, and proceeded to talk a lot about the freeze-dried food they were eating on Dunagiri. He had organised its acquisition. We told him about our route and our hammock epic, but he did not seem particularly interested.

"Oh yeah, we knew you were here, of course, we've been walking backwards and forwards for days. Oh well, I'd better move on. The leader of our expedition is coming now. He'll be here soon. He's bringing down our Indian liaison officer who ain't feeling too good. The height, I guess." Neko moved off down the valley and disappeared around the corner.

"He had nice new gear, didn't he?" I said.

"He seemed a bit old," said Joe.

When our next two visitors arrived, we were ready for them.

"I'm Graham Stephenson," said the tall man, "from Los Angeles." He was bearded and in his mid-fifties. "And this here's our liaison officer, Mandip Singh."

Mandip Singh did not look very well. I asked Graham why they had chosen to climb Dunagiri. Apparently Eric Shipton had given a talk to the Sierra Club whilst on a lecture tour of the States, and Graham Stephenson had asked him at the end of the evening if he could recommend a good peak to climb in the Himalayas. Shipton, who attempted Dunagiri in 1936 with the Sherpa Angtharkay, recommended the South-West Ridge, that he had so nearly climbed, as a reasonable objective. We asked Graham about other expeditions in the area. He told us of the death of Nanda Devi Unseold, and that some Italian climbers were due in the area soon, intending to climb Kalanka. We absorbed the news avidly, it was like arriving in the Chamonix camp site, fresh from England. Joe was swearing obscenely whenever he spoke. I do not think he realised. We had been alone together for so long that our language had deteriorated—there had been no one to offend. I was embarrassed. Graham was confused, but courteous. We showed him a picture of Changabang and indicated our high point. He was impressed. We wished him the best of luck and he said he would see us later, when we were down from the summit—they were planning to leave around the 12th October. Then he left us, taking Mandip Singh down with him.

Joe and I sat for a few minutes, savouring the minutiae, every word and gesture, and hint that had been said and made during the previous half hour. The whole tenor of our conversation, of our relationship with each other, changed. We no longer felt isolated as we had been for the previous twenty-seven days. We were almost performers again —someone knew what we had been doing. The mountains had people in them. As we shouldered our packs we continued to discuss the meetings endlessly, digesting all the nourishment from them before they became a mere memory.

"Did you see that Chouinard ice hammer Stephenson had?"

"It looked brand new."

"I wonder if they realise what they're tackling?"

"He seemed as if he'd been around a long time though."

"It's difficult to judge American climbers—there are so many types.

Have you heard of the gear freaks, the 'Sierra Cup' types—people who buy these aluminium cups that burn your mouth and hang them from their waists?"

"Communication between different areas and groups of climbers in the States is so bad that there is very little interrelation of climbing standards. Each little group creates its own experts."

"And I thought they were going to be Californian surfing girls."

We were assessing the people we had just met, making gross generalisations. We were full of a sudden confidence generated by the contrasting boldness of our own adventure. We had summed them up as if they were opponents. We were both well practised at assessing climbers, by the way they talk about climbing and the equipment they choose. In particular, I had learned from instructing with a mountaineering school in the Cairngorms, how to categorise people quickly before going out for a day on the mountain with them. We had judged them solely in the narrow terms we ourselves prescribed.

"They must have had a lot of porters," said Joe, as we walked up the valley.

Now I realised that I had not been imagining all the scuff marks on the ground before. They had been caused by the passing of the feet of the porters hired by the Dunagiri expedition to help them establish Base Camp. But our ways parted. The tracks turned left up the glacier towards Dunagiri, and we turned up onto the moraine towards Changabang.

We were talking to each other unguardedly, chatting naturally all the way up the glacier, even though we were approaching seventeen thousand feet. We felt perfectly acclimatised, and fit. We were at that optimum point of acclimatisation, after about four weeks at high altitude, which seems to precede the onset of gradual deterioration.

The sun set whilst we were half way up the glacier, and we sat for half an hour and watched the shadow line racing up the Western Wall. The longer retracting rays of the sun turned the upper part of the Wall through gold to rich red. Then the light faded and froze and we began to shiver. As we picked our separate ways over the ice towards the tent, the moon took over the lighting with silver brightness. It was Bill Murray who had described moonlight as the eye-fang: "Changabang . . . shone tenderly as though veiled in bridal lace . . . seemingly as fragile as an icicle; a produce of earth and sky rare and fantastic, and of liveliness unparalleled so that unaware one's pulse leapt and the heart gave thanks—that this mountain should be as it is." Happiness was welling inside me, and I wondered if Joe felt as deeply content as I. Surely the radiant fall of night stirred his imagination too?

On the following day, the 6th October, as planned, we went across to the ropes hanging from Shipton's Col. After rice pudding for breakfast we left at 11.30 a.m. and enjoyed moving off the beaten track of our route up from Base Camp to explore a new corner of the glacier, to get to know the area better by seeing old familiar mountain shapes from new angles.

There was a long snow slope to the foot of the Wall below Shipton's Col. It felt good to move finally up to it, unburdened for once from the heavy, crippling sack that had accompanied nearly all our other efforts in the previous weeks.

We were disappointed when we arrived, for the ropes hanging there looked as faded and unreliable as washing lines. There was some old polypropylene, white and bleached by the sun. Next to that was some red nylon line. In the autumn of 1974, after the Indo-British Changabang ascent of the spring, an English expedition led by John Prosser had attempted Kalanka. They had been unable to persuade their porters to take their gear round into the Nanda Devi Sanctuary and up to the Changabang Glacier to the foot of Kalanka, because of the extra three days' walk it involved. Instead, their porters had dumped them in the same place as the Bonington expedition. There had, therefore, been a painful re-enactment, with a smaller team, of the trip over Shipton's Col. In the lower places they had reinforced Bonington's polypropylene with their nylon rope. Later, however, hampered by bad weather, an extended supply line and a tight time schedule, Prosser's expedition failed on Kalanka after running out some fixed rope up the mountain. Joe and I looked at the rope. In many places it disappeared, and then reappeared behind feet of ice. We scrambled a hundred feet up. We could never trust this rope. If we came over from the other side, we would have to arrange our own abseils.

"We must be really close to the others," said Joe. The South Face team Advance Camp must have been just over the other side of the col. We shouted their names—but it was only a gesture.

There were a few pegs not yet buried under the ice. It was a haunting thought—hands I knew had placed those pegs, two and a half years ago. I wondered if it had been Martin, or Doug, or Chris, or Dougal. All had been my companions on Everest since. It was an archaeological dig of mountaineering history with a difference—I had known the hands that had used the tools we were uncovering. We cut some lengths of rope.

Woke up (alarm) around 5.30 a.m. and had a couple of brews and porridge. We've brought the Advance Camp tent inner up with us, also a load of food and the little stove. So we had a lot of packing to do. Away around 8.45 a.m., wearing our windsuits—which we were glad of when we reached the Ridge. I'm feeling fit—hence hungry all the time.

When we arrived here we sorted the tent out—which seems to have sunk! Incredibly stable though, considering how long it's been up. We had dhal with some rice I'd brought up frozen in a poly bag —cooked last night. We've enough fuel up here to last for days. I re-dressed my thumbs and fore-fingers and spent a tedious afternoon mending my overboots—finished off the strong twine, Evostik and Araldite. Worked from about 1.00 p.m. until 6.30 p.m.! And now my head aches. Just eaten corned dog and rice—as usual, but it's filling—followed by a cuppa and Mars Bar.

But the main thing to write about is today's weather—such a contrast to the last three or four days' still sunshine. Early this afternoon, a dramatic two-hour electric storm—and after I'd been telling Joe that you don't get storms like the Alps in the Himalayas. "Is it the Chinese then?" he asked. When it cleared, it just moved back like a curtain, leaving the whole valley down to the Rishi plastered in snow. Perhaps it's the same as 'Termination Dust' in Alaska—the first snowfall of the winter season and a sign that summer is over. And now there is a very violent wind, rattling noisily, with occasional lashings of spindrift. All reminiscent of our days a week ago in the hammocks. Still, we are secure down here in the tent—glad we're not up there, but rather apprehensive about how we're going to build an effective shelter up there when we go up.

It's quite chilly—I'm glad I've brought my down suit. Our route seems to be in a very exposed position. 7.55 p.m.

There followed an uneasy day, which held us in a void. We discussed whether to move—as always, each of us took opposing points of view and tested them out on the other. Joe was for staying and, after a few minutes, it was evident that he was right. We had woken late and it was blustering outside. It would be madness to risk being caught out on the ropes again—particularly since we had not even brought the hammocks with us. We had left them at the high point on the icefield. We resolved to leave very early the next day, whatever the weather.

"Ah well," I said, "we can eat the other half of that Christmas pud in comfort."

By mid-morning, the weather turned out not to be as bad as we had feared. It was too late to alter our decision. We had brought some books up this time. Joe settled back to read *Germinal* and I tried to start Steinbeck's diary. Some publisher had decided to print verbatim all the warm-up pages that Steinbeck wrote every morning before he started writing seriously. It seemed a bore, snapping and biting at trifling worries and obsessions about his accommodation and family. I felt that Steinbeck had been cheated by the publisher and that he would never have allowed such material to be printed if he had been alive. Having brought this book to such a remote place, I felt in a position to judge quickly and harshly many values of the civilisation that had governed it. Filled with the hubris only wilderness can bring, I stuffed it to the back of the tent. The books we were reading always had a strong effect on our moods—it was as if they brought new personalities into the tent.

For the rest of the day I pottered about sorting the tattered bits of rope we had recovered from Shipton's Col. My mind was too busy thinking itself up the sides of the mountain to concentrate on subtleties. Back home I had never been very practical, I could never see the point of wasting time on tasks that I knew other people could do much more quickly than I. Here it was different—there were no helpers. Four years before, I had been on a one-year outdoor activities course at Bangor University, and part of this course was learning to sew and make equipment. Over the year, I had produced a misshapen pair of overtrousers, and cut out the pattern for a rucksack. I had kept the unfinished rucksack material for mending purposes and had brought it with me to Camp One. For three hours I cut out strips of it and sewed lengths of polypropylene to them. These would be the marker flags with which we would guide ourselves on our descent, if we decided to come down the West Wall. At the back of my mind, I was coming round to thinking that would be the case. When we picked up the ropes as we went up the next day, we would leave most of the anchor pegs in place. If, when we eventually came down, some of them were hidden by overhangs, or by mist or storm, then the blue flags would help us find them. I knew from personal experience how important markers can be. On the descent from the summit of Everest, I would never have survived if I had not stumbled across the near-submerged shape of an oxygen cylinder marking the end of the fixed ropes. Lying beside me in the enforced closeness of the tent, Joe was feeling depressed:

"I was not feeling well for some reason, either just general weariness or something I had eaten. Camp One was becoming a little squalid. I hoped my anxiety was simply due to our bad experience in the hammocks. I reasoned with myself that Dick and I had spent ten nights bivouacking on the Face of Dunagiri only a year before. But my earlier enthusiasm to be back on the route seemed to have tarnished. I was back in the old going through the motions routine, doing what I was there for without knowing why.

"In the confines of the inside of the tent we were aware of every movement, action, thought even, of each other. There was no argument, no need for words, the mute passivity, clipped and curt responses, non-volunteering 'find out for yourself' attitude, were sufficient indications to each other of our feelings.

"For a full month, we had been alone together, working virtually every day, the whole burden of the Expedition resting on both of us. We could not succeed alone, we needed each other."

When I had finished making the marker flags, I started reading *Nana* but the light was fading and I was so wound up for action that I could not concentrate on Zola. If we could move up and establish a well-stocked and secure camp at the top the following day, then battle could commence. This was like war: we were living under constant threat and danger, our cunning and stealth were being stretched as exactingly as if we had been commandos beyond enemy lines. Except here there could be no victors or conquered—but perhaps we could sneak up and down whilst the enemy was sleeping?

CHAPTER SEVEN

The Upper Tower

9th–13th October

Camp One shrank below me, a blue dot on the curve of the ridge that swept from far beneath my feet towards Bagini Peak and Dunagiri. The only sounds were the wind whipping the corners of my down hood, and my own heavy panting as I pushed and pulled myself up the rope with the jumars. I was returning to the problem, feeling strong. Everything around me was pure in the light of receding dawn. The fresh powder snow, the harsh crystalline granite, the air itself, seemed newly created. There was even a terrible cleanliness about the danger to which I was exposed.

Two hundred feet below me, Joe was fixing a few short lengths of the rope from Shipton's Col, over the rock steps above Camp One. He had agreed to continue up behind and do the finger work of dismantling the fixed ropes beneath the Balcony and bringing them up with him. To compensate his extra burden, I was carrying all the down epuipment.

It had been the earliest start we had ever made on the mountain. I had not slept well. I had kept on waking up and thinking about the route. At three in the morning I had decided I was certainly not going to get any more sleep. Silently resenting Joe's peaceful doze, I had leant out of the door in the darkness and smashed some snow off the ever-retreating section of the cornice outside the tent and put the brew on. 'Typical!' I had thought. 'I bet he hardly stirs for another three hours.' And he did not. Nevertheless, we had moved off by half past six, at first light.

The plan was to pull up all the six terylene ropes hanging below the spike beneath the Balcony, where we had spent our first hammock bivouac. These, combined with the ropes on the icefield, ought to be enough to fix the Upper Tower. In this way we could still leave two ropes tied through the overhangs. We knew that if we retrieved these, we could never get back again. We had mused morbidly that it was retrieving the rope after the first crossing of the Hinterstoisser traverse on the Eiger that had cut off the retreat and precipitated the tragic deaths of the four climbers in 1936, including Toni Kurz. Joe and I were not prepared to cut off our retreat completely. If the hammock plan had worked, then we would have moved slowly up the mountain, stopping whenever we finished the day's climbing. But now, if we could establish the tent on the icefield, we would have to work every day from there, and take all the risks of jumaring and prusiking that it entailed.

I was astonished how smoothly the jumaring went. I was carrying two long sticks of bamboo that we had rescued from one of the Japanese expedition camps. I had pushed them as far as possible to the bottom of my sack. Now their ends wavered in the air above my head like bizarre antennae, as if they were rendering mysterious aid to my progress. I was wearing my one-piece down suit, yet even when the sun came out I was not too hot. The weather was steadily becoming colder. As I negotiated the vertical jumaring onto the foot of the icefield above the Toni Kurz pitch, I was bouncing about as usual when I ripped a large tear in the suit. For the rest of the journey up the ropes, I was accompanied by a trail of down, which rose, hovered and plummeted on the up-and-down draughts of air that sailed around the West Wall. Now, instead of staring glumly at the ice as I recovered between bursts of effort, I watched feathers soar hundreds of feet, with the intensity of a child at a balloon competition at a fair. Yet this was a more expensive game. I decided, and determined to wear my oversuit on top of my down suit in the future.

I reached the high point at half past two in the afternoon, thankfully to find that all the equipment, food and fuel we had left there was still intact. Combined with the food and fuel we were bringing up with us, we had a week's provisions – or ten days in an uncomfortable emergency. We were still feeling fit and fresh. I knew that I had lost a lot of weight, and that my body had become hardened and sinews become wiry with the effort of the previous few weeks. And I knew, also, that this feeling might not last for long. However, for the moment my mind and body felt in perfect accord, as if my will could force my limbs into any situation, as long as it entailed reaching the summit of the mountain.

The critical problem then was to find a site for us to pitch Camp Two. I unclipped from the rope and started soloing around the mixed ground above the fixed rope. After climbing about fifteen feet, I came to my senses and decided to clip back on. It was stupidity to deny myself some sort of chance if I were to slip. Joe was still a long way behind me on the icefield, so I pulled through fifty feet of the spare rope we had left up there and tied on to it. Then, with more confidence, I started climbing. I ran half the rope out, by which time Joe had arrived. Joe belayed me and I looked at all the area within seventy feet above our high point. Every time a line of rock promised a ledge, on inspection I always found its top stacked steeply with hard water ice. I crept back to Joe. I could not talk to him because of the wind, until I had reached him.

"Well, there aren't any good ledges. We might as well try and hack a platform out of this bit of ice as any other."

We tied off to fifteen-foot lengths of rope and started slicing into the ice with our axes.

We set about the work with enthusiasm. This was mountaineering at its most basic; serious play. As a child I had loved building tree-top dens and digging dug-outs. This was similar elemental home building, except the difference was the situation and the materials. Now we had the threat of bad weather and avalanche hanging over our heads if we did not do a good job. Secure shelter would make the difference between success and failure.

The ice-cutting was exhausting work. We hacked furiously until stopped by shortness of breath or cramp in the forearms. We soon hit the rock of the slab under the ice, and this forced the limit on the width of the ledge. By the time the sun was sinking into the cloud beyond Dunagiri, we had enlarged a ledge six feet long, two feet six inches wide at one end and tapering to two feet at the other. Whilst I tensioned the tent off from a system of nuts, spikes and rock and ice pegs I had fixed above, Joe lashed two sticks of the Japanese bamboo together and bent them across the entrance like a hoop. He improvised guylines from little stones knotted into the walls of the tent and hammered our hammock spacer bars into the ice for tent pegs.

Before the afternoon sun disappeared, I finished off the pitch I had started leading earlier. The climbing was quite awkward, but it was mere scrambling compared to that beneath the icefield. My thoughts raced ahead with the hope that the Upper Tower would be quickly climbed if it were all like that.

The last rays of the sun had moved off the Wall high above us and 'home' was ready.

"There doesn't seem to be much room in there," I commented.

"We'll have to tie on well," said Joe.

"Yeah, that's a drag, we'll have to leave part of the tent open to let the line through. And we'll have to keep our harnesses on inside our sleeping bags."

We had left our full body harnesses at Camp One, and put on our sit harnesses, hoping to save weight and also because the full body harnesses got in the way of the pockets of our oversuits. Now we regretted having made this decision, for the point of attachment of the sit harnesses was so low down. Outside the tent there was a chaos of equipment, slings and ropes, and after we had sorted them out the question that had been in the backs of our minds came out into the open. "Who's going to sleep on the outside then?" If Joe was still insisting that I cooked breakfast, then I was not going to give in on this question. To my surprise, he agreed to sleep on the side of the tent overhanging the edge.

"Only for a couple of nights, mind you," he said.

The tent was so cramped there was only room for one of us to sort himself out at a time. I went in and laid the insulating mats and the hammocks down, took off my boots and got into my sleeping bags. Joe squeezed in and did the same.

"Christ, my knees protrude over the edge," he said.

"Isn't it cosy?" I said.

"Good job we've got our pee bottles with us," said Joe. "I wouldn't fancy getting up in the middle of the night for a piss!"

"Make sure you pour it out on the left-hand side, we don't want our cooking ice polluted," I said.

We wedged the stove in between the soles of my boots in the tent entrance and put a brew on. The wind did not seem to be penetrating the thin fabric.

"You taking Dalmane or Valium tonight?" asked Joe.

"Dalmane, Dalmane, all around my brain, please."

Saturday, October 9th. I had missed the BMC Peak Area Meeting!

The improvised tent was protecting us—the problem of shelter had been solved, and my heart warmed to the action to come.

We had decided that on the Upper Tower we would do two leads each in succession. We expected to go just as slowly on the Upper Tower as we had done below and had found that leading four rope lengths each was too much—two days' consecutive leading had been exhausting, and if you were seconding, you lost a feel for the action.

The next day I was intending to run out another rope length before Joe took over.

It was an exciting change to start climbing in the cold of the morning, straight from the camp and without any jumaring. But the optimism of the previous afternoon was short lived.

The only line that offered any feasibility of progress was a bottomless groove that was guarded from me by a bulge of ice. As I moved up to the bulge I started feeling tired. The climbing became hard and the wind and cold were sapping my strength. I was now wearing both down and nylon Ventile oversuits—far more than I had ever found it necessary to wear on Everest the year before. With my overmitts off and dangling from my wrists, and wearing only the pairs of gloves underneath, my fingers quickly became cold. I wanted to avoid making them colder by trying to put my crampons on. I traversed left on the rock to below where a bulge turned into a rock overhang. This was slit by a ramp, which I managed to step onto, and I traversed across to the side of the ice that filled the back of a hanging groove. Rather than put crampons on, I tapped a drive-in ice peg into the ice. It went in a couple of inches before stopping against the rock underneath. I tied a nylon rope sling around it where it came out of the ice, and stepped into it. Then I repeated the same movement further up the groove twice, before I could bridge out with my feet on either side on to rock. A few feet of climbing and I had reached the top of the groove.

The groove was capped by a six-foot overhang. I saw one ledge eighteen inches wide over on the left that ran around the corner onto the North Face and, after shouting a few warning words to Joe, I crawled along it. The wall above me bulged out and I was virtually on all fours. The ledge was in a horrifying position, without the ice-field to soften the view downwards. Below me was a sheer drop of four thousand feet onto the Bagini Glacier. By curling my fingers around narrow sideholds, I braced myself sideways and peered round the corner. We had seen, through our binoculars from the glacier, a long slanting groove line high on the edge of the Upper Tower between the West and North Walls. It had been the only obvious feature on the Upper Tower and we had hoped it would offer some straightforward crack climbing. We had called it 'the Niche'. Looking upwards now I could see it, and it scared me even to look at it! The corner was vertical, ice-smeared and two hundred feet high. I shouted down to Joe.

"I've seen the Niche. It's around the corner. It overhangs the North

Face and looks bloody impossible – to reach it, climb it, or get upwards from the top of it. We'll only get up if we climb the right side of the Upper Tower for the next few pitches!"

It was a measure of our trust in each other's climbing judgement that Joe accepted all this immediately, without demanding a look of his own.

The right-handed exit offered the only option – a fifteen-foot leaning crack. I tried to climb it by artificial aid, but none of the pegs or nuts I had with me would fit the crack. 'Don't be such a chicken,' I told myself inside. 'If this was on gritstone you'd bomb up it. It's obviously a lay back crack and doesn't look as if it'll play any tricks. Just take a few deep breaths and fight up it.'

I felt as if I had lead in my boots and my weight had doubled as soon as I swung my weight onto my arms. Half-way up the lay back, my fingers started to unfold from the edge of the crack so I rammed my fist round and into the back of the crack and squeezed it in a hand jam. I locked my arm straight from the jam and hung there until my breathing returned to normal. Then I returned to the lay back position and fought, with continually draining strength, upwards. My fingers curled over the edge of the arête that bounded the top of the crack. The arête rocked a little – it was a granite block of dubious quality. But I was past caring about that. One last heave and I swung up onto some footholds and gasped for air. A momentary feeling of nausea welled up from my stomach; I thought I was going to vomit. I managed to bang a peg in, tied the rope off and shouted down into the wind to Joe that he could start jumaring.

'That would have been quite a respectable grade on gritstone,' I thought, and resolved to avoid such strenuous climbing in the future. I looked down past Joe at the buff-coloured tent of Camp Two, now two hundred steep feet below. Beyond that was the sweep of the ice-field and then nothing. The Wall seemed to breathe in under that. There was only the Rhamani Glacier, and the tiny dot of the Ridge Camp Ore was just visible. Joe was dangling beneath me, all arms and legs, braced across the groove, hanging from a thread. He was unscrewing the ice pegs.

"A pity you'll miss the lay back," I said.

It was an uncharitable sentiment which back home on rock I used to relish when I watched seconds struggling up something difficult that I had led. Joe heard me from beneath his layers of balaclava, helmet and hood.

"It looked quite hard," he muttered. With a few upward strokes of his jumars, he had joined me. Now it was his turn.

With confident balance, Joe moved up a few feet above my head and then traversed diagonally rightwards under a line of overhangs, placing his feet carefully on a narrow sloping granite shelf. He placed a runner around a spike and looked around, obviously enjoying himself:

> "The climbing was delicate and thrilling, tip-toeing up the edge with stupendous exposure below. At the end of the shelf was a magnificent groove, steep and reminiscent of a Scottish climb. I put on my crampons. I found it hard, but on the right side of the borderline. Rocks frozen in place provided welcome holds and, when loose, added an extra thrill to the climbing. I was bridged across the icy runnel for most of the way. It was just the kind of pitch I enjoyed most, varied, intricate, uncertain."

I was watching the progress of the sun. The shadow crept back towards me imperceptibly, but inexorably. It had long since moved down the Bagini Peak and past Camp One. As the Wall steepened, so its speed increased. For a few moments I could see the icefield crystals shimmering in the sun's halo above the windswept South-West Ridge. Then the sun came out and the shadow ran away up the Wall. But the wind and the altitude were fighting away the warmth that should have come with the light.

The rope stopped moving, and there was not much of it left. The restless wind swept our shouts aside and threw them around the mountain. I decided that Joe must have tied on. I pulled on the terylene rope. Yes, it seemed secured. I shouldered the sack and moved off.

I was tense with concentration as I crossed the shelf that Joe had appeared to stroll across with such ease. 'Perhaps my boots are too big. Perhaps it's the weight of the sack. Perhaps I'm having an off day. I wish he'd put more runners in, I might swing off,' I thought. The thought that Joe was climbing well, was not allowed. I swallowed my moans.

The groove up which he had disappeared looked as if it had been fun to climb, with a succession of spikes to haul up on—held on to the mountain by hard water ice. But now I had swung into the line of the rope and was jumaring past them. Above the groove there was some easier angled rock and the rope whipped back left around the edge of the Upper Tower. I followed it and found Joe standing at the bottom of an overhanging groove that split the edge of the mountain for about three hundred feet. We both hoped it would not be necessary to climb that, and called it the 'Big Groove'. However, the alternative over on the right did not look much more attractive—massive blank walls stepped by overhangs looming upwards for over five hundred feet confronted us.

"There might be some easier angled ground on the left between us and the top of the Niche," said Joe. And he disappeared round the corner, leaving me standing at the foot of the Big Groove.

For two hours, Joe fought a hard and cunning battle with the rock and ice of the North Face on the left of the Big Groove:

"I came to a long, slightly overhanging crack. I chose to look further left. The crack was feasible but would have been very strenuous. Another corner had a tongue of ice running up into it— this seemed a better proposition. The ice was steep, a lot steeper than it had looked from below and, as I gained height, the tongue of ice became narrower and thinner. I had difficulty in maintaining my balance. I hammered a thin blade piton into a crack above. It only went in an inch, but gave me a little more support. I wondered whether to come down and try the other corner. It would be time-wasting to start again; I could see nothing of Pete. He would be wondering at the slow movement of the rope. I hoped he had secure hold of it. The next few moves would depend on everything working together just right.

"I hammered the pick of an axe into the ice; carefully, I balanced up and stood on the head of the axe protruding from the ice. Gently I reached down and undid my crampons. With my boots free of the crampons I stepped up onto small footholds on the rock, feeling strangely naked. I bent down and yanked out the axe.

"There were some delicate moves to make on the rock, but the friction of the rope pulled me back. I had to strain furiously to pull sufficient rope through to allow me to move up a few feet.

"Above was another ice slope. It seemed like a haven of security. On the rock I had been exposed and vulnerable. I drove the pick of my axe into the ice and went through the procedure of refixing my crampons.

"With my crampons on, I climbed up the ice to a grotto where I could see some boulders to which I attached the rope, and relaxed."

It was obvious that this lead had been desperately hard and, for Joe, the most demanding of the climb so far. I found it very difficult leaving Joe's last runner without swinging off further over the North Face like a pendulum — a sixty-foot swing could do a lot of damage and I would have difficulty getting back. I felt mentally and physically tired when I reached Joe. "It's getting late," I said.

Joe, full of accounts of sliding feet and frightening hops with ice hammers, was obviously thirsting for more action. It was 4.30. We had not far to descend back to the tent, but we knew it would start getting dark at five. There were seventy feet of steep ice above us on the North Face. It was my turn to lead but Joe was obviously more in tune than I. He set off up it, after agreeing to stop at five. He climbed it carefully but quickly and hammered in two pegs. The shadow that had climbed upwards six hours before was now returning. It was good to have snatched those extra feet at the end of the day. We swung quickly down the ropes to Camp Two, feeling happy. Things were going well.

Back in the tent, we peered at our photographs of the Face, trying to calculate our latest high point. We knew that we could not continue up the North Face any further, for we wanted to reach a feature which we had named 'the Ramp' — a thin line of snow that appeared from our photographs to stretch down from the summit snowfield, through an area of steep rock to the top of the Upper Tower. If we became committed to the upper section of the North Face, we would inevitably miss that exit. We only had five lengths of rope left which we could fix in place. After that we would have to climb away from our lifeline, and the Ramp seemed to be the only feature that would not trap us on the Wall or dangerously slow us down, but would offer us a slim chance of success. So the next day we would have to try and regain the crest of the Upper Tower above the Big Groove. And that would be my task.

It was morning.

"Bloody hell, no lumps of ice left." I swore violently.

Joe's eyes shuttered open briefly. "What's up, hasn't it been delivered?"

All my pent-up fears and frustrations were being released in curses into the morning wind. I had forgotten to break any ice the night before for the breakfast cooking and, in the darkness, was having to stretch out and claw at the ice hanging above the tent. Slowly, I accumulated a pile of ice chips on the side of the level patch outside, shouting loudly and angrily at the fragments that splintered off into the air and bounced down the mountainside. Back inside the tent, I tried to warm myself up again and started melting the ice, chip by chip. "I'll be glad when we've got up this mountain!" I mumbled, as it started becoming lighter. "I'm fed up with this view, I hope we can see Nanda Devi from the top."

The reality that soon I was going to have to do two hours of frightening jumaring was gnawing at me and I was irritable. I crushed thoughts that Joe, lying snoozing peacefully, was deliberately obstructing my cooking, and felt embarrassed about my morning moaning. I had not been shouting at him; I wanted to say I wasn't blaming him for suggesting this climb, for not cooking breakfasts. I was just exploding with the tension and shouting at everything – it did not mean anything and I was all right now. But our conversation had died to a basic minimum. I tried to rouse him with some talk about how settled the weather was. I felt that we ought to talk about something. But Joe hated small talk and platitudes, and felt as if I were treating him as if he were on one of the BMC Committees. He preferred to keep his brain ticking over in neutral.

It was the lonely hour of dawn. Joe went down to the icefield to pick up three ropes which we would need for climbing on and fixing on the Upper Tower. We had done a lot of diagonal climbing backwards and forwards the previous day, and I went up to straighten out the first three rope lengths. By removing the first two anchors, I hoped to be able to save a hundred and fifty feet of rope for higher up. It all seemed feasible in theory. On reaching the second anchor, I wanted to swing the rope into line below Joe's shelf pitch. I took the peg out and leaned sideways on the rope. But I had miscalculated the distance I was going to swing. Time closed up before me, like the progression of incidents in a split-second dream. I was soon hurtling through the air with a momentum that would not have been out of place on an Outward Bound ropes course. Too late I tried to spin my legs round to take the impact, but was not fast enough and I crashed into a wall, vertically below the next anchor, with a sickening thud that squeezed all the wind out of me. I had swung forty feet – half a pendulum, stopped abruptly by a rock wall.

I wriggled as much as I was able, whilst suspended from my jumars. No, nothing seemed to be broken. My mind shrugged grimly, 'Well, I'm still here.' I looked down at Joe, a tiny dot on the icefield. He probably had not seen my mishap, and why should he bother about it anyway? There was nothing he could do. We were further apart than we had been for a long time.

It was strange deciding the line of the ropes, by myself, after days of deciding all tactics by consultation. I laughed at how dependent I was becoming, and moved on. I chose to keep the line of the rope going through Joe's groove in the overhangs, so as to avoid any overhanging jumaring. Soon after eleven, I was established at the previous day's highpoint and waiting for Joe, feeling determined to maintain the momentum he had set in his lead the previous day.

The problem was to try and move back right to the edge of the Upper Tower. There was a line of cracks stretching across a steep wall in between us and the sky line. Guarding any entrance to them was an enormous flake. It was angular and about ten feet across, and it was possible to see light behind it in places. It seemed to be glued to the side of the mountain by a few patches of ice. Wearing my crampons, I front-pointed up to it and thumped it hard with my hammer. 'BOOMM!' it replied threateningly.

"What do you think to this, Joe, do you think it'll be safe? It might skate off with me riding it."

"Oh, it'll be all right," he replied. "It must have been there long enough. Anyway," he added reassuringly, "it's not my lead, is it?"

Nervously, I draped a sling over the top of the spike, as if I were conferring a holy order. I curled my fingers around the edge of this spike and swung my weight onto it. Nothing moved, except my mind, which was whirring with thoughts of the sweeping action this great tonnage of rock would have on us if it decided to detach itself. What would Joe do with me if I broke my back up here?

I slotted the front points of my crampons into a tiny lip of granite on the block and edged across. Leaning across the wall I could just reach a crack about two inches wide. At full stretch, I managed to prod a large bong peg into it, and this I patted in until it seemed to stay there by itself. Using this as a hand hold, I traversed out a little further. I reached high above my head with my hammer pick and hooked it into a little niche in the rock, then, pulling myself up onto this, made a lunge with my feet for a foothold on the edge of the buttress. Gently, I eased my weight over my feet until I was in balance. The foothold was a good one and I relaxed, detachedly amused at myself for reaching such an extraordinary position.

The sun had moved onto us whilst I had been climbing and I could see my shadow silhouetted on the rock above Joe. Beyond his self-absorbed form hanging in slings, I could see the forbidding sweep of the North Face and the brown lines of moraine on the Bagini Glacier, far below. I was directly above the Big Groove, and could now see parts of the West Wall again. I leant across and screwed a good hand jam into the top of the crack at the back of the Big Groove, and bridged across. A few feet above, the Big Groove reached an apex, like a pea pod, and I swarmed up to it. Above this, there was a ten-foot-high iceslope and I planted my ice axe and hammer into this and pulled up until I was teetering on the ice with my front points. My calves were quivering with the strain and I battered the ice with my axe until a foothold splintered into existence and I could rest my foot sideways. Above me, the Wall reared up again, split by a thin crack. Longing for security, I pounded three pegs into it, a blade, a soft steel blade and a leeper. These three pegs provided a welcome refuge after the sixty feet of instability beneath me.

Joe jumared up to me and we quickly discussed the situation. We had generated such unified intensity of purpose that whatever Joe said I had been thinking at the same time. Yes, we would straighten the fixed ropes the next morning. Yes, the next pitch should bring the Ramp into view. Yes, the crack looks the best line to follow until I can tension around the corner. The wind and the sunshine were forgotten.

The crack line became continually thinner, but there were no other features to use to climb this blank wall. After twenty feet, it faded out among the granite crystals. I leant down and sideways until it seemed every muscle in my body was taut. My balance was wobbling on the point of swinging me round and off the rock like an unfastened barn door in a draught. I was able to place a one-inch long knife blade peg in upside down, and this enabled me to reach another crack line which took me around an arête into a groove. For twenty feet I was able to establish a pattern of movement as the pegging became straightforward, and there was no hope of free climbing, since the rock was either vertical or overhanging. However, soon I was running out of equipment and above a short overhang I could see the back of the upper part of the groove gleaming with bulging ice. 'Nothing's ever simple,' I thought. I took out two pegs I had used below me and placed them, and then knocked two ice pegs into the ice-filled crack. As I moved my weight onto them, I was not quite sure if it was the rock, ice or just a lot of luck that held them there. Now I only had small angle pegs left, and there were no ledges in sight.

Our route seemed to be forcing us up into ever more bleakly exposed fly-on-the-wall situations. However careful we always were at retrieving pegs, there were always some that were dropped or were left behind, and now we were running short of many sizes. The three angles that I had hammered in did not inspire my confidence, but I convinced myself that, on the law of averages, one of them would stay in, and I tied the rope off. 'Joe can sort it out from here in the morning,' I decided.

"Can you see the start of the Ramp?" shouted Joe.

"Yes, I think so." I returned to him, de-pegging as I descended and it was nearly dark when I reached him. We were late and, for the first time, I realised the full consequences of the loss of my descendeur as I struggled down with my complicated karabiner brake, past pegs and knots. The difficulty of this descent was a harbinger of the nightmare descents to come.

Dawn, the following morning, was the time of reckoning. I was going to have to go to the loo. I had been fighting this moment off all the previous day. Crawling out of the tent was a problem in itself, there were so many things I could knock over, including Joe and the tent. Only one person could move at a time and it was my turn. I imagined that I was at the fairground, trying one of those games where you have a circle of wire in your hand which you have to thread along another meandering piece of thicker wire without touching it. If you do touch it, a buzzer rings and you lose your money. Joe, the tent door, the pan on the stove, I thought, would all buzz loudly if I touched them as I threaded myself past them. Once outside the tent the game was just as delicate. On the third night, in Camp Two, we had not bothered to tie ourselves on whilst we slept, because the criss-crossed ropes inside the tent made the simplest movement too complicated. Once outside, however, to move anywhere you had to climb, and it was important to tie on. We had cut a line of steps underneath the tent and these I followed until I reached the back of the ledge. There, leaning out on the rope, I wrestled with the specially-designed zips of the oversuit, down suit and polar fibre undersuit. As soon as they were undone, my trousers started flapping agitatedly upwards, like medieval streamers in the bitter wind that was rolling up the Wall. Occasionally, my face or backside was lashed by a volley of spindrift or a flailing zip.

Local transport to the mountains. (JT)

Photo Credit Code:
    JT = Joe Tasker
    PB = Peter Boardman
    DS = Doug Scott

Spinning men of the Garhwal. (PB)

Torrents above the Rishi Ganga. (PB)

Base Camp pay off. (PB)

Flight Lieut. D. N. Palta. (PB)

The massive inhospitable face of Changabang West Wall. (JT)

Joe at Advance Camp, Trisul behind the tent. (PB)

First steps on the Begini Ridge. (JT)

Tracks from a night visitor to Advance Camp. (JT)

Steep granite climbing, Camp One a tiny dot on the ridge below. (JT)

The Tony Kurtz pitch, the first overhangs. (JT)

Approaching the overhangs
of the Barrier. (JT)

Jumaring up the wall above. (PB)

Controversial resting position on the icefield. (JT)

Climbing the Icicle after the
tension traverse. (JT)

Hanging belay next to the Icicle. (JT)

Nanda Devi. (DS)

The first hammock bivouack, Joe suspended from eight-millimetre terylene. (PB)

Four-star recovery at Base Camp. (PB)

Joe following the layback pitch on the Upper
Tower. Camp Two is just visible bottom left, with
Camp One over 2,000 feet below. (PB)

**The belay below the Booming Flake, the Begini
Glacier curving away beneath. (PB)**

Evening sun on the icefield. (PB)

Camp Two with Tibet beyond. (PB)

Through the Keyhole. (PB)

Pete following the Exit Gully. (JT)

Joe on the summit with Nanda Devi beyond. (PB)

The whole bizarre procedure took half an hour and, at the end of it, the word 'masochism' had taken on a new meaning.

We had decided it was Joe's turn to go up the fixed ropes first that morning, and this gave me a feeling of relief—we were sharing the risk. Joe was to go up and straighten the fixed rope and sort himself out at the high point of the previous day. The first one up always took the risk that the wind might have frayed the rope against a sharp edge of rock somewhere. Nevertheless, following him I was still apprehensive, even though he had tested the rope and anchors like the jester sampling the king's food for poison. When we had climbed the rock below the icefield we had thought it steep, but it seemed that now the Wall was rearing even steeper. The jumaring was correspondingly more exhausting. My thoughts, refreshed by the night's sleep, were alert to all the dangers. I was delayed by still having some rearranging of the anchors to do on the ropes above Camp Two, and when I arrived at the foot of the Big Groove a shock was awaiting me. Joe had de-pegged the anchors from the three rope lengths above me and, on reaching the three peg crack, he had swung all the rope round in a great loop like a four hundred-foot skipping rope until he had lodged them in the Big Groove. Then he pulled them up tight. As a result I was confronted by nearly two hundred feet of eight-millimetre terylene rope hanging out from the rock down towards me.

'Joe's put it there, so he must be prepared to jumar it,' I thought as I started up, the competitive urge the only motivation. All the instances I had ever known of ropes snapping flashed through my mind like slides on a projector on autochange, interspersed with pictures of me spread out in the air in the apparent standstill of a free fall. 'Still, at least terylene doesn't saw up and down,' I thought. But as I got higher, this rope started to shudder sideways on an edge of rock at the top of the Big Groove. The apex was far away. I moved very stealthily, trying not to jerk the rope, looking at my jumars, eyes focused only on the umbilical cord that held me. The uncanny double-take, a constant companion at altitude, moved in. Was my mind here? My body seemed to be, but my mind felt free and uninvolved. Suddenly it was the top of the apex—there was the short ice slope, Joe, and the three peg crack. Joe was preparing to jumar up the last pitch to our high point.

"That last bit was exciting—it's in a good position," I said.

"It's saved a lot of rope," said Joe.

I knew that we could not afford to go up and down that length of rope many times without it wearing through, but did not mention it. Joe could see it as well as I, and he would find out all about what it was like to jumar the Big Groove when we next came back up! But did he worry as much as I did? I was filled with envy—I was seeing his existence from my separateness, and it seemed to possess a coherence and unity that mine did not.

I followed Joe up to the high point I had reached the previous day. It was a tangled procedure, interlocking me onto the hanging belay. I noticed he had only clipped into two of the three angle pegs I had placed so apprehensively before.

"Why have you only clipped onto two, Joe?"

"They look all right. Two should be enough," he said.

I hastily clipped into the third one. Pegs always give an illusion of safety if you have not put them in yourself.

The sun was filtering around on to us, as Joe set off in the lead. At first the climbing was almost identical to that of the pitch before. Joe did a few feet of pegging until the crack disappeared. He drove a blade peg until it stopped half way, and then passed the climbing rope through a karabiner on the peg. As I held the rope taut he leaned across rightwards, his weight supported by the tension in the rope. Using tiny flakes on the slab, he pulled himself across to the arête. Soon all that I could see were his left hand and foot, scything the arête. It was a fascinating puppet show. The hand and the foot jerked up and then scuttled down. Up, and then down. Up, and then down. Then suddenly they disappeared.

Around the corner, Joe was having a grim struggle:

"From the arête I could see a groove with a crack in the back about six feet away. The groove continued upwards towards the corners above.

"I pulled myself round the arête. The rope was horizontal between my waist and the peg; it was still holding my weight. I tried to reach the groove but as I stretched further right I tended to swing away from the rock. There were no holds big enough to hang onto; I relied on friction to keep me in place. Moving further rightwards round the arête was to move beyond the balance of friction maintained by the rope taking much of my weight and the rugosities of granite beneath my boots and hands. If I parted company, I would swing back twenty feet and the peg would probably come out.

"I juggled with the precarious balance for a while, stretching slightly further each time by clinging to tiny flakes discovered by my groping fingers. My body was almost horizontal and still I could not reach the groove. I glanced at the rope—it was rubbing, every time I moved, up and down the sharp edge of the arête. There was a sense of detachment about this observation; I wondered if I would reach the safety of the groove before the rope was cut through.

"I was quite exhausted by now and as a final resort took a nylon sling from around my neck. It had an aluminium chockstone on it, which I threw towards the crack. It lodged there first time, and I pulled myself to the crack on the nylon tape. The groove was overhanging; I didn't look down to soak in the atmosphere, but hammered in a peg immediately, fastened myself to it and rested."

A few feet of free climbing took him to a large granite block, which he flopped his arm around and rested again.

From the block Joe could see on his right an enormous hanging corner, two hundred feet high. Above that hung tendrils of ice, signifying the start of the Ramp. Towards the middle of this corner, across an overhanging wall, ran a two-foot wide sloping ledge, thirty feet long and banked high with ice. Joe gingerly put his crampons on and kicked his way across it until he was barred by an overhang. This he pegged over. Then he hammered two pegs in to hang from, and waited:

"I shouted for Pete to follow. When I remembered to examine the rope which had been wearing away on the arête I saw that it had been half cut through. I felt a lot more frightened now that I was safe and just thinking about what could have happened, than what I had actually been when involved with the situation. I cut away the frayed part and re-fastened the good rope to my waist."

Joe's tension traverse was difficult to follow, and I moved the diagonal line of his ropes by a series of swings as I knocked pegs out. It was acrobatic, and I felt like Tarzan swinging on a long vine that kept on snagging amongst twigs and branches. When I reached the big block, I peered around the corner and could see Joe, roosting forlornly above the overhang, like a big black hooded bird.

"Where are you going from there?" I shouted.

It looked like a dead end to me. The corner above him that stretched up to the Ramp would take a whole day to climb, if it was possible at all.

"Don't worry," came the habitual reassurance, with its over-emphasised, patronising tone. "I can see a way."

Feeling thankful that he did not sound frightened, I tightened up the rope along the ledge like a handrail on a catwalk, and set off along it. I had decided not to waste time putting my crampons on and my feet felt very insecure in the footholds Joe had hacked in the ice. Most of my weight was on the rope, which felt even thinner than normal, since it was stretched sideways. I remembered that the breaking strain of the rope was even lower when it was stretched horizontally. It had started to snow, and Joe was busily recording the dramatic situation and the snow and cloud effects with his camera.

Joe was right, there was a way out. Between the overhangs, and out of sight from below, a stepped corner reached up leftwards for sixty feet back to the crest of the Upper Tower. "Good route-finding," I complimented him, wondering if he had been led there by his sixth sense, blind luck or just because he could not climb up anywhere else. At first the crack in the corner was blind and he reached another crack on the left wall by a tension traverse. This crack he followed into the corner, and proceeded to climb it by a series of delicate free moves. After an hour he reached the crest. "Can you see the Ramp? Will it go?"

"Yes, it only looks one rope length away. Hurry up, it's a hell of a way down and it will be dark in a minute."

The snow shower had passed and rock was turning red around us. But I felt relaxed. I took some pictures of Joe, varying the exposures so as to catch the lighting.

"Hurry up, there's no time for taking photographs." It was the first time Joe had sounded angrily impatient.

"Don't worry," I shouted back. "You'll be glad of them when you are an old man!"

It was another diagonal swinging pitch to follow. I retrieved all the pegs and nuts so that we could fix the edge out straight down the overhanging wall to the big block. Joe was perched on one foothold and I hung off the slings of his spike belay whilst he sorted the equipment out for his descent. I had taken half an hour longer than he did the day before to descend back to Camp Two, because I had to use a karabiner brake.

"Don't forget to put the brew on," I reminded him.

"See you soon," he said as he reeled off down the rope and out of sight.

Irrationally, I did not share Joe's sense of urgency. I looked up and saw an overhanging groove reaching up to the Ramp. For me it was a golden line of promise through an area of turmoil, as if parted by the rod of Moses. At the top it was crowned by an enormous block of granite bridging across the walls of the groove like a beam across the corner of a roofless house. Perhaps we could peep beneath the crown? Nothing could stop us now.

The rope that had been my tormentor in the harsh light of early morning awareness, had now become a friend. I was descending in a trance. The swooping slides, the dancing traverses and swings, were part of the pattern deeply hidden within the game of the descent. The complicated procedures for passing knots and pitons were factual procedures to be mastered as part of the choreography. The consequences of a mistake were forgotten. The emphasis of progress and the numbness induced by the cold, altitude and fatigue had put me in a state of reverie. A fantasy world had grown around me assuming nonsensical names and nationalities. The knots in the rope I called 'cows', the pegs became 'Americans', the karabiners at my waist all took the names of different girls. I was a big spider scuttling down.

There was a blue light inside the tent, telling me that the stove was purring. The brew was on. I crouched in the darkness, sorting and clipping my equipment to the slings outside, ready to crawl in for shelter.

"I nearly left you to finish the climb on your own, whilst I was up there," said Joe. He was shaken and unnerved.

At the point where there were three pegs together, the rope was criss-crossed between them. Whilst Joe had been passing this section, he had realised something was amiss, and had noticed that his jumar had become unclipped from his waist, his descendeur was in his right hand and all his weight was hanging from his left hand on the jumar.

"It was really weird, odd thoughts kept on spinning round like 'Is this it?' and 'Is Pete going to have to finish the climb on his own?' and 'I don't want to drop my descendeur.' Eventually I fumbled a nylon sling from my neck, wrapped that round the rope and put my arm through it, so that I could get myself clipped in."

Joe said little as we ate our evening meal. It was the usual Oxo with freeze-dried meat and mashed potato and a cup of tea, followed by a nibble of chocolate. I dozed out of his way, as he cooked. What a day it had been—from doubt and fear to resolution. Then from intense effort to joy—all the emotions of a lifetime had been carried to my heart with extraordinary power. Yet our conversation reflected no more than a quiet, calculated hopefulness. In the morning we would move away as early as possible, pack food for two days, and push, alpine style, for the summit.

It was as if our subconscious was plugged into the same internal clock. We both woke late, having already made the decision whilst we were asleep to have a rest day. Now we were waiting for the other one to suggest it. Eventually I asked Joe what he thought about the idea since I had to decide whether to start cooking or not.

"I'm glad you suggested that," he said. And we laughed and slid back onto our imaginations, comforted by the thought that we could wait for the sunshine before starting the cooking or venturing outside into the wind to go to the toilet. That morning at least our internal clock could rest unwound.

During the afternoon, I started to feel claustrophobic inside the tent. When crawling out I accidentally knelt on some of Joe's camera equipment. He snapped at my clumsiness. I had not understood until that point his enthusiasm as a photographer. He had brought his lens tissues and brush up with him and was fastidiously cleaning his equipment.

"I had to buy my cameras," he said. "They weren't given to me, you know."

I had been given an Olympus OM1 camera for the Everest climb, which I had brought up with me, fitted with a wide-angle lens. But I wasn't lavishing it with the attention that Joe thought it deserved. As usual, Joe's precise, orderly approach to bivouacking and equipment made me feel muddled and clumsy, like a small boy told off for touching in a china shop. Some people judge mountaineers by their speed, and by the difficulty of the rock they can climb. But on Changabang the real test was more how efficiently you could put a brew on, warm your fingers or take your boots off.

Outside I drank in the view in the afternoon sunshine. All the mountain shapes nearby were so familiar. Was that the Holy Kailas I could see, I wondered, looking at a solitary white-topped mountain above the distant brown plains of Tibet? Kailas—the throne of Shiva, the precious ice mountain, the crystal one, the centre of the universe. The waters of Kailas fed some of the greatest rivers of Asia and before politics and a war changed borders and religions, thousands of pilgrims travelled to walk or crawl around it. To me it was a white signpost to a forbidden land. Soon, I thought, I would see Nanda Devi from the Summit Ridge, and we would have worked hard for that view. It was now the 13th October, and soon the winter would come. We had not much time.

As I began to squirm back inside the tent I noticed some dark stains on the snow just outside the door, where Joe had been coughing. He had been spitting blood. Since he had not talked about it to me, I decided not to mention it. Inside the tent he was lying in his sleeping bag with an ecstatic look on his face.

"What's making you look so pleased with yourself?" I asked.

"Ooh," he said, "have you felt the tent fabric? It's sort of billowing down over my face, and when you touch it it sort of bulges in soft round yielding curves. Ultimate Bill says that it's the same material used for making women's underwear."

The rest of the day floated past in idle banter. Changabang did not worry us any more.

CHAPTER EIGHT

Beyond the Line

14th–15th October
> White hovers away and near
> Brushing and sliding a solution above fear
> In clouds that pierce and sway
> Through solids inside, beneath and away
> As feathers of needles
> Caress in a groan of silver
> Who am I here? Alive yet apart
> Without and within the wings of the earth.

Outside the night roared. Winds were breaking around the great white rock of Changabang, and then retreating, drawing in their breath with anger, gathering their frustrated powers beyond the mountain, to return again through the darkness. And the mountain rolled on. Only dreams of the summit helped us cling to its side.

It was three in the morning, and pitch black. "It sounds bloody awful out there," said Joe.

It always did from inside the tent—the crackling walls seemed to be shaking with the constant threat of imminent disaster and were turning the tent into a sound box. Joe was still lying on the outside, and only the bulging nylon of the walls was holding him in place. When the wind gusted violently, the side of the tent tried to roll him over. Fortunately, I had chipped the ice ready for melting for breakfast, the night before, and soon had a pan on the stove. The flame of the stove reasserted our defiant right to be there. The tent walls moved the air inside, and the flame swayed slightly from side to side, as if it were continually slipping and righting itself—shaken but always recovering its balance.

We were ready to move at half past six. We had very little equipment, just a climbing rope, a sleeping bag and a bivouac sack each, and a stove, a pan and a little food.

"It's going to be a long, cold haul back up there," I said. "Do you want to go first and sort out the rope just below the high point? Then you can get belayed ready for me to lead the top pitch. The Big Groove jumar might get you buzzing."

Joe agreed and I was thankful. I did not want to be the first to jumar the Big Groove, and wanted him to find out what it was like.

The wind was gusting up to fifty miles per hour, and it was agonisingly cold. Every fifteen minutes I had to stop in my jumars, undo the zip on the front of my oversuit and down suit and thrust my hands deep under my armpits, gripping my fingers firmly under my arms. 'If this goes on any longer I soon won't be able to warm them back up again,' I thought. It demanded a disciplined effort to recognise when my fingers were reaching the danger zone, because many of the ends were numb already.

Joe had forgotten to tighten the rope below the high point – it had been a misunderstanding. Still, it did not matter. We had an old hawser laid rope which we thought would reach the Ramp, and probably would not need any more. I took off my sack and left it with Joe, and set off up the pitch. A day's climbing was ahead, and we had no idea where we would be at nightfall. A day to hold in the front of my mind, to pace myself through. But the immediate problem was the Groove.

There was a lot of ice on the rock but I wanted to avoid using crampons. First I had to reach the foot of the Groove by crossing its right-hand wall from Joe's stance. There were some good incut holds for my fingers, and soon I was fifteen feet above his head. However, my fingers had lost all sensation again; I clipped an etrier in to a spike runner, stuck both feet in it and tried to warm them up. I knew I could keep on climbing with numb fingers, but that would do permanent damage, and we had a few days to keep going yet. If Joe resented having to wait in the cold during my re-warming antics, he never complained. However, this was the first time we had been forced to do desperate climbing out of the sun – it was a good excuse.

A flake of rock curved into the Groove and I hand-traversed across this, finding little flaky holds on the granite beneath to support my feet. Soon I was poised next to the Groove, uncertain whether my legs would stretch to a small foothold on the other side, if I launched myself across it. I took a deep breath and, feeling as if I were stepping from a secure quayside into an untethered rowing boat, lunged across. My foot missed the hold but, with my hands, I steadied myself against the left-hand side of the Groove, and eased myself carefully into a bridging position. After twenty feet the Groove moved from the vertical to overhanging. The right-hand wall had become blank and I could no longer bridge across. I placed a nut in the crack and clipped into it, gasping for oxygen. I twisted my head back and looked around.

It was the most amazing, exhilarating situation I had ever been in. I looked down and across at Joe, who was hanging on the edge of space. Directly below me almost our entire route fell sheer away. Over a thousand feet below was Camp Two, and yet the Upper Tower was so foreshortened beneath me, and the air so clear, it felt close enough still to be our home. Beyond the icefield, the undulations and peaks on the ridge between Rhamani and the Bagini Glacier were flattened by the perspective of my height. The ridge drew a vertical line across the earth beneath my feet between light and shade, white and brown, known and unknown, explored and forbidden. The black spot of Camp One on the ridge was the only sign of our passing in that wilderness. The rock of the Groove seemed poised on the edge of the mountain. I was directly above that tent nearly four thousand feet below. For a moment I was speeding through the skies above the wrinkled world.

Above me, a great arc of colours stood across the sky in a rainbow around the pool of white light of the hidden sun. The ice crystals in the air of the upper atmosphere were forming a halo around the sun, the classic herald of an approaching front. I wondered if Joe had read the signs as well, and when the storm would arrive; I hoped it would not be a big one.

The big block crowning the Groove was suspended above my head. I leant out on the nut I was hanging from and pushed it. It did not tremble, so I moved up onto another nut higher in the Groove, pulled a leg clear and kicked it. I did not want to dislodge it in case it chopped the ropes or hit Joe. It probably weighed half a ton. Since there were no signs of it moving, I decided it would be safer to try and squirm behind rather than risk levering it away by pulling around its outside.

As soon as I had wriggled my shoulders through the hole my feet swung out into space. After a lot of undignified wriggling and heaving, I suddenly popped out onto some snow. From above, the block seemed to be balanced on a perch that defied gravity, and I quickly moved my weight off it. I looked upwards and saw snow, the easiest angled snow I had seen for four thousand feet. I had popped through the Keyhole that, at last, seemed to have opened the door to the climb—surely nothing could stop us now?

"I'm on the Ramp," I yelled into the wind.

Within seconds the sun moved onto me, to help match an outer with inner warmth. I tied off one of the ropes for Joe to jumar up, and started hauling up my sack. As Joe neared me, he had to take his own sack off and attach it to mine, so that he could squeeze the sacks and himself separately through the Keyhole. He was pleased to join me in the sunshine.

"Reaching the Ramp was tremendous. That was the real conquest, the imponderable difficulties were over — the summit was 1,000 long, cold, weary feet away."

The sun was weak and watery, but now we had movement to warm our limbs. We shed most of our hardware and took with us two ropes and a handful of pegs, slings and karabiners. We were still adhering to the pattern of leading two pitches each at a time, and I quickly set off, kicking steps up the snow above us, plunging the spikes of my axe and hammer with a steady rhythm. It was a joy to be able to move so freely, to begin to gain height with such ease. Dumping most of the hardware had made a big difference.

Another buttress of rocks towered above us, rearing its head between us and the summit slopes. The snow I was climbing was powdery and unstable, and I decided to aim for these rocks to gain the security of a rock belay. To reach their nearest point, I had to climb diagonally across the slope. I touched the rock at the same moment the rope stopped coming to me from Joe. It had just been long enough.

Joe soon joined me. We had left the jumars behind and were now climbing in the Alpine style with which we were familiar, moving as a fluid, integrated unit, our sacks geared for survival. We had cast off from the fixed ropes and the rope between us had been demoted from master to servant; for a while, at least, the mountain would be our total support, and we were reprieved from the hanging, fragile line. The leader and the second could share the climbing movement, no longer were we jumaring past the verticality of each other's achievement. The movement had become all-important. The afternoon was ticking past — we were committed to the summit and our speed would be our only defence.

"This must be the Ramp," I said, "and so we ought to keep on traversing right. It should curve up through this buttress on to the summit snowfield."

Joe, however, thought we should go straight up, following a more direct gully line through the rock buttress. "It looks all right, it'll be much shorter, and it'll be easier to abseil down," he said. Also, he didn't like the state of the snow, and considered that a lot of traversing without the assurance of there being good rock belays would be more dangerous. I was worried that the gully might be too difficult, and that we would waste too much time on it. But it was Joe's lead and so it was his decision to make. After taking a few slings from around my neck he moved off and, after hugging the foot of the rock, led a difficult diagonal pitch over mixed ground up into the gully.

The upper section of the gully was out of sight from us, hidden by an ice slope fifty feet wide, that bulged at eighty feet. Joe pulled over a short rockstep and climbed steadily on the ice up to and over the bulge. Many ice fragments started falling down and the rope stopped moving out so evenly. The texture of the ice had changed from being white, aerated and firm to black, hard, unyielding water ice. Joe climbed for thirty feet up this sixty degree, steely surface towards the left-hand side of the gully at a point where the gully walls closed in. As he climbed he tried to protect himself by hammering in ice pegs. The ice was so hard that it splintered after the ice pegs had entered more than a couple of inches, and he had to tie them off. They offered him little more than psychological protection. His axe and hammer picks and crampon points were blunt after all the previous climbing and demanded heavy swings before they penetrated enough to offer any support. It was mentally and physically an exhausting pitch, and by the time Joe hammered in a rock peg, he had cramp in his forearms and calf muscles. He managed to nick a small foothold in the ice to stand on, and pulled the rope in.

"I found that quite hard," said Joe when I eventually reached him. There was not much room, and I found I became spread-eagled around him, with one foot on the ice and one foot on the gully wall. I had enjoyed the pitch immensely. It had been the first time on the route I had been able to relish hard technical climbing under the safety of a top rope.

"Excuse me," I said, since I was half hanging from his harness in my attempts to pass him.

"It's about time you had a wash," said Joe.

I returned to the original subject. "Yes, that last bit was rather tricky. Where do we go now—over there on the right?"

Joe agreed, he had been weighing up the next section whilst I had been climbing. On the right at the back of the gully was a line of apparent weaknesses in the broken ground, where the rock and the ice met. It was impossible to judge its angle and difficulty from where we were.

Trying to appear as confident and forceful as possible, I took a few deep breaths and vigorously front-pointed for fifteen feet across the gully until I could brace a foot across a spike and scrape my other crampon against the ice until I was in balance.

For me, it was a perfect pitch. Every move was intricate, technical and yet I could recapture my balance after every two or three movements. Every technique I had ever used was tested and applied, half consciously—bridging, jamming, chimneying, lay-backing, mantle-shelfing, finger pulls, pressure holds all followed in a myriad of combinations. The struggling rope acrobatics of the Upper Tower were forgotten, for this was mixed rock and ice-climbing at its finest. I felt in perfect control and knew the thrill of seeing the ropes from my waist curl down through empty space. I was as light as the air around me, as if I were dancing on tip-toes, relaxed, measuring every movement and seeking a complete economy of effort. Speak with your eyes, speak with your hands, let it all flow from your heart. True communication, true communion, is silent. Chekhov once said that when a man spends the least possible movement over some definite action, that is grace. This was my lonely quest, until the jerk of the rope reminded me that I must stop and secure myself—and that I had a companion. Looking back at Joe, I realised how late it had grown. The gully had turned into a golden amphitheatre, poised on the edge of darkness.

It was an awkward pitch for Joe to follow:

"The rope was pulling me rightwards; I had to climb into the back of the gully but was pulled off balance each time by the rope. I shouted to Pete but he did not seem to hear and I could not pull any slack down. With a fervent prayer that he had a good belay, I swung on the rope across the gully and grabbed the rock on the other side."

Our awareness of each other, and our strength, flowed between us in waves. Now, when Joe arrived, I realised with an almost physical sense of shock that he was tired. For a few moments the mask of silence between us fell aside. Nearly three hundred feet above us, the gully seemed to finish in a crest against the summit slopes. There were no ledges where we could spend the night around the narrow snow slope, broken by rocksteps, above us.

"I'll take us to the crest if you like," I said.

"Yeah, I'm a bit tired," said Joe.

I was filled with urgency, and determined to stay in the sun until I reached the crest. It was an invented game, to pluck us from the grasp of darkness. It gave me a surge of strength, keyed up as I was by the rhythm of the action. The gully was sheltered and, as I churned up-wards with my feet, the powder snow poured straight down. The air was becoming colder but the light was warm and red. The sun was pushing me upwards as if I were soaring on particles of solar light.

Ten feet beneath the crest, I plunged a deadman into the snow and pulled the rope in, but Joe was already moving. I saw his red helmet bob over a rock step, lassooed by the evening light. For the first time since I had followed Joe's pitch up the gully, I could look around me. But night was quickly closing its doors and only the sun held my gaze. It was a glorious sunset that spread its calm into me and abstracted me from the time and space below us. Numb toes and racing heart were forgotten. But these were moments I could not savour. The advent of Joe, darkness and cold stopped our upwards motion. We had to bivouac.

The crest of snow where the gully met the summit icefield was on the edge of the mountain. We reckoned we were at 22,000 feet—with about 500 feet to gain to reach the summit. As soon as we moved onto the crest, the whole atmosphere of the evening changed, for we moved from the shelter of the gully into the wind. The wind was blowing agitatedly across the crest, as it accelerated around the top of the moun-tain. The temperature was plummeting as the sun disappeared.

"We'll have to stop here," I said, "we might be able to dig in." I felt unusually assertive, as if it was my job this time to organise the bivouac. I fixed up a belay line to some nuts and a piton I had placed in a rock that poked out of the snow, and we both tied on to it. I traced out the area of snow that we ought to excavate, with the pick of my axe, and Joe started digging at one end and I at the other. It was becoming colder by the minute, and soon we were digging with the feverish haste of gold-crazed prospectors, using feet, hands and axe, and throwing up clouds of snow into the wind.

Rock was disappointingly near the surface, and our hopes of a snow-hole faded. Eventually we managed to gouge a tiny platform. We were now dangerously cold and it was vital to warm ourselves up. We had brought two small bivouac bags with us in case we had been unable to

find a ledge and had to bivouac separately. This meant we had no
shelter large enough to cook inside, out of the wind. There would be
no evening drink or meal.

"It's your turn to sleep on the outside," said Joe.

"Are you keeping your boots on inside your pit?" I asked him. Yes,
he was. We only had our two-pound, lightweight sleeping bags with
us, and would need as much warmth as possible.

With his habitual bivouacking speed and catlike search for comfort,
Joe was soon ensconced in his green cocoon.

"Our values had sunk ever further. Tonight, bliss was cessation
of activity, a place out of wind and warm sleep."

I was struggling with my sleeping bag, feeling angry at my own
comparative ineptitude. I felt very insecure, as if I were only preventing
myself rolling off the shelf by keeping my muscles tense. I was lying
on my side, facing into the slope which was not quite long enough for
me. My feet were poking out over the crest and the wind was
tearing at them so fiercely, it felt as if there were no layers protecting
them.

Joe seemed to gain a few inches of the ledge every hour. An irrational, miserable little corner of my mind started resenting him. 'I bet
he's really warm. I bet he's fast asleep. Why does he always seem more
comfortable than me? Why does he need so much room?' Every time
I dozed off and relaxed, my back and leg muscles would jerk back
awake as gravity started to topple me off the ledge. There is a bivouac
story of a climber who stayed awake all night so as not to wake his
sleeping leader who had slumped against him. Well, that was not me —
and I had had enough.

"Hey, Joe, you're pushing me off!"

"Oh, sorry." He sounded wide awake, and immediately made some
room for me.

I must have fallen asleep. I pushed the tiny hole left where the draw-
cord had been drawn tight at the top of the bivouac bag, round to my
eyes. It was still dark. It was even colder, and the wind felt as if it were
blowing through me like a sieve. Then I realised. My feet. I could not
feel my feet. I fought the overwhelming desire to flop back to sleep
again, and struggled into the foetal position and started taking my boots
off. One foot, and then the other; I tried to warm them alternately by
pushing both hands down the sock and rubbing and holding the base

of the foot and then the toes. It took two hours to bring the feeling back into them.

Dawn meant nothing to us and we were not ready to accept it. I was wincing uncontrollably with the cold.

"Shall we wait for the sun?" I bawled into my bivouac bag, hoping that the sound would manage to escape somehow through the hole above me.

"Yeah," came the strains of a reply. "We should be on the top in an hour or so from here."

I was too cold to think. Two hours later, however, the bivouac king was bored.

"I'm making a brew," he announced, the trade union job differential forgotten. An hour later, a lukewarm mugful of something nondescript was thrust through the gap and I downed it in a couple of gulps.

"The sun's out you know," came the second announcement. And so it was, but all its power was filtered by a high veil of cloud, and it was not warming the day up as we had hoped. I counted up to ten, steeled myself and started getting up.

"Could you tie my bootlaces, Joe?" I knew if I tried to do it my fingers would never recover.

Joe stooped down without a word and tightened them up for me. I felt like a pathetic little child — but Joe did not take the opportunity to throw a gibe. 'He must have had a lot of practice doing this for all his little brothers and sisters,' I thought.

"We'll leave all the gear here, shall we?" said Joe.

So we were not going to descend the other side. "We'd better take a rope and a couple of deadmen," I said. And we were ready.

It was as if I had done all this before, in a dream, but now I was in the dream itself. We quickly climbed through a short rock step above the bivouac site and started moving together up the 50° snowfield. Joe was in the lead.

"I wanted to get it over with. The romance for me was gone . . . the fatigue of altitude and exertion were familiar and not disconcerting. I never looked back to see how Pete was doing, whether he was moving faster or slower. I could feel the rope tug at my waist and I would wait, but did not know if it was Pete on the other end or whether it was just dragging in the snow . . . The 'Horns' of Changabang were now below us and faintly, in the depths of my consciousness, was the awesome thought that at

long last we were clawing our way up a slope, poised breath-
takingly above the precipice of the West Wall, 5,000 feet above
the glacier. A few points of metal on our boots, a couple of
metal tools in our hands and a rope tying us together, were all
that were holding us in place."

The light, like an over-exposed photograph, now had no warmth,
no colour, no perspective and the snow could have been of any angle —
except my gasping breath and heavy feet told me of its height. The
wind bowed my head. My eyes were lowered to the moving ground.
Wind buffeted, powder snow scurried past in an endless stream. The
standstill feeling had returned, which I had felt so many times before
when climbing on snow. I was inside a shell that moved in slow
motion, with a steady mechanical high-lifted step.

I was blinkered in mind and vision. Clouds were surrounding us.
This was Changabang, soon I would be able to see its other side. Would
I be able to see Nanda Devi and the Sanctuary of my childhood dreams?
It seemed simplest to stay in a single, intense thought, to feel the prospect of a wider horizon draw me like a magnet towards the summit
ridge. The memories of a month's struggle on the West Wall lay
beneath my feet and the summit was the distillation of all my hopes.

Joe was sitting on my horizon line. He had reached the ridge and
was pulling in the loops of rope between us. For the final fifty feet
there was a wind-carved crust of hard snow on top of the powder,
which collapsed under my weight. I steadied my impatience and
kicked through it carefully. Joe was as relieved as I was excited at the
view. "Don't worry, you can see it," he said as I arrived. It was as if
he would have felt responsible if I could not but, so reliable, had
managed to arrange a convenient break in the clouds. And there it was.
Nanda Devi, the bliss-giving goddess.

Clouds plumed horizontally from its summit above its shadowed
North-Eastern Walls. These 8,000-foot walls formed a vast, forbidding
amphitheatre of swirling mist. To the west, however, the sun picked
out a silver track along the Northern Ridge that threaded its way to
the main summit. And the summit was clear. Below the spaciousness
between our spire and the twin-peaked mass of Nanda Devi, stretched
the upper arms of the promised land. Long, orderly brown moraines
lined the sides of the glaciers, as if fashioned by giant hands. It was the
15th October and winter would soon cover all that wilderness. No
man slept there.

The summit, the highest point on the whole of the ridge, was thirty feet away.

"You might as well move across," said Joe. The top was only a few feet higher than the point where we had reached the ridge.

I thought we would at least shake hands, but Joe did not make any gestures. I wondered if he felt he had just done another climb and that life would just go on until he did his next one. Perhaps wiser than I, he had already started focusing his concentration on the problems we were to face in the descent—perhaps to touch each other would have broken the spell of our separateness. I took some photographs of him sitting on the ridge, with Nanda Devi in the background. His beard and mouth were encrusted in ice and his mirror sunglasses hid any feeling in his eyes. In the mirrors I could see my own reflection. How could I ever know to what depth he was retreating? His few words seemed so inadequate. I could not know if practicality did rule him, or if he was concealing his emotion. Was it that we had different attitudes to expression? Or were we really living at different levels?

It was difficult to judge the size of the cornice and we belayed each other and peered alternately over the edge and down the upper ice slopes of the South Face. We could see about two hundred feet, and then the Face cut away into the unknown.

"There don't seem to be any tracks anywhere," I said, "perhaps the lads haven't done the South Face."

I was glad there were no tracks, for they would have taken the edge off our isolation. To the north-east, we could see Kalanka Col, with Kalanka rising from it. Beyond that more white mountains, and I photographed them, determining to discover their names later. But they were tame to our eyes, after the vertical world we had left beneath us. I wished we had decided to descend the other side, to bring a new dimension to our experience of the mountain.

I sat in the snow and changed the film in my camera. But now Nanda Devi and Kalanka were obscured by cloud. "Have you seen over there?" asked Joe.

The storm cloud which had been darkening the northern sky over Tibet all day, had suddenly grown and was moving towards us. The coming of the storm had been announced by signs in the sky, twenty-four hours before. Now it had arrived.

I did not want to leave and hated the prospect of descending the West Wall. The sight of the other side had liberated my spirit. The isolation of our situation, and the size of the wilderness beneath us, intensified our strength. For a moment I felt omniscient above the world. But this feeling of invincibility was an illusion of pride, for we had yet to descend. It was two in the afternoon and we had been on the summit for half an hour when the first snow flakes began to fall.

CHAPTER NINE

Descent to Tragedy

15th–19th October

"We might as well unrope for the first part of the descent," said Joe.

"What — with this storm coming in?" I was incredulous.

"Well, there's not much point in keeping it on if we're not going to belay. If one slips, he'll just pull the other one off."

"I prefer to keep it on and move together, so that it's there and ready in case we come across any tricky bits," I said.

"Well, there aren't any tricky bits and we'll have to abseil as soon as we reach that rock step above the bivouac," said Joe.

"All right then, but you go first and I'll carry the rope," I agreed. 'If he can do it, so can I,' I thought. Although I could understand Joe's cool rationale, I was repelled by the idea of soloing above the five and a half thousand feet of the West Wall of Changabang. On the summit Joe had become assertive, whilst I had been preoccupied with the view and our arrival. A wave of purpose had rippled between us and I was happy that he led down.

I finished coiling the rope. Joe quickly moved back along the ridge and started down our line of tracks that stretched down the snow-slope. As I looked across at him, I could see under the cloud the familiar sight of the Rhamani Glacier, twisting down towards the Rishi Ganga. The walls of the Rhamani before had oppressed me, but now we moved above them, and they were reduced to geographic details. The moraines of the Rhamani, that broke through the ice like the bones of the earth, were now the highways of our return. The beginning of the dark sheltered vegetation of the Rishi Ganga was a promise that sprang from a kindlier planet. There, only treetops would be swaying.

The snowslope was easier to climb down than I had feared and, in descent, the altitude had lost its enfeebling effect. Soon the falling snow had imprisoned us in mad, whirling whiteness and we kicked and plunged downwards with increasing urgency. Joe reached the rock

step and hastily fixed a sling. I uncoiled the rope and we flung it below
us. It snaked out into the cloud and writhed down among the falling
snow and spindrift. The air and snow around us were in constant
downward dance, and as we slid down the ropes we joined their
momentum.

As we picked up our sacks and sorted our gear at the bivouac site,
spindrift was pouring everywhere, into our sack, into our gloves and
down our necks. We were retreating under bombardment. The hardware was so cold it stuck to our gloves. 'Let's get the hell outa here,'
echoed a thought in a voice like a John Wayne movie, and with it
came the return of the strange realisation that I was actually enjoying
myself.

The next two abseils went quickly. By the time I arrived next to Joe,
he was fixing the anchor for the next abseil and he threaded it through
as I pulled one end of the doubled rope down. The previous time we
had used this abseil procedure had been five years before, when we had
first met in the Western Alps. Now it was automatic.

We had reached a point half way down the steep pitch I had led the
previous day. As I swung down the rope towards him, Joe said, "If I
direct the rope right, we should make it in one go to the bottom of the
gully from here." He was perched on a couple of footholds and I held
on above him. After I had pulled the ropes down I saw his anchor. He
had tapped a one and a half inch knife blade into a thin diagonal crack
in a rock inlaid in the ice. It had gone in about an inch of its length.
And he was about to slide off on it!

"You're not going to just abseil off that are you?" I was aghast.

"Can you suggest anything better?" he replied coldly.

We had left most of the pegs at the top of the fixed ropes and now
only had two left with us. The other one was of the wrong size. I could
not suggest anything better, and off he went without an upward
glance. I clung on to the peg with one of my hands, hoping it would
not lever out. Joe did not seem worried:

"I believed that the piton was just adequate to take our weight.
I had the impression that we would be all right. We had put
everything possible into making sure it was safe, we could do no
more; we needed now a little bit of luck."

Joe, out of sight beneath the bulge of the gully, shouted to me that
he had reached the snow, and that he was swinging across to the side

of the gully to fix an anchor. I was still frightened about the peg, because of my extra weight. However, I knew that once Joe had tied off the end of the rope there was chance of a fall being held after 300 feet.

I went springing over the bulges, and the sun started fighting through the snow clouds. The storm was passing and I knew that with the improving visibility we would find the end of the fixed ropes. But it was a declining sun and brought to the amphitheatre lighting identical to that of the afternoon before; except we had reached the summit in between, and now golden particles of snow were falling through the light.

Reaching the fixed ropes felt like coming into the mouth of the harbour out of a storm-tossed sea. Our faces and clothing were encrusted with ice from the struggle. As we arrived, it stopped snowing but, unfortunately, it also became dark.

"Go and get the brew on, Joe," I said. We had eleven hundred feet of abseiling to do. It would be too dangerous to try and retrieve the rope, and, so, sadly, we would have to leave it behind. Joe went first:

> "We did the long, lonely abseils in the dark, without seeing or hearing each other. There was just an awareness, a mental, psychological bond between us . . . In the thirty-six hours since we had been on the ropes they had been, in parts, affected by the wind. One anchor point on the big flake had lifted off. I had to haul, drag and claw my way back onto course. I replaced the anchor point to make it easier for Pete . . . Then on down, with my hands stiffening into cramp with the strain of hanging on, finding my way by touch and memory."

We had climbed the West Wall when nobody had thought we could do it, and now I was grimly determined that the mountain would not have the last word. Every knot, peg and ropelength that I unclipped and clipped and heaved my way past was another piece of mountain that could not capture me. Every foot I descended was taking me further away down the mountain that was now an enemy that was trying to cheat us. The circling voices, faces and names returned, accelerating around in my head.

The descending traverses that reversed the tension moves were desperately complicated to negotiate, because the rope was tied off in so many places. I was thankful to reach the three peg crack above the Big Groove. On reaching the top peg I leant down and clipped an etrier into the lower peg and put my foot into it. Then I clipped my waist into the middle peg with a fifi hook and leant out on it and extricated the karabiner brake from the rope above. Suddenly I was being propelled backwards, flopping over head-first, as helpless as a rag doll. 'I'm dead. How did that happen? Thwack!' I was winded but I had not fallen. My foot had caught in the etrier. Without a thought, I scrambled and pulled myself upright. The middle peg had come out. It was one that I had put in. 'Well, I'm still here—better get moving.' This was not the time for prayers of thanksgiving.

Wind and cold were forgotten. The rope in the Big Groove only had to hold my weight once more: and it held. Long engraved disciplined skills took me past obstacles and my detached mind was half-surprised at my progress. Trained homo sapiens, the tool-user, had taken over.

Far below me, Joe had reached Camp Two:

"Half-way from the summit, half-way to safety. As usual, I hacked some lumps of ice and put them near the tent doorway, then tumbled into the tent, feeling more exultation than I had ever permitted myself on the summit.

"Warm inside my sleeping bags, revelling in the sensual ache of relaxation after exertion, I melted ice, preparing a hot drink for Pete when he came in. Without a descendeur, it usually took him much longer to descend than it took me to have the water hot. I listened for him, full of things to say for once, wanting to share the satisfaction of knowing we had succeeded. He seemed to be taking longer than usual. The water was hot. For some curious reason, I delayed having a drink myself until he arrived.

"I waited. There was no tell-tale jangling of hardware to herald his approach. I looked out into the blackness. Not a sound. I called out. Nothing.

"Back inside, I mentally went over the last hour—one and a half hours—to see whether I could recall any sound which might have been Pete falling. With this, I admitted the possibility to myself of what might have happened, but could recall nothing.

"Still there was no sound. I asked myself what the hell could I do? I longed to hear the sounds which would banish these morbid thoughts from my mind.

"Then the sounds came—a rattling and jangling, a scraping of crampons on rock; not in the sudden rush of catastrophe, but slowly, in control. My fears vanished, but I could not find again quite the same exultation which I had wanted to share two hours earlier."

I saw the fragile, flapping nylon of Camp Two, fifteen feet below me in the darkness. It looked deserted but I knew Joe would be inside, crouched over the stove. Then, far below on the glacier, I saw a green light.

"Hey, Joe," I yelled excitedly. "There's a green flare on the glacier. Can you see it?" But he was too late, for by the time he got his head out the tent door, the light had faded. "Pass me your torch, Joe." I flashed it back down towards the glacier, but there was no reply. I insisted that I had seen it, but Joe was guarded—like a doctor suspecting a patient of concussion.

Inside the tent we talked compulsively, our minds unwinding the elation of success. We laughed unashamedly at the terrible warnings other climbers had given us. For two hours our egos reigned supreme. We were not off the mountain yet, but the dangers below us were all on known ground.

The morning sun thawed us slowly into action. There was no sense of urgency. The view from the door seemed as friendly as a loved and familiar face. It was not the mountains around us that had changed, but our attitude to them. The cold camp we had left with tense resolve two days before was now a warm and comforting haven. We talked on the surface, but there was no need to express the deep contentment that flowed between us. There was no need for blunt confrontation any more, because all the important decisions had been made.

"I suppose we'd better get moving, or we'll get benighted again."

"I don't like the idea of having to hump all this stuff down on our backs."

"We could always roll some of the gear down from here, it'd only bounce a couple of times before landing at the bottom of the Wall, and there aren't many crevasses for it to go in."

"Yes, and it'll be fun to watch too."

"We'd better hang onto our survival gear though, just in case the stuff disappears."

We rolled up the superfluous equipment including the tents, the hammocks and the three remaining Gaz cylinders we had left, into red stuff bags and strung them together until they looked like a string of floats for lobster-pots.

"Remember to let go of them when you throw them."

"I wonder what the Mars Bars-eater'll make of these when they plunge out of the sky and land around its ears."

The stuff bags slid off down the icefall with the confidence of an Olympic ski-jumper, launched out above the Barrier, hung momentarily in space, and disappeared from view.

I had to rebandage my three fingers that were most damaged. Once again, Joe offered to go first and rig the abseils on the icefield. He would find it easier than I to find the anchors we had left behind, since he had led this section of the climb.

I am always scared unless I am abseiling off at least two pegs, even if one apparently is a perfect placement. But it did not seem to bother Joe to abseil off just one. Halfway down, he set off on another solitary knifeblade. It was flexing as he went down. This time I was not going to say anything, but I unclipped from it, so that I would not be pulled down after Joe if it came out. At that moment, Joe looked up and saw what I had done.

"Well, if it does come out, you'll be a bit stranded up there without a rope," he shouted cheerfully.

"I'd take my shirt off and wave for help," I shouted back.

Fortunately it was an obedient peg, and stayed where it was to Joe's apparent confidence and to my whispered incantations. I suppressed my worries and drew strength from his attitude. I did not know whether this bluffing of each other was based either on mutual deception or on mutual support. It was like being in a platoon of soldiers, in which nobody really wants to fight, but everybody is doing what he imagines his comrade expects him to do.

Soon we were at the bottom of the icefield and Joe disappeared down the overhanging wall next to the Guillotine. It was half an hour before he shouted for me to come on down. As soon as I moved down over the lip of the icefield I saw the reason for the delay. The abseil rope had not been long enough to reach the end of rope we had fixed through the Toni Kurz pitch, and Joe had found himself dangling and sliding towards the loose ends whilst still a few feet out from the rock. He had tied some slings together and, after knotting them to the end of the abseil ropes, he had swung in and grabbed the peg.

I found it difficult to retrieve the ropes. Joe pulled me into the rock with the slings on the end of them and held me there whilst I hammered in some pegs. I then hung off these and pulled the ropes through and then abseiled from there down to Joe.

"I'd better go down the Toni Kurz pitch first, in case I get tangled up in karabiners and need to be extricated," I said.

"Don't worry, Uncle Joe'll look after you," came the reply.

It was the first time on Changabang that I had abseiled whilst wearing such a heavy sack. Halfway down I lost my balance and turned completely upside down with a squeak of fright. I hoped that Joe had not heard it, and painfully righted myself. I floundered and thrashed about, trying to unclip and clip the mess of karabiners around my waist so that I could pass the pegs, hoping that I was not unclipping the wrong ones. The torques and tensions the heavy sack had introduced were enormous, it felt as if I were trying to couple up the trucks of a heavy goods train single-handed. But I reached the Balcony before I realised that I could have saved a lot of energy.

"It'd be best to come down on your jumars, Joe. It'd make it much easier getting past the pegs. It's bloody desperate if you try to abseil."

The afternoon had rushed past, and granite was turning red around us as Joe bounced into sight around the overhangs.

"It looks easy angled down there," he said, looking past me at the rock below us. I looked round at it. Yes, compared to the rock and the risk of the Upper Tower, its angle looked gentle. And to think how awe-struck we had been on those early pitches! If only we had known what was to come—how our sense of judgement had changed.

"We'll have to find all the abseil placements in the dark now, though," I said. I was cursing myself for the conceit of our leisurely morning. We had completely underestimated the time the descent would take. 'Why does everything always turn into an epic?' I thought. 'Why can't anything be simple?' Then Joe announced that while he was overseeing my descent, his descendeur had become unclipped from a karabiner and had bounced down into the shadows. A nasty thought sneaked into my mind and had its say before I slammed the door on it. 'At least he'll find out how desperate it is abseiling with all these karabiners.' It did not matter now who went first, we were both equally slow.

As quickly as we could, we made three abseils in the waning light and were five hundred feet above Camp One when it became dark. The remaining problem was to find convenient abseil points on this mixed ground of snow and rock without straying so far to our right that we went over the North Face, or so far to the left that we missed the ridge altogether. The short sections of rope that we had gleaned from Shipton's Col and hung over some of the rock steps were hidden by the darkness.

One hour after nightfall, the wind started to carry snow with it. Steadily the wind became stronger and the amount of snow in the air increased. Now we had reached the change in angle where the ridge started out of the Wall.

"You'd better go down first," said Joe. "Your eyesight's better than mine in stuff like this. My contact lenses aren't infra red."

"It's finding the point where we go down through that first rock step above the camp that's going to be the tricky bit," I said.

We decided that we would move together, to save time, and I would go first and place as much protection as I could.

I kicked off down the slope. The visibility was so bad that I could not see Joe after the first ten feet. I was scared that I might go through the cornice, and tried to sense that I was just below the crest of the ridge by the angle of the snow. After seventy feet I placed a deadman snow anchor as a runner and, after ninety feet, I stumbled across the blackness of a short rockstep with one of our pegs and marker ribbons in it. I clipped the rope into this and kept going. Soon I felt the rope tug gently, as if there were a fish on the end of the line. Then it slackened off again. Joe was coming.

It was a bitter ordeal—feet frozen, legs shaking with cold, bodies screaming 'no more!' Yet we were completely in control, treading the fine line that separates the difficult from the dangerous. It was impossible for us to feel tired whilst we still had one more obstacle to overcome. We knew we were probably only a couple of hundred feet above the camp, and thrilled to the action, for success could not be far away. I was playing to the audience of my mind. The situation was drawing from me the utmost of my skills and strength, and yet more seemed to rush in to compensate, as if I had been created to struggle through to life. 'If I've got any sixth sense, it had better start working now,' I thought. We were so keyed up by our tantalising position that nothing could have stopped us from finding the tent.

"The rock step must be just below." Joe's voice was muffled by the snow and wind.

I moved down and a few feet below me the slope sheered away. I lowered myself down from my ice hammer and axe, and lunged at the ice below with my feet. It was like kicking concrete. The crampons bounced off hard granite beneath the ice.

"I'm just above it now, I'll traverse around till I find the polypropylene," I shouted. If only it were daylight! Then I recognised something about the way the black outline of rock curved into the slope. I stepped down and brushed away the snow. I could feel two pitons and a length of polypropylene rope. I clipped into them and belayed Joe until he joined me. We quickly rigged an abseil and sped off down it.

"We'll pull the rope down in the morning."

The dark shape of the tent loomed up in front of us through the drifting curtain of snow. We tumbled inside. It was 9.15 p.m. We had been descending for three hours in darkness. We prepared a quick meal with the scraps of food that were there. The air inside the tent quickly warmed up. We started to feel drowsy, and soon flopped into exhausted sleep.

It had been the 17th September, exactly one month before, when we had erected the tent at Camp One. Now it had sunk deep into the snow of the ridge and, in the morning, we hacked it out and packed up all the equipment we had accumulated at the camp.

"To think we carried all this lot up," said Joe, as he thrust the pressure cooker into the top of his bulging sack. I chipped out the sweet papers that were inlaid like a mosaic under the groundsheet.

"We could always do another trundle," I suggested.

Joe seemed slightly shocked. Dropping anything, whether it's part of the mountain or equipment, is frowned upon as bad practice in the crowded Alps, when it is likely that you will hit someone. This accounted for the sense of guilt we had felt when we dropped the gear down from Camp Two. We both peered over the edge of the ridge, like a couple of small, mischievous boys planning to drop something on a train.

"We'll have to throw it well clear of these first rocks," said Joe. We wrapped the tent and our outer sleeping bags and duvets in the foam mats and hurled them into the air. Long seconds later, many objects appeared back into our view on the glacier a thousand feet below. Our carefully tied parcels had disintegrated and now all our jettisoned belongings were running all over the glacier like startled sheep. We tried to watch them all until they stopped, memorised their positions and then shouldered our sacks. We then climbed down the ridge and, taking one last look towards Tibet, started to climb down the ice slope towards the Rhamani Glacier.

It was an effort to summon the concentration to descend the ice slope. Our crampons were worn into blunt and stubby points and hardly bit into the ice. The slope had disintegrated beyond recognition and was still poised on a layer of loose rubble that threatened to behave like ball bearings and roll the sheets of ice off. Joe moved quickly below me, to get out of the way of the stones I was dislodging. He was down it half an hour before I was and, as I descended the last dangerous section, I looked down at him collecting our fallen belongings, envying his safe world of the glacier. At last I was stumbling over the lumpy avalanche debris at the foot of the slope. 'Nothing can kill me now,' I thought as I walked across the glacier to help him.

"It kept us on our toes till the very end didn't it?" said Joe.

We managed to find nearly all our equipment. The Mars Bar-eater had covered the glacier with more of its tracks whilst we had been on the mountain, and now we added to them in our search. Our full body harnesses and the tent had disappeared.

"We'll come back and look for them in the morning," I said.

"It kept us on our toes till the very end, didn't it?" said Joe.

There was only a tin of corned beef to greet us inside the tent at Advance Camp, and we soon demolished that. Now that we were safe, thoughts of food started to obsess us. It was eleven days since we had eaten our last big meal at Base Camp. However, we knew that we could manage another day without much to eat. There would be plenty of time to celebrate later. It was a marvellous luxury to slide into our sleeping bags before it was completely dark, and to fall asleep without the fear of rolling over.

We woke up hungry, but there was no breakfast. I decided to start on a course of Ampicillin to prevent my fingers from rotting.

"Who's the junkie now?" said Joe, as I took the first pill. "I bet they haven't any calories!"

It was the 18th October, the day the flight we had booked left Delhi. Our parents and our friends would be starting to worry about where we were, since they were expecting us on it. They would not have heard from us since we had sent letters back with Palta for him to post for us, early in September. Obviously, it was a priority to reach Joshimath and send some telegrams. Also, we were bursting to tell someone we had climbed the West Wall. We wondered how the Americans had fared on Dunagiri, and if there would be any of them around at Base Camp. Joe was longing for a change of company as much as I:

"That would be good, to go and relax amongst other people . . . Able to laugh and joke in the knowledge that I had earned the right to laugh completely, that it wasn't a false façade I would be projecting. We had earned the right to relax."

We had wound down from the effort of the route into a lazy passiveness, when it came to turning our talk of descent into action. Food is fuel and we had none, and our stomachs were rumbling as we walked up to the foot of the West Wall to look for the gear we had lost. Joe saw the harnesses, half buried by snow inside the bergschrund, and lay flat across a snow bridge so that he could lever them out with his ice axe. There was no sign of the tent and, after extensive searching for it, we assumed that it had disappeared down a crevasse.

The amount of equipment at Advance Camp seemed enormous, after we had taken the tent down and accumulated it all in a big pile. We realised that we would not be able to carry it all back down to Base Camp that afternoon, and determined to return for the remainder the following morning. We did not contemplate leaving any behind.

"Ever a little further . . ." muttered Joe, as he hitched his sack up.

"It's 'always a little further', actually," I said — the title of a book by Alistair Borthwick, from a line in a poem by Flecker.

"Pedant," said Joe. "Typical English student!"

The sun was low in the sky by the time we left the moraine of Advance Camp. Imperceptibly, the days had become shorter with the coming of winter. Our departure offered a scene that would have gladdened the heart of any film producer, had he been there. Our sacks were piled high on our backs and the sun was glittering on the ice of the glacier, casting our long shadows into the shadows of the mountains around us. We crunched downwards with slow, wandering steps, whilst white-walled Changabang loomed high behind us, cold and aloof, looking as awe-inspiring as it had on first sight.

It was dark when we reached the top of the valley. I always regarded Base Camp with a strange mixture of feelings, for it was both a welcome home and a misty Bleak House at the same time. It had been a refuge of recovery, but also a hiding place after defeat. Now I was in a silent mood of trepidation, although we had both just been complaining to each other about being ravenously hungry. As the angle of the descent changed, and our feet started thumping the soft earth of the moraine instead of harsh grey ice and stones of the glacier, Joe suddenly stopped.

"Can you hear voices?" he said. We both listened, but there were no living noises in the eddying air. "I'm sure I heard something. Oh well, perhaps not."

We were walking closely together, as if for security. A few hundred feet lower down, I was convinced I could smell woodsmoke. Then we both definitely heard voices. Our pace quickened involuntarily. We

rounded the boulders abruptly and saw a hillside aglow with lights and
fires. Our forty days of self-imposed isolation had ended and we
were back in the world of people. We shouted hallos. No reply. We
became dubious. "Perhaps someone's raiding our tent," I said.

We approached with caution. Nothing seemed out of place. The
tent was still fastened up. The note was still underneath the stone. We
dropped our sacks and hurried, tripping and falling, and a little uncertain, across to the fire. A large tent loomed up; there were lights inside
and voices chattering away. "They sound Japanese," said Joe. I pulled
back the flap.

The inside was bright with candlelight, and I saw a blur of red
sweaters and dark, bearded faces. It was a big tent and they were all
sitting around the sides. In the middle of them was a table made of
boxes, with an enormous primus stove belching away with a large
pot on top of it. Everyone shuffled around and room was made for Joe
and me. Rabbi Corradino introduced himself as the leader of the
Italian Garhwal expedition, from Turin, and then introduced his seven
fellow-members. Joe and I found ourselves sitting next to a woman,
who told us she was from the American Dunagiri expedition. Cups of
hot tea, biscuits and Italian cheese were thrust into our hands and we
chatted in a mixture of broken French and English.

The Italians had come to climb Kalanka, but their porters, disliking
the idea of the long trek around into the Sanctuary and up the Changabang Glacier, had brought them here to the foot of the Rhamani. The
Italians had tried to cross the ridge but had not realised the circuitous
manœuvres that the Indo-British expedition had made to cross Shipton's Col. Two of them had reached the ridge by a snow slope between Shipton's Col and Rishi Kot, but the other side had been too
difficult for them to contemplate descending. Then the expedition had
seen signs of fixed rope on the Japanese route on the South-West
Ridge and, hoping that it was all in place, had been across to attempt a
second ascent. However, the ropes had stopped after a few hundred
feet and so they had not got very far. And now they were going back
and their porters were due in two days' time. It had not been a very
successful expedition for them, but they did not seem too bothered.

Yes, they knew we had climbed the West Wall, they had seen us
coming down. Had they any news of the South Face expedition?
Apparently they had reached the summit about ten days before we had,
by a new route on the south side, although they did not think it was
the actual South Face. We were hungry for more news, and our

achievement and experiences were changing in value to us, for the
outside was bringing new perspectives. I had organised a climbing trip
to Britain, the previous year, for eight Italian mountaineers from all
over Italy, and now I repeated their names to them. Yes, they knew
them all, and it was good to talk about mutual friends. Joe they knew
of by his reputation, mainly because of his second ascent of the Gervasutti route on the East Face of the Grandes Jorasses. It was an ascent
that had been widely acclaimed in Italy, and an article by Joe about it
had been published in an Italian mountaineering magazine.

And what of the Dunagiri expedition? Had they climbed their
mountain? Why was the woman next to us the only American here?
Where were the others? We thought that they would have left days
before. Had they been delayed? The American woman, Ruth Erb,
had a quiet voice and it was difficult to hear her against the background
hubbub of the Italians.

"We had an accident," she said.

"I'm sorry to hear that," said Joe. "Was anybody hurt?"

"Yes, four of us were killed three days ago. I'm the only one left."

Slowly her words penetrated our bemused confusion of fatigue and
elation. I winced as if I had been slapped in the face. Had we heard
correctly? Her voice seemed so calm, so measured, it seemed to belie
the content of her words.

"Was anyone related to you?" asked Joe.

"Yes, my husband."

"How did it happen?" I asked, suddenly unsure of myself, not
knowing if she would want to talk about it. Our happiness, our intoxi-
cation at our success, started to feel inane.

Ruth talked objectively, as if with an enormous effort she was holding the full implication of the tragedy off from her consciousness. On
12th October they had established a camp at 19,850 feet, at the foot of
the rockstep on the South-West Ridge. By the 15th, the day Joe and I
had reached the summit of Changabang, six of the team had to leave
because their available time was growing short or for various other
reasons. Ruth had stayed at the 19,850 foot camp while the remaining
four climbers, Graham Stephenson, the leader, Arkel Erb, John Baruch
and the Mexican climber, Benjamin Casasola, had set out to establish
a camp on the ridge above, from which they hoped to reach the summit the next day. On the afternoon of the 16th, Ruth had been watching Arkel and John descending the snow ridge between 21,000 and
22,000 feet, when she saw them slip and fall. They had appeared to be

trying to brake their fall with their ice axes on the slopes but had failed, and had disappeared from view. They fell about two thousand feet. Ruth had moved to a point on the edge of the ridge where she could look down onto the glacier below, and saw not only the bodies of her husband and John, but also those of Graham and Ben.

Ruth had spent the next two nights alone at the camp, hoping that the expedition porters at Base Camp would come up to see what was wrong and to help her down. The previous day, the 17th, she had noticed someone about a thousand feet below her. She had shouted and whistled and thought he had heard her, but was shattered when he went back down. However, the man (Yasu) had gone down to Base Camp to get help. He had found the Italian climbers and that day three of them had gone up with Yasu and helped her down. She had arrived at Base Camp one hour before we had.

Joe stumbled out of the tent, in search of Yasu, who was a good friend of his. For me, the Italians had drifted into the background. They were tactfully talking amongst themselves. I asked Ruth if she had any children. She had a twenty-two year old son. Had she thought what she was going to do now? She hoped there might still be some members of the expedition in Delhi, and would leave the mountains with the Italians. However, she was worried about the bodies. Someone ought to go up and find them. I felt overcome with the pain of listening to her and hardly dared look at her face. I told her I was going to get something to eat and left the tent.

Outside, I stretched upwards into a clear, starry night. I shivered from the cold and went to our tent, which was still in darkness. Joe appeared.

"Hey, Pete, come over here to Yasu's tent," he said. "He's got masses of food. His mate Balu's here from Joshimath."

We wanted to talk the whole thing over together, and as we walked over to Yasu's tent Joe told me what he had been able to find out. Yasu had been able to see the bodies in the distance on the glacier, below the South-West Ridge, and they wanted Joe and me to go back up to them the next day. Joe's knowledge of the geography of Dunagiri would be a great help.

"Yasu was incredibly pleased to see me," said Joe. "I think that since they'd acted as agents and negotiated porters for the expedition, they feel responsible about the whole thing. I don't know how experienced they are, and they seem a bit subdued. Yasu's only about twenty and Balu must be around the same age. Somebody has to take decisions for

Ruth at the moment, and its easier for us to discuss with her since she speaks English."

Yasu gave me some packets of freeze-dried food that the Americans had left behind. "They have no need of it now," he said.

The stream that flowed through the meadow had dried up and Joe set off up the hill to fetch some water. I flopped inside the tent with a confusion of thoughts racing through my head. I put on my down suit and lay down, looking at the pattern of the candlelight on the tarpaulin of the shelter. It was half an hour before Joe arrived.

"Haven't you got the primus lit? What have you been doing all this time? I had to go bloody miles to get the water." He was furious.

I shook myself into action and rushed about, lighting the stove and preparing the meal whilst Joe crouched outside self-righteously. Yasu had come over to talk to Joe and I saw the teeth of his smile gleam in the darkness.

"You know the Monkey God, Hanuman? He has servants who are also monkeys and who rush about and do everything for him. Just like Pete is for you!"

Joe had quickly focused on a plan of action. I was amazed at the speed with which he had absorbed all that had happened, and had decided exactly what we had to do. We would leave at seven the next morning with Yasu and Balu, climb up to Dunagiri and reach the bodies. If it seemed the best thing to do, we could bury them in a crevasse after collecting as much of their personal belongings as possible, and after photographing them in case there were any legal problems about proving their deaths. We considered walking up the Changabang branch of the Rhamani Glacier, and collecting the rest of our equipment afterwards, but realised we probably would not have enough time. Joe went and consulted Ruth about the plan. She was desperately anxious that the bodies should not be just left on the glacier. She could only speak for her husband, but felt that the other relatives would, if they knew, entrust us with the task and the decisions that would be involved.

I was in awe of Joe's honest compassion and the direct simplicity with which he had immediately offered to help. How crass my bumbling professions of sympathy seemed in comparison!

"It could be a bit gruesome," I ventured.

Joe just shrugged a sigh. "It's just something we've got to do," he said.

Before we finally settled down and tried to snatch some sleep before the morning, a new sort of conversation started up. The crazy hours of the evening had shaken us out of a groove into a frank realisation of how deeply we understood each other, and what a solid team we had become. Now that we had met other people and climbed the mountain, we were no longer so committed to each other. The squeamishness with which we had previously steered conversation away from discussing our relationship was forgotten. However, our conversation was not painful or probing—it was a frank development of ones we had had before. The darkness suspended time and made it easier to say exactly what we thought of each other. We discussed our experiences on the mountain, revealing our moments of greatest effort and deepest depression. We both agreed that it was the hardest route either of us had ever done, or particularly wanted to do. We told each other exactly what judgement we had reached about each other's abilities.

"You're a funny bugger," said Joe. "I mean, back home your job thrusts you into the limelight and you have to be diplomatic with all these different types of people, and yet somehow everyone seems to like you because you don't pose a threat, you're so mild and trusting and seem so naïve—and yet when you're climbing it's a different bloke. You're confident and can be bloody arrogant."

Joe said that he had been surprised at my persistence, and that he thought I was probably a bit stronger than he was. I told him how much better I thought he was at looking after himself, and how much I had learned from him. "I don't think I could have done the climb with anyone else," I said.

"You scratch my back, and I'll scratch yours," said Joe. The conversation had only been a momentary thaw—we could not resist teasing each other for long. "I didn't think I'd have anything to teach a Superstar," said Joe. "They'll be expecting great things from you on K2 now."

He knew that he was just as good as I, if not better, and he gibed me slightly about the fact that I had climbed Everest and had been asked by Chris Bonington to go on an expedition to K2, the second highest mountain in the world, in 1978. I mocked Joe in return, sharing his amused distrust of the outside world's attitude to mountaineering achievement.

"Never mind, Joe," I said. "You can relax now for a bit. You've made the grade. You're bound to hit the big-time soon and join the hall of heroes."

"No thanks, it sounds a real rat-race."

Strong moonlight was filtering through the tent. I looked at my watch. 5.30 a.m. I had hardly slept and since I was feeling thirsty, I decided to put a brew on. We had no water left, so I crawled past Joe and out of the tent, past the still-sleeping tents nearby, and walked up the river bed in the hillside towards the sound of running water. It was a long way up and I did not hurry, but savoured the calm, colourless light of the moon that seemed to flatten the ground around me. When I found the water it was a dark pool, and I had to stoop deep into the ground to scoop it out. As I descended, carrying icy water that slopped painfully over my fingers, the sky was becoming lighter and the ground was gaining relief. I saw the figure of Joe standing outside the tent. "I couldn't sleep either," he said.

We ate some porridge and then Yasu and Balu arrived. Soon we were ready, and the four of us set off over the frozen ground towards the moraine valley and Dunagiri.

It had been many days since we had seen the morning sun on night-frosted grass, and we stopped to enjoy its arrival as we neared the top of the moraine valley. The sun helped to warm our stiffened limbs. The days at high altitude had taken their toll and our muscles had shrunk into stick-like arms and legs. Once at the top, we turned left up the Dunagiri branch of the Rhamani Glacier. It was of a very different character to the Changabang branch. Here, instead of massive blocks of milk-white granite, the moraines were of dark reddish brown smaller blocks and shale. We climbed these steadily onto the glacier. It was a relief not to be carrying heavy sacks and we moved over the ground quickly.

The route was well cairned and it was not long before we passed the Americans' Advance Camp. All that remained of it were two derelict boxes on the moraine and an American flag, erected on a tall pole. The flag had no meaning, its sadness lay too deep for comment and we moved on.

As we gained height, the moraine we were following dwindled into the snow of the glacier. We followed the tracks of many footprints in the snow as they wound past crevasses up the mountainside. We were following the outside edge of the glacier as it curved around from the cirque formed by the South-West and South-East Ridges of Dunagiri. On the inside edge, where the corner was much tighter, the glacier had been squashed and jostled into an icefall. Once we were above the level formed by the bulge of this icefall, we could see the whole southerly flank of Dunagiri. The great sweep of the South-West Ridge nearly filled the entire skyline and it was stepped by the projected ends of layers of rock that inclined downwards from left to right beneath the snow of the flank. The mountain was considerably foreshortened because we were so near its foot. The South-East Ridge, which Joe had climbed the year before, looked deceptively easy angled.

Yasu pointed to where the bodies had landed. They must have fallen from a point much lower down the ridge than we had expected from Ruth's description, and we would have to go up a tongue of glacier, skirting through an upper icefall below the lower part of the South-West Ridge. We scanned the area through our binoculars and picked out the tiny dots of the bodies and scattered equipment below the bergschrund. They lay just above a heavily crevassed area.

At midday, we reached the tent that the expedition had established on the glacier, before their route had turned up to the foot of the South-West Ridge. We looked inside and found some books—one of them in Spanish, and evidently the Mexican's. Also, there was some food, and amongst it some peppermint indigestion tablets. I had a queasy feeling in the pit of my stomach and took a packet and started chewing them. Balu said he was feeling ill, and dropped behind. Soon after he had left us, the slope we were climbing steepened.

"Balu has my crampons, will I be safe without them?" asked Yasu, who was trailing behind us.

We were just about to put our crampons on, and told him he would not be safe. Joe and I climbed over a bulge in the glacier and both Yasu and Balu dropped from our sight.

"I think they're both a bit superstitious," I said. But my plodding pace lacked the forceful purpose of Joe's stride and I lagged behind him.

This was not like the death of Mick Burke; I had not known these climbers, they had not been my friends. I had been on mountain rescues before, and knew what bodies looked like after they had fallen a long way. I had nursed a dying man by a roadside after he had been knocked off his bicycle. But this was different, just as terrible. We were alone, in the sunlight in the middle of a wilderness of mountains, and the drama of the situation overpowered my attempts to rationalise my frame of mind into the matter-of-fact, hardened attitude of a hospital casualty officer. The fact that we had not known them seemed to add to the sense of pathetic waste. Every piece of scattered equipment seemed to unfold an aspect of the tragedy as we walked past it. The bodies were close to each other, still roped in pairs, at 20,000 feet. On reaching them we saw that they all had severe head injuries and must have died instantly. There was no indication as to how the accident had occurred. We gathered all the pieces of equipment from the slope and went through their pockets and rucksacks for items that might be worth saving. Only John Baruch, the nineteen year old boy tied to Ruth Erb's husband, had a diary in his rucksack. It was soaked in paraffin from a smashed bottle, also in the sack. I put it in my rucksack to give to Ruth. It was not my business to read whatever story was told inside it. "He seems a good-looking lad," said Joe.

We agreed to slide two bodies each down the slope, using the ropes to which they were attached and to bury them in a crevasse. Joe took the bodies of Arkel Erb and John Baruch and I took Graham Stephenson and Benjamin Casasola. The bodies were twisted and stiff and it was awkward and dangerous sliding them into the narrow neck of the first crevasse we came across down the slope.

We couldn't judge how stable the edges of the crevasses were. "Watch what you're doing, Joe!"

I was feeling sick and Joe, noticing I was fighting back tears, came over to help me. But this was an overwhelming sorrow that weeping could not symbolise. "I suppose we ought to say a prayer or something," I said. We had never discussed religion or beliefs before.

"We'll stop for some moments," said Joe.

All around us, the peaks of the Garhwal glittered in the late afternoon sunshine, Changabang, Rishi Kot, Nanda Devi—we were seeing them all from a different angle, and this fresh perspective heightened the impact of their beauty on us. Our sense of the area fell into a new pattern. The deaths of the four climbers had made us feel alive with every breath. This was the sensation of life—the sense that we remained. The four climbers were now part of the Rhamani Glacier, and 'Rhamani' meant 'Beautiful'. The legend told that the Rishis were troubled by bad people and demons, but they came to this place and found a refuge. Surely there could be nothing mean or sordid about death in such a place?

We trudged down, into the gathering shadows. Yasu and Balu had packed the equipment at the camp and, when we arrived, they looked at us as if we had come from the moon.

It was long after nightfall when we approached Base Camp. There was a great fire burning and around it many people were silhouetted. It was the Italians' last evening, and their porters had arrived, ready for the departure the next day. The porters had just finished singing a song of the Garhwal, and the Italians had launched into a song of the Dolomites. Joe and I walked into the light of the fire and the singing stopped abruptly. I was sorry—we had not wanted to stop it. I felt all the eyes of the Italians and the porters on us. We went over and talked to Ruth. There were the lines of tears on her face.

"I'm sorry about these," she said, brushing them away, "all that lovely singing made me kind of forget myself."

CHAPTER TEN

The Outside

20th October–1st November

Wewantedtobehome.Theintensityandsinglemindednessofpurpose that we had generated in our adventure were ebbing away. The immediate priority was to get word of our safety back to our relatives and friends in Britain. Also, I started to worry about my job, since I was three weeks late for work at the BMC. The Italians did not have enough porters to help us; some of them were already being used to carry the American equipment and we could not move ours straight away because there was still about fifty kilograms of it up at Advance Camp. We decided that one of us should go out immediately with the Italians and Ruth, to Lata, send five porters back from there, and then go on to Joshimath to send telegrams.

Joe had spent six days by himself in the same place the previous year, not knowing if the porters whom Dick had promised to send were going to come or not. He did not relish the prospect of a repeat performance. I did not mind staying behind, and looked forward to some quiet, undisturbed hours during which I could recover my thoughts. Although I wanted to be home, I dreaded the noise and bustle of the return journey, which I knew would bring complications before it brought comforts. Early on the 20th October, the morning after we returned from Dunagiri, the porters were rushing around the Italians, trying to get everything ready to leave. They wanted to reach Lata in two days, in time for the Diwali Festival. We negotiated with Tait Singh, who had been so dynamic on the walk in, that he would return as soon as possible with three Lata men. He realised that there was no time to lose, since a winter storm would make the whole route impossible. I thought the return journey should take them about five days.

Yasu, Balu and the porters were very worried that I was intending to stay at Base Camp alone, and urged me to come with them. They seemed superstitious about the deaths of the four climbers on Dunagiri. But having been there and buried them, I did not share their sense of mystery. The Italians gave me some potatoes and biscuits and shook my hand. As soon as they started moving away, all the individuals I had just been talking to seemed to melt into the crowd of thirty people. 'It looks quite a horde,' I thought, as they walked down the meadow. I stood and watched them until all the dark woollens of the Garhwalis and the red sweaters of the Italians had disappeared down and round the corner between the moraine and the flanking hillside. It was many minutes before the noise of their shouting and laughing died away. Joe threw a few pieces of equipment into his rucksack and was ready.

"See you soon."

"Cheerio for now." He hurried away, trying to catch sight of those in front, looking fit, strong and capable. It was a beautiful day. Silence surged back around me.

The expeditions had wreaked havoc in the area. There was a litter of discarded and broken equipment, and tent platforms hacked out of the slope with stone walls built around them. Now I was alone it looked like vandalism. I spent the morning tidying the meadow up and lit a big fire of rubbish. I was worried about spending the long hours of darkness inside the tent without any light, for our supply of candles and batteries had long since run out. Fortunately I found some candles whilst rummaging around the Italian camp. Once the meadow was as near to normal as it could be, I started feeling more relaxed, for now there were no distractions. I started sorting out our equipment, and found the medical box and a mirror. I bathed and bandaged my finger ends and trimmed my beard. It was the first time I had seen myself soberly for weeks. I sat on a kit bag just outside the tent, under the tarpaulin that we had arranged as a large awning over the entrance, supported by an improvisation of sticks and tent pegs, line and boxes. I felt like Robinson Crusoe, for I had built the boxes up around me into a protective wall. I had stocked up inside with food and two big Italian tins full of water, so that I would not have to wander in search of the stream at night.

At dusk I started to feel slightly threatened as the shadows closed in around the tent. I decided to light the primus stove and make myself a mug of tea, hoping that the flame and purr of the stove would dispel the sense of loneliness. It was the small primus stove which we had bought especially for the expedition, and had used constantly at Advance Camp and Camp One. As usual, I put some solid fuel on the preheating cup and lit it, closed the valve, gave it a couple of pumps, put a pan of water on top and waited for it to light. As I was rooting out the sugar and teabags, I heard a bubbling, rasping noise and turned around. It was the stove, behaving rather erratically: little blue flames were coming out of the point where the top unit is screwed into the bowl. Then a swirl of flame started to come out of the safety valve and pump. 'I'd better leave it outside,' I thought and put it on the grass near the entrance. I watched, fascinated as flames started to lap all around the stove, gaining size rhythmically as if fanned by bellows. 'That's getting a bit too dramatic,' I thought. 'I'd better kick it farther away.' I started to get up. There was a flash and the air was filled with flame.

When I came to, I didn't know where I was. It was completely dark and my face was smarting with pain. 'I'm blind,' I thought. I reached up instinctively. I was enveloped in fabric and I realised that I had been blown back into the back of the tent which had collapsed on me. I struggled out into the night and knew immediately that I was not blind because I could see the burning remains of the stove. I threw some water over it to stop the fire spreading. I felt myself all over, and decided that I was not seriously injured. I lit a candle and found the mirror, and looked at my face. My beard had virtually disappeared and my eyebrows, eyelashes and the front of my hair were singed. My neck and wrists were slightly burnt and I cleaned and dressed them. 'How ironic,' I thought as I recovered the tarpaulin from where it had landed and re-erected the boxes and shelter, 'to have climbed Changabang and then to have nearly been killed by an exploding stove at Base Camp.' All that remained of the stove was the mangled, steaming wreckage of its base. The top part, pump, legs and panful of water had been blown into the night. I was determined that the incident would not upset me and managed to extricate a stove left by the Italians, and tried to light that. It gave off a sooty, weak flame but at least—I hoped—seemed fairly safe. It was a long time before I had cooked and eaten an evening meal, crawled into the tunnel tent and painstakingly fastened the door, shutting out the night. It was a slow, lonely discipline the next day to summon the energy to climb back up to Advance Camp and I did not leave until midday. I was feeling very weary, and hoped that Joe was faring better on the walk out, and that he was feeling more wound into action than I. I did the walk as quickly as I could push myself, but still could not carry the load back down before it went dark. I ate a cold meal of Italian biscuits and cheese before dropping asleep from fatigue.

The next morning I felt more enthusiastic, because I knew it would be the last carry I would have to do. I left much earlier, determined to return in daylight. The fact that I was alone and dreamily tired made me feel self-conscious, as if I had been on a stage too long, walking in front of a giant insubstantial backcloth of mountains. The previous day I had felt in a grim mood, and had stared only at the ground. But now the persistent sight of Changabang once more took my breath away. Had I really been up there? Well, I need never go there again. At Advance Camp I packed the remains of the equipment into my sack and collected all our rubbish together. There was a bottle of paraffin left and I poured the liquid all over the rubbish and then set it alight. Flames leapt up and licked the sky. I tended the fire for a while, until I was sure that everything would burn into disintegration. Then I knocked over the cairns that had marked the site of our camp and guided us towards it across the glacier. I was determined, if at all possible, to leave no sign of our passing. As I walked away across the glacier I kept on looking back, to see if the fire was still burning. There was a sacrificial quality about leaving it burning beneath the West Wall; the flames seemed to be stranded on the moraine imbued with life.

That night I had a terrible dream. I was at a party and did not know anyone and people were dissecting each other coldly, clinically, in fun and without any trace of fear. In my dream I cried out in horror. I woke up, mouthing dumbly into the darkness of the inside of the tent.

When I awoke in the morning, I looked at the date on my watch. It was Saturday, 23rd October, the day after the great Hindu Festival of Diwali. 'The porters'll probably arrive tomorrow evening,' I thought. 'I bet they can't drag themselves away from all the drum beating in Lata.' I got up and made myself some porridge. Then I found some pliers and levered off the supergaiters that were nailed around the soles of my boots. It had the nature of a symbolic act, for nothing would induce me now to leave the ease and safety of low altitude to go amid the hazards of the glacier and mountain where I would have to wear them. I filled out the rest of the daylight vaguely sorting out the equipment into porter loads—the only important task left. My mind was marking time and I just wanted to leave the mountain. I was yearning for the contrasts of home in Derbyshire. The longing I felt was not for any particular things. It was nostalgia that defied analysis, but was just there, as a dull ache.

In the evening I decided to cook some of the Italian potatoes but was too scared of risking another explosion to use the pressure cooker. I had forgotten how low the temperature of boiling point is at 15,000 feet and, after boiling them for over an hour, they were still hard. Nevertheless, I ate them.

I had been so intensely caught up in the climb and descent and aftermath, that I had not written my diary for sixteen days. Now I got out a piece of paper and tried to reconstruct the main events of the missing time. As the evening went on, I was looking at my watch, thinking what time it would be back home. It was the evening of my local climbing club, the Mynydd's dinner—the first time I had missed it for years. As I lay in my sleeping bag, the numb parts of my fingers and toes were tingling with growing nerve ends and improving circulation. Yes, I had a lot to be thankful for, and there would be some good booze-ups when I got back.

I woke suddenly, sure I had heard a shout. It was daylight, 9.00 a.m. —I had overslept! Yes, there it was again, a great, long drawn out shout that echoed around the mountains. Excitedly, I struggled out of my sleeping bag, pulled on some clothes and rushed out of the tent in the full light of the early risen sun. I could see no one. It was as if the sound had come from the mountains themselves. Then I heard the babble of voices and, moments later, the porters rounded into view, moving very quickly over the frozen ground.

First I felt delighted, then guilty, as if Joe were telling me off for being dozy. The five porters had arrived a day earlier than I had expected, and I had not got the loads ready. I rushed around, flinging things into boxes, for it was evident that Tait Singh was in a hurry and the other Lata men jumped about as he ordered them to help me. The tent was suddenly ripped up from the ground and shaken inside out and disappeared inside a kit bag. My packing stopped abruptly, so that I could ensure that they did not pack my books and other things I would need for the journey out. I was impressed to hear from Tait Singh that they had left Lata only the day before, and had bivouacked just below the left turn up the Rhamani. And tonight we could reach Dibrugheta!

Before we left, Tait Singh handed me a note which Joe had written to me on his arrival at Lata.

Dear Pete,
    The porters will bring the gear to Lata for 640 rupees and Tait Singh will bring it to Joshimath if we give him one of the tarpaulins.
                                                                    Joe.

I laughed. I was used to Joe's ways now. No news, no platitudes, just a statement of fact—and why not? All this adventure was perfectly normal was it not?

The porters were happy, because their loads were light, and I was happy because I was leaving. The descent to the side of the Rishi swept past and soon we were picking our way along its side. It was good to be alone with the porters, because I could laugh and joke with them in a more relaxed way than when I had been with Palta and Joe. Also, they seemed to have gained respect for us now we had climbed the Shining Mountain. We were no longer just some more western trekkers to fleece.

Now the flowers had gone and the Rishi Ganga had faded from greens to mellow autumnal tints. What had been misted over on the walk in was now clear. I could see the whole height, now, of the mountains on the other side of the Rishi as they rose from the warm forests of the river bed to their high snows. Behind us, standing at the head of the gorge like a sentinel, was Nanda Devi. Details of the ground, shapes of rock, and patterns of tiny gullies, areas of level ground encouraging a rest, had lain dormant in my mind for many weeks, but now rose up to be remembered. The change in visibility was a revelation and it was only these little details that anchored my sense of place.

That night we reached Dibrugheta. I was going to sleep out in the open, but Tait Singh insisted that I slept in the 'member tent' and he quickly erected it. The porters built a fire and sat around it. The flames held their eyes into the night. The temperature was way below freezing point and they did not have many blankets with them. I took a gulp of the tea they had made and nearly scalded myself. We had descended 8,000 feet that day and, for the first time for nearly two months, I was drinking tea that had reached something near the usual boiling point temperature. I could not gulp it down, but had to sip. It felt as if I were learning to taste again.

There were also hostile signposts to the life to which I was returning. The track had been beaten even broader by the passing of expeditions back from the Sanctuary. And along it was a trail of metallic foil, tins, empty Gaz cartridges and food wrappers. I could see from the wrappers which expeditions they had come from. And now the Indian Government is mooting plans to build a catwalk through the mouth of the Rishi Ganga, to make the area even more accessible for tourism and hunting. Nature's best defence that held back explorers until the 1930s cannot withstand the might of bulldozers of the 1970s. And what will happen then to the Sanctuary of Graham, Longstaff, Tilman and Shipton?

Many tales and legends, linked through all cultures, carry poignantly within them a sense of loss, of a glory that has gone, an Eden unrecovered and yet also convey the implicit promise of renewal, return, recovery, the Eden which will again be found. Perhaps the Sanctuary of the Bliss-Giving Goddess would one day recover from its imminent devastation—but in what way I could not guess.

As we climbed steeply up the slope towards Dharansi Pass, the porters were reacting differently to the effort. Dharam Singh, sporting a brown balaclava and yellow anorak from the American Nanda Devi expedition, was always in front, effortlessly singing at the top of his voice whilst climbing the steepest sections. Tait Singh, always the leader, decided when to rest. Immediately they would dump their loads with a whistle of relief, and light a beedi or leaf cigarette. The beedi finished, he gave a sharp nod of command and they jumped into action. They had a good rapport with each other and worked well as a team. They were forever laughing and chatting together, as though they had just met after a prolonged absence. I could not understand the language of their banter, but slotted them into caricature—one big, strong and aggressively reliable, one cheerful and worldly, another with a sharp, dry wit and a wizened face. One of them, the dozy fall-guy, was always lagging behind—he had a deep, rattling cough and seemed ill. I think he had T.B. He was probably in his late thirties.

On the ridge we paused for a while. Dharam Singh unfolded a grubby teacloth and handed me two chappaties. "Packed lunch," he announced.

The view was fantastic and I felt I had seen it before with the same amount of fresh snow covering. Virtually the same panorama was in the long, fold-out photograph in the book *Five Months in the Himalayas*, which had been written by Arnold Mumm about Longstaff's 1907 expedition. I asked the porters the names of some of the more distant peaks to the north and west, but I could not decipher their words and they disagreed with each other. To the east, I could see Dunagiri from a new angle. It looked deceptively low and accessible. Having climbed the West Wall of Changabang, my whole attitude to these mountains had changed. I thought continually of the early explorers of the Garhwal. In earlier days a trip to the Himalayas had

involved far more in travel. The boat journey to India had given those
expeditions a different attitude to time. It had only been worth the
effort of coming out if you had a six-month plan including many objec-
tives. In 1939, André Roche's Swiss expedition had attempted many
peaks in three different areas. In 1950, Bill Murray's Scottish expedition
had walked around three ranges. As Eric Shipton had said, "A lifetime is not enough to absorb the wonder of that country." The experiences of modern politics would, of course, now prohibit such wandering. But Joe and I had spent forty days clinging to one side of one
mountain. We had exalted the idea of climbing the Wall. For two
months, it had given us something to believe in. It had acquired a
permanence—a hold on our lives. As I took one last look at Nanda
Devi and the white rims to the great space around me, I could not help
worrying that our single-mindedness had been unhealthily tinged with
fanaticism. 'Monomaniacs, that's what we are,' I thought. 'We've
proved nothing that hasn't been proved before—if you want to climb
something enough, you'll end up climbing it. Perhaps I'll go round a
mountain in the future, instead of pushing an irrational way up one
of its sides.'

The porters had left, moving nimbly over the icy slopes of the north
side of the ridge, down towards the first trees that promised the hillside
above the Dhauli Ganga. My legs felt emaciated and my knees were
rattling together as I jolted in hot pursuit to rush down the 3,000-foot
slope to Lata.

Little boys and girls peeped shyly from doorways—they were the
first children I had seen for two months. Below me, on the stone-
flagged courtyard, Tait Singh's wife was threshing grain, ready to be
stored for the winter. That night I slept on Tait Singh's balcony. The
festival was still in progress and, late into the night, I could hear the
throb of drums and the wild cries of dancers.

In the morning the porters turned up again at Tait Singh's house and
carried down the loads to the roadside. It was eight o'clock, and Tait
Singh and I sat on the boxes waiting for the bus. But the bus was full,
and the next three buses also refused to stop, as did every vehicle that
passed us. For the following eight hours we sat by the roadside. The
sun moved onto us and moved off. High above the opposite hillside,
a great lammergeyer, with a wingspan of at least nine feet, wheeled
and swept effortlessly backwards and forwards, hunting the ground
below it. I admired its self-discipline, but drew no comfort from it.
During the day a succession of characters, families, flocks and herds

walked past us at biblical pace, in marked contrast to the roaring dirt of military jeeps and wagons heading to and from the north.

By four o'clock the vehicles were becoming less frequent, when a truck stopped in front of our desperate flaggings. Tait Singh pleaded with the driver for ten minutes. Instead of just slamming the door, as had happened before, the driver eventually agreed to take us as far as the military camp near Joshimath. I found myself sitting next to a Sikh soldier whose mouth was masked by a fold of his turban to keep out the dust that billowed into the back of the truck. On the way we stopped for petrol at Tapoban. The soldier spoke some English. He came from the plains, and was just going home for two weeks' leave.

"Do you like being in the mountains?" I asked.

He laughed. The question was a foolish one. "My family lives in the south," he said.

Once more we were by the side of the road, but this time we were outside Joshimath. There were soldiers everywhere. Tait Singh looked slightly lost, and it pained me that someone who was so competent on the hillside and respected in his village, should be swept up by a civilisation that seemed to reflect him as a simpleton. I offered to walk to the Neilkanth Hotel, and to send back some porters to help carry the gear.

As I strode through the main street I started to feel, for the first time, unkempt and strangely dressed. But no one was noticing me and I felt confident. So this was the outside—were its preoccupations off-centre or were mine? Did I need it? It was twilight, transistor radios were blaring and naked bulbs were flickering dimly in the shops and sweet-meat stalls. It was crowded, and I had to jostle past through the crowds of shoppers, pilgrims and beggars, carts and dogs. My senses were stormed by a confusion of images, intense, momentary 'takes' freely flashing by the corners of my eyes.

I walked into the rest house. Joe was there, looking washed and rested. I was still carrying with me the wilderness of mountain life and the aura of one newly returned amongst people.

"Where's the gear?"

"Don't worry, Tait Singh's waiting with it at the top of the main street." I was pleased with myself—I had actually done something without Joe's initiative.

"That's a relief, I thought you'd got stranded on the other side of the Dharansi Pass by all this fresh snow."

"No, it was O.K., actually—most of it must have fallen on the other side of the Dhauli Ganga. Did you send the telegram?"

"Of course."

"To the BMC and to me mum and dad?"

"Yes, don't worry."

We had not seen each other for a week, and we talked incessantly, bringing each other up to date. Joe had been in the outside world for five days, so more had happened to him, and I soaked up his ramblings. His words tumbled out.

"It was bloody desperate getting here. I felt really fit after I'd left you, but Ruth had quite a hard time and I stayed with her. We camped at Dibrugheta and I was determined to catch the last bus to Joshimath, so I ran ahead of all the others on the descent to Lata. I just got to the road in time to see the last bus disappearing around the corner. So I kipped by the roadside. But of course, the next day was Diwali and it took me ages to get on a bus. I got the telegram off, virtually straight away. That first American we met, Neko Colevins, came up here to meet Ruth—he was still in Delhi when he heard about the accident. Some bastards have broken the news of the deaths worldwide, so that families'll hear about it over the media in the States before they're told. Ruth'll be swamped by reporters when she reaches Delhi—it'll be a hell of a strain for her. The two of them left two days ago. I had to go to the Police with them and make two statements. The Italians left this morning. I went to Badrinath with them a couple of days ago on the bus. It was an amazing journey, crammed packed with pilgrims, all spitting red betel juice out of the windows like blood. Oh, and I met Jimmy Duff—they didn't do the South Face—got to the headwall and ran out of time, so they did a new ice route to the right in a four-day round trip. Pretty good effort, eh? They reached the top on October 2nd, so they must have done the route during that bad weather, whilst we were in the hammocks. The big snow storm whilst we were at Camp One must have blotted out their tracks on the summit, so that's why we didn't see them. Oh yes, and you've got some letters."

I seized the bundle greedily and Joe went off to ask Bhupal Singh to fix me some food and to send some porters to help Tait Singh with the gear, and to buy the bus tickets for the next morning's return to Delhi.

Tait Singh arrived and we had a long argument over the money we owed him. We knew he was not well off, but he had put up the price and we felt we had a responsibility to future expeditions to the area, and ought to be hard bargainers. It had only been the large-monied expeditions of recent years that had disrupted a long-surviving tradition of fair dealing by distributing lavish baksheesh and thus sowing the seeds of greed. We wanted no part of that. I hated the confrontation, because Tait Singh and I had shared such a grim day together. Eventually, Bhupal Singh smoothed a compromise by paying Tait Singh a few extra rupees out of his own pocket, and everyone shook hands.

It was a long bus ride. In the early morning the bus side-slipped down and around the steep bends, blaring at the migratory families and live-stock that were strung along the road. The inhabitants of the high villages of the north were descending to the Chamoli district for the winter, carrying with them their pots and pans and valuables. As we roared past, little boys hurried their goats and sheep to one side with their sticks, and old men stood, staring impassively. On mothers' backs were child-shaped forms, swathed in cloth, waking and sleeping to their life on the move.

After twelve hours we were down onto the plains and into the heat.

"Back into Coca-Cola country," said Joe.

In Rishikesh I bought a newspaper and we met another European, dressed in Asian fashion. "You guys know a place to hang out for the night?"

"Sorry, I don't," I replied. "We're just moving through. Are you going anywhere in particular?"

"No, I'm just travelling around, stopping wherever it takes my fancy."

"That's hardly wandering in the Shipton style," I said to Joe when he had gone. "But then, there's a shortage of blanks on maps nowadays — that's the problem."

The bus journey seemed interminable. We hung on through the night for another six hours, sitting upright on scarcely padded seats, in silent agonies of piles, diarrhœa and stomach pains.

"Never thought I'd be glad to see Delhi," said Joe.

We must have smelt — only money persuaded the Y.M.C.A. to let us in. It was four in the morning and we flung our skinny frames under hot showers. Old skin peeled off my fingers and new skin appeared underneath.

Five days later we arrived at London Heathrow Airport and a Swiss diplomat from Kuwait gave us a lift into the gleaming lights of central

London in a taxi. We had a few hours to kill before the overnight sleeper left for Manchester, so we found Charlie Clarke, on night duty at his hospital.

"Can I use your 'phone?" I asked.

"He's going to 'phone Dennis, to find out if he's lost his job," explained Joe.

The Yorkshire twang of Dennis Gray, General Secretary of the BMC, answered the 'phone. "Peter Pan Boardman—am I glad to hear your voice? Come back, all is forgiven."

Charlie told us that his wife, Ruth, had had another little girl and we told Charlie all about our adventures. Joe and I had thrashed out our opinions about the climb so closely that they had become almost identical, as if we were presenting a solid front to the world.

Charlie sniggered. "You two both give exactly the same answer to a question—it's like talking to the same person."

"Don't worry," said Joe, when we were on the train, "it'll wear off. You'll regain your sense of identity. It's only your sense of humour that's the same. That's why I asked you along in the first place."

"The next time I go on a two-man expedition," I said, "it's going to be a two-person one. I've had enough of tough-guy talk and cold toes. I'm going to find a young lady and go to the tropics."

"Mmmm yes," said Joe, "that'd be a pleasant change."

When we left the platform at Piccadilly station in Manchester the following morning, we saw a line-up of men in blue overalls sitting on a bench in the entrance hall. The entire night shift from the Salford deep freeze had come to meet us. Our grins matched theirs.

That morning I was back in the office.

Epilogue

I first met Pete Boardman in the summer of 1974. He was a candidate for
our expedition to the South-West Face of Everest; the almost token new
face that we felt should be added to the old-timers who had been with me
on the South Face of Annapurna and on Everest in 1972. We had tossed
around several names, but although none of us knew him, Pete seemed to
have the best credentials—steady on rock, with routes like Bitter Oasis on
Goat Crag, Borrowdale, in the English Lake District, to his credit, a good
Alpine background, with several first British ascents on long mixed routes
behind him—the North Face Direct of the Olan, the Gervasutti Route on
the North Face of the Breithorn, the North Face of the Nesthorn and the
North Face of the Lauterbrunnen Breithorn. But most important of all he
had been to the Himalayas on a university expedition and had been the
driving force in a particularly bold style of climbs in the Hindu Kush,
making fast Alpine-style pushes on the North Faces of Koh-i-Khaaik
(19,226 feet) and Koh-i-Mondi (20,450 feet), both of them being first
ascents.

When he came to my home in the Lake District for a climbing weekend,
I instantly took a liking to him. There was a combination of surprising
maturity and steadiness for someone who was only twenty-three, combined with a boyish, fun quality that made him good and easy company. I
felt that he would fit into the expedition and immediately invited him to
join us.

He was the youngest member of the Everest team and, as the newly
appointed National Officer of the British Mountaineering Council, was
on the receiving end of a certain amount of teasing from a group of
climbers who regarded all forms of bureaucracy, particularly in the climbing sphere, with a cynical suspicion. Pete stood up for the BMC, and, with
a quiet humour, deflected the jibes.

On the mountain he performed well and was a member of the second

summit team, paired with our sirdar, Pertemba. The other two were
Martin Boysen and Mick Burke. The story is well-known. Pete and
Pertemba made a fast ascent of the peak from their top camp, and then on
the way down met Mick Burke, who had plodded on for the summit after
Martin Boysen had turned back. They agreed that Mick would go for the
top, while Pete and Pertemba continued down to the col below the South
Summit to wait for Mick there.

Shortly after this a violent storm engulfed the mountain and Mick
Burke never returned. Peter waited for almost an hour before making the
agonising but inevitable decision to descend while it was still possible. The
only explanation for Mick's failure to catch them up was that he had
walked through the cornice on the very narrow ridge in the white-out
conditions that prevailed in the storm.

Pete had to relive that terrible decision time after time at press con-
ferences and lectures following the expedition. The entire experience
undoubtedly scarred him, and his two-man trip to Changabang helped to
heal those wounds. The smallness of the party, the immensity of the
challenge and the richness of the achievement—not only in climbing
terms, but in ones of human relations and the creative quality of the
book—all contributed to the healing process.

His career had also been developing steadily and in sympathy with his
love of climbing. After leaving Stockport Grammar School, he went to
Nottingham University to take a degree in English. After a post-graduate
course in outdoor education at Bangor University, North Wales, his first
job was as an instructor at Glenmore Lodge, the Scottish Council for
Physical Recreation centre in the Cairngorms. Just before joining us on
Everest, he became National Officer of the British Mountaineering Council, a job entailing sitting on endless committees, demanding a great deal of
patience and powers of diplomacy.

In 1977, the year after his return from Changabang, came the most
important development in his career; he took over the International School
of Mountaineering in Switzerland, after Dougal Haston's death in a skiing
accident. It was a great challenge but, at the same time, gave him the
freedom to go on expeditions, climb to the full and also satisfy his creative
drive in writing.

In 1978 he joined me on the West Ridge of K2, where tragedy once again
struck, when Nick Estcourt was killed in an avalanche and the expedition
was abandoned. In 1979 he had his best year ever, going on three wonderful expeditions: firstly to New Guinea with Hilary, his wife-to-be, to make
an exacting new route on the Carstensz Pyramid; then to Kangchenjunga

with Georges Bettembourg, Doug Scott and Joe Tasker, making the first ascent of the North-West Face and Ridge; and finally, in the autumn, to Gauri Sankar with John Barry, Tim Leach, Guy Neithardt and Pemba Lama, to make the first ascent of the South Summit by the heavily corniced four-kilometre-long West Ridge.

In 1980 he returned to K2 with Dick Renshaw, Doug Scott and Joe Tasker and made three very determined attempts on the mountain, on one of which their top camp at 26,000 feet was destroyed by an avalanche forcing a desperate retreat in a storm. Then in 1981 came a successful and happy expedition to Mount Kongur in China, when Alan Rouse, Joe Tasker, Pete and I reached its 25,328-foot summit on our first ascent. This led to our expedition to the unclimbed North-East Ridge of Everest in 1982, when Pete and Joe made their bid for the summit and were last seen at a height of around 27,000 feet before disappearing round the back of one of the pinnacles on the ridge. They should have come back into view after only a few hundred feet and it therefore seems almost certain that they were involved in a fall or avalanche on the very steep, and probably unstable, snow that was on the other side of the ridge.

Their deaths meant the loss of two fine friends, outstanding mountaineers and very talented, creative people. Pete Boardman was the strongest climber that I have ever been privileged to climb with. He had exceptional stamina, and I am convinced he was fully capable of reaching the summit of Everest without oxygen. He was extremely bold in his climbing concepts but at the same time was very levelheaded and cautious in his appraisal of climbing difficulties. He had a romantic love of the mountains, of their history and their topography; he liked his creature comforts, almost to the degree of appearing quite soft, and yet he had a hard resolve that made him one of the most formidable British climbers of the postwar generation.

He will be greatly missed as an outstanding mountaineer and creative writer, but most of all as a warm, compassionate human being.

Glossary of Mountaineering Terms

PREPARED BY LOUISE WILSON

Abseil Method of quickly descending steep ground by sliding down a doubled rope using a device, such as a karabiner brake, to create friction and control the rate of descent.

Acclimatisation The process of gradually becoming accustomed to climbing and living at altitudes where the air is thin.

Aiguille (French) A needle-shaped mountain or pinnacle.

Alpine-style ascent Method of climbing a mountain in a single push, carrying all the necessary gear, rather than by gradually setting up and stocking a succession of camps in a series of forays from a base camp.

Anchor The point where fixed ropes, abseil ropes or belays are secured to the rock, snow or ice by various means, such as a sling, piton, ice screw, etc.

Arête (French) A ridge; often used to describe a narrow, very sharp ridge.

Artificial climbing A method of climbing steep, ungrippable rock or ice, which it is not possible to ascend otherwise, using mechanical aids such as pitons or bolts driven into the rock to form artificial hand or footholds.

Avalanche A sliding mass of snow or ice.

Belay The means of attaching a stationary member of a climbing team to the mountain to prevent his being pulled off should the leader fall or be hit by any falling debris, etc. It also helps safeguard the lead climber, as the second should be able to arrest the slide of the rope, should the leader fall, by having it passed around his waist, for example, thus creating friction. *See also* **Running belay/runner.**

Bergschrund (German) The last large crevasse at the head of a glacier, usually dividing it from a rock face or steeper slopes above.

Bivouac A temporary encampment without a tent and usually with some makeshift kind of shelter.

Bridging A technique for climbing chimneys and corners by using opposing pressure of arms and feet against the two sides—in other words 'bridging' the gap between the two chimney walls.

Bulge A rounded overhang.

Buttress   A section of a mountain or cliff standing out from the rest and often flanked by a gully on either side.

Cairn   A heap of stones built to mark a summit, pass or other salient feature; also used at intervals along paths to aid navigation in misty weather.

Chimney   A fissure in a rock or ice wall large enough for a person to climb inside.

Chimneying   The method of climbing a chimney by opposing pressures of feet and back on opposite walls.

Chockstone   A rock or boulder wedged in a crack, chimney or gully. These can be used as hand or footholds, anchor points, belays or running belays. Artificial chockstones can be created by wedging aluminum nuts into cracks or fissures. *See also* **Nuts.**

Cirque (French)   A steep-walled natural amphitheatre at the head of a valley, formed by erosion by snow and ice.

Col   A pass or major scoop in a ridge which usually has access on at least one side.

Cornice   An overhanging bulge of snow along the crest of a ridge caused by the wind constantly banking up fresh snow to form a lip that projects out into space beyond the edge of the ridge. It is essential to take a route well below the crest of the ridge in case the cornice breaks away.

Couloir (French)   A gully.

Crampons   A set of metal spikes which are strapped to the soles of climbing boots for climbing snow or ice. They usually have twelve points—ten pointing downwards and two sticking forward beyond the front of the boot for use on very steep ground. *See* **Front pointing.**

Crevasse   A fissure in the ice of a glacier caused by a change in the angle of the ground beneath it. Crevasses can be any size from very small to immense and are particularly dangerous when hidden by a covering of snow.

Deadman   An alloy plate, shaped like the blade of a shovel, which is driven into the snow to form an anchor point in the absence of any rock or ice belays. The blade has a wire threaded through it, on to which the climber attaches himself; any downward force on the wire has the effect of pulling the blade deeper into the snow, thus making it more secure.

Descendeur (French)   A friction device used for abseiling.

Étrier (French)   A short, lightweight ladder of three or four steps used to provide footholds on holdless or overhanging rocks, and to assist climbing by artificial means. Étriers are usually made either from alloy rungs fixed to a thin cord or from a length of tape sewn, or knotted, to form loops for the feet.

Expansion bolt   A bolt which expands and locks when screwed into a pre-bored hole in the rock. Used when a rock face has no cracks into which a nut or piton can be inserted.

Exposure   A long drop beneath the climber's feet; also the condition of hypothermia caused by exhaustion and exposure to severe weather, which can lead to rapid collapse, especially at high altitudes.

Fifi hook   A small hook designed for permanent attachment to an étrier, making it easier to pull up for further use than when the étrier is used with a karabiner.

Fixed rope   Method used on long climbs to enable climbers to ferry equipment up a mountain, or to pass up and down over a period of time. Once a pitch has been climbed, a rope is anchored in place for continued use throughout the climb.

Friction brake   Device, such as a bar mounted on a karabiner, or several karabiners with the rope threaded over and under them, designed to produce friction when abseiling.

Front pointing   A method used to climb steep snow or ice by kicking in the front points of twelve-point crampons, using the pick of an ice axe in one hand and an ice hammer in the other as handholds.

Frostbite   Gangrene that results from the freezing of tissue. Fingers and toes are particularly vulnerable.

Frostnip   Less severe form of frostbite.

Glacier   A river of ice.

Hand jam   A method of wedging a hand or fist in a crack to form a handhold.

Hand traverse   A horizontal movement across a rock face where the body is supported mainly by the hands.

Harness   Name applied to a nylon webbing or tape harness worn by a climber, to which he attaches the climbing rope. It can prevent him from turning upside down in the event of a fall, absorb the shock of a fall, or enable him to abseil in comfort.

Ice axe   A tool for cutting and scraping steps in hard snow and ice, consisting of a blade (adze) and pick mounted on a wood or metal shaft.

Ice hammer   The same as an ice axe but with a hammer head instead of an adze. The hammer head is used for driving in pitons.

Ice piton   A piton that is hammered into the ice, specially designed for use in hard snow or ice.

Ice screw   A piton equipped with some kind of screw formation so that it can be screwed into the ice and easily removed by unscrewing. It makes the most secure ice anchor.

Jamming   Term used to describe the method of climbing by jamming hands or feet in a crack line. *See* **Hand jam.**

Jumar   A device for moving up fixed ropes. It works on a ratchet principle, sliding up the rope by gripping it under tension to prevent its sliding back down.

Karabiner (krab)   An oval or D-shaped snap link made from steel or alloy with a spring-hinged gate in one side. It is used to clip the rope into pitons or anchors and for carrying other gear. Several linked together can be used as a friction brake while abseiling *See* **Friction brake.**

Knife blade   A long thin piton.

Layback   A method of climbing flakes and cracks by gripping the edge with the hands, leaning back and setting the feet on the rock opposite, using opposing pressure to move up.

Leader/lead climber   The climber who ascends a section of a route first, leading out the rope for subsequent climbers.

Mantleshelf   A technique used to surmount a narrow ledge with a flat top and no positive holds. The climber pulls himself up on his arms, transfers his weight over his hands in the press-up position and then hooks one leg on to the ledge and carefully stands up.

Monsoon   Annual front of warm wet winds which hits the Himalayas around the end of May, making climbing virtually impossible.

Moraine   Piles of rocks, earth and rubble brought down by the movement of a glacier.

Nuts   Small alloy blocks, with one or two holes drilled through for a sling, for jamming into cracks to form anchors or running belays. *See also* **Chockstone.** A climber normally carries a selection of different-size nuts.

Overhang   Rock or ice beyond the perpendicular.

Peg   *See* **Piton/peg.**

Pitch   A section of a route between belays.

Piton/peg   A piece of metal consisting of a blade with an eye at the end, through which a sling or karabiner can be attached; designed to be hammered into a crack to act as a belay, anchor point or running belay. Pitons come in many shapes and sizes, e.g. the **Knife blade.**

Powder slide   A small avalanche or 'rush' of powder snow.

Powder snow   Very light, fluffy fresh snow which has not thawed or been refrozen.

Prusik   A special knot tied in two slings on to a rope (or friction device); used to ascend a rope.

Running belay/runner   An intermediate belay point where the rope runs through a karabiner attached to an anchor point so that a fall by a climber, usually the leader, is shortened. For instance, if a leader is forty feet above his second, he would fall eighty feet without a runner. However, if there is a running belay five feet below him, even though he is still forty feet above his second, he will fall only ten feet on to the runner.

Saddle   A broad shallow col.

Siege tactics   Method of climbing a mountain by setting up and stocking a series of camps along the route in preparation for an assault on the summit.

Slab   An expanse of rock inclined at roughly between 30 degrees and 70 degrees to the vertical.

Sling   A short length of very strong nylon tape or rope tied or stitched to form a loop and used for belays, running belays, anchor points, etc.

Soloing   Climbing unroped.

Spindrift   Powder snow being blown by the wind.

Stance   The place where a climber makes his belay, ideally a ledge where it is possible to stand or sit comfortably.

Step-cutting   Cutting steps in snow or ice with an ice axe.

Step-kicking   Kicking the feet into firm snow to form steps.

Tension traverse   A technique used to edge across a holdless section by leaning against the tension of the rope paid out by the climber following.

Tie-off   A method of reducing the leverage on a piton which has not been fully inserted by tying a sling to the piton blade, close to the rock face.

White-out   A condition caused by driving snow or mist that makes it impossible to distinguish anything around you.

Wind-slab   A crust formed on the surface layer of snow, caused by wind action, which, because it is on top of soft snow, is very unstable and prone to avalanche.

Index

Advance Camp, 51, 52, 54, 61, 63, 73, 77, 85, 86–88, 100, 107, 108, 113, 115, 159, 160, 170–173
Afghanistan, 29, 42
Alaknanda River, 36, 37, 41
Alaska, 23, 54, 58, 115
Alps, 14, 15, 23, 59, 70, 85, 89, 115, 151, 158
American S.W. Ridge of Dunagiri Expedition (1976), 55, 101, 109, 111, 159, 161, 162, 166, 179
American Nanda Devi Expedition (1976), 42, 45, 48, 176
Angtharkay, Sherpa (1936 Dunagiri Expedition), 110
Argentière Glacier, 15

Badrinath (Hindu shrine), 34, 41, 179
Bagini Glacier, 58–60, 63, 81, 122, 129, 140
Bagini Pass, 51, 59, 62
Bagini Peak, 60, 113, 118, 124
Balcony (on the Barrier), 72, 74, 75, 90, 94, 95, 118, 156
Balu (porter), 163, 164, 166–168, 170
Bangor University, 116
Barclays Bank International, 27
Baruch, John (American Dunagiri Expedition), 162, 163, 168
Base Camp, 39, 45, 47, 48, 50, 53–55, 59, 85–87, 98, 101, 102, 105, 106, 108, 109, 159, 160, 168, 170, 172
Beaumont, Rosemary, 28
Beaumont, Tony, 28
Bethartoli Himal, 44
Bhiundar Valley, 45

Bhupal Singh (Neilkanth Hotel), 37, 179, 180
Big Groove (on Upper Tower), 125, 126, 129, 131, 132, 139, 140, 152, 153
Birtles, Geoff, 20
Bleak House *see* Base Camp
BMC *see* British Mountaineering Council
Bonington, Chris, 16, 18, 19, 51, 53, 63, 112, 165
Boysen, Martin, 51, 63, 112
British-Indian Expedition (1974) to S.E. ridge of Changabang, 19, 51, 112, 161
British Mountaineering Council, 11, 14, 17, 24, 35, 68, 102, 121, 127, 170, 179, 181
Brocherel brothers, Henri and Alexis, 53, 59
Brown, Joe, 20
Bruce, Charlie, 59
Burke, Mick, 13, 167

Cairngorms, 111
Camp One (Ridge camp), 88, 99, 114, 116, 118, 121, 123, 124, 156, 158, 171
Camp Two, 119, 123, 126, 130, 131, 134, 140, 153, 154, 158
Casasola, Benjamin (Mexican member, American Dunagiri Expedition), 162, 163, 167, 168
Chamoli district, 180
Changabang South Face Expedition (1976), 17, 39, 40, 42, 43, 63, 108, 112, 148, 161, 179
China, 30, 36
Clarke, Dr. Charles, 25, 181
Clarke, Ruth, 25, 181

Clothing, 22, 23, 31, 58, 65, 93, 108, 109, 115, 119, 122, 130
Clough, Ian, 20
Cohen, Anthony (Cambridge University student), 43
Cold store *see* Frozen food centre
Colevins Neko (American Dunagiri Expedition), 109, 179
Corradino, Rabbi (Italian Garhwal Expedition), 161

Delhi, 11, 14, 25, 27, 28, 32, 159, 163, 179, 180
Dharam Singh (porter), 176
Dharansi Pass, 44, 176, 178
Dhauli Ganga, 41, 43, 177, 178
Dibrugheta, 42, 44, 45, 174, 175, 179
Diwali (Hindu festival), 173, 179
Doss-house, Janpath Lane, 27
Droites, 14, 15
Duff, Dr. Jim, 42, 179
Dunagiri, 51, 52, 55, 58, 60, 81, 118, 120, 163, 164, 166, 170, 176; Ascent of S.E. ridge by Tasker and Renshaw, 11, 13, 15, 16, 27, 42, 48, 49, 56, 83, 100; American Dunagiri Expedition, 109, 110, 111

Eiger, 15, 78, 81, 119
Erb, Arkel (American Dunagiri Expedition), 162, 163, 168
Erb, Ruth, 162–164, 167–170, 179
Estcourt, Nick, 19
Everest, 60; South-West Face Expedition (1975), 11–17, 23–25, 27, 35, 44, 59, 65, 77, 80, 84, 86, 93, 108, 112, 116, 136, 165

First aid *see* Medical supplies
Food, 32, 34, 39, 47, 49, 56, 64, 65, 67, 73, 86, 89, 90, 94, 97, 99, 100, 102, 108, 109, 112, 114, 115, 116, 136, 146, 159, 171–175
Frozen food centre (Salford), 18, 21–23, 181

Ganges, 36

Gangotri (Hindu shrine), 34
Garden of the Himalayas *see* Garhwal Himalaya
Garhwal Himalaya, 11, 18, 19, 30, 33, 36, 41, 45, 60, 92, 106, 168, 176
Gervasutti route (Grandes Jorasses), 162
Glencoe, 24
Graham, W. W., 42, 43, 176
Grandes Jorasses, 15, 162
Gray, Dennis, 11, 14, 16, 181
Groove *see* Big Groove
Guest, Keen and Nettlefold, 28
Guest, Keen Williams, 28
Guillotine (on the Barrier), 77, 78, 80–82, 84, 95, 99, 155

Hall, Brian, 20
Hammocks, 21, 22, 107; first hammock bivouac, 90–93; second hammock bivouac, 96; third hammock bivouac, 97–98
Hans (Swiss trekker), 41, 44, 45, 49, 51, 87
Hanuman (the Monkey God), 48, 164
Hardeol, 58
Hardwar, 33
Haston, Dougal, 16, 19, 112
Hill, Dr. Andy, 23
Hindu Kush, 64, 73, 89, 103
Hinterstoisser traverse (Eiger), 119
Horns of Changabang, 58
Hutchinson, Pete (Mountain Equipment), 22

Icicle (on the Barrier), 78, 79
IMF *see* Indian Mountaineering Foundation
Indian Government, 17, 175
Indian Mountaineering Foundation, 17, 20, 28, 31
Indian Trisul Expedition, 42
Indo-British Changabang Expedition *see* British Indian Expedition
Indo-Japanese Expedition, 42
Inner Line, 31, 36, 43, 58, 81
Italian Garhwal (Kalanka) Expedition, 110, 161, 168, 170, 171, 179

Jagat Singh (headman of Lata), 42
Japanese Base Camp, 61
Japanese Ridge, 97
Japanese S.W. Ridge of Changabang Expedition (1976), 19, 42, 97, 107, 161
Joshimath, 36, 37, 40, 43, 45, 159, 163, 170, 178, 179

K2., 165
Kabul, 14
Kailas, 136, 137
Kalanka (The Destroyer), 48, 58, 110, 112, 148, 161
Kapoor, J. D., 28
Karakorum, 20
Kedarnath (Hindu shrine), 34
Keyhole (to the Ramp), 140, 141
Kharbir (Gurkha), 53
Kohi Khaaik, 64
Kuari Pass, 41
Kurz, Toni, 78, 119; see also Toni Kurz pitch

Lammergeyer (bearded vulture), 177
Langdale, 21
Lakeland team see Changabang South Face expedition
Lata, 40, 42, 43, 170, 173, 174, 177–179
Lata Kharak, 43, 44
Latak peaks, 58
Liaison officer see Palta, D. N.
Link pitch (ramp of snow), 48, 54
Llanberis, 20
Longstaff, Dr. Tom G., 33, 44, 48, 51, 53, 59, 60, 70, 176

Mana Pass, 41
Mandip Singh (Liaison officer to Americans), 110
Mars Bar-eater, 56, 62, 155, 159
Matterhorn, 15
Medical supplies, 23, 63, 65, 73, 89, 91, 100, 102, 114, 121, 159
Mount Dan Beard (Alaska), 23
Mount Everest Foundation, 17
Mount McKinley (Alaska), 23
Mumm, Arnold, 176

Murray, W. H. (Bill) (Scottish Himalayan Expedition 1950), 36, 41, 43, 111, 177
Mynydd Climbing Club, 15, 174

Nanda Devi, 40, 42, 45, 48, 127, 137, 147, 148, 168, 175, 177
Nanda Devi Sanctuary, 18, 33, 41, 45, 47, 49, 52, 59, 112, 147, 161, 175, 176
Nanda Ghunti, 44
National Mountaineering Conference (Buxton), 19
Nehru, Jawaharlal, 29
Neilkanth Hotel, 37, 178
Nepal, 27, 29, 42, 60
New Mills, 24, 25
Niche (on the Upper Tower), 122, 125
Niti Pass, 30, 41
Nottingham University, 14

O'Donovan, Roger, 23

Palta, Flight Lieutenant D. N., 31–36, 38–40, 42, 44, 45, 47–49, 108, 159, 175
Pearce, Dave, 19
Pertemba, Sherpa, 13
Prosser, John (Kalanka expedition 1974), 112
Purbi Dunagiri, 58

Ram, Munshi (Secretary of IMF), 31
Ramp (above the Upper Tower), 126, 130, 133–135, 139, 141
Ranikhot, 33
Renshaw, Dick, 11, 13–17, 49, 50, 64, 83, 93, 100, 101, 170
Rhamani Glacier, 16, 47, 48, 51, 52, 54, 59, 84, 95, 123, 140, 149, 158, 161, 164, 166, 168, 175
Ridge Camp see Camp One
Rishi Ganga, 41–45, 47, 53, 59, 87, 115, 149
Rishikesh, 33, 34, 37, 180
Rishi Kot, 48, 52, 59, 84, 106, 161, 168
Rishi Pahar, 58
Roche, André (Swiss expedition 1939), 48, 58, 177

Rogers, Ted (Changabang South Face expedition), 17

Sanctuary *see* Nanda Devi Sanctuary
Scott, Doug, 16, 19, 112
Scott, Rosemary (Cambridge University student), 43
Scottish Himalayan Expedition (1950), 36
Shipton, Eric E., 18, 33, 50, 110, 176, 177, 180
Shipton's Col, 51, 52, 63, 108, 112, 118, 157, 161
Shrines, sacred, 34
Sierra Club (U.S.A.), 110
Sleeping pills *see* Medical supplies
Smythe, F. S., 45, 48
South Face team *see* Changabang South Face Expedition
Spider (Eiger), 81
Srinagar, 34, 36
Stanage Edge, 17
Stephenson, Graham (American Dunagiri Expedition), 110, 162, 168
Stewart, Ian, 23

Tait Singh, 42, 45, 170, 174–180
Tapoban, 41, 178
Tasker, Joe, contributions by, 11, 16, 24, 51, 53, 59, 65, 71, 73, 76, 80, 81, 82, 83, 90, 92, 94, 99, 103, 107, 113, 117, 124, 125, 132, 133, 135, 141, 143, 145, 146, 151, 152, 153, 179
Tibet, 31, 36, 41, 43, 58, 60, 69, 136, 148, 158
Tilman, Bill, 18, 33, 42, 176
Tirsuli, 58
Toni Kurz pitch, 78, 80, 81, 84, 94, 99, 119, 155, 156
Trango Tower, 20
Trisul, 53, 59
Troll Mountain Products, 21, 22

Ultimate Bill *see* Bill Wilkins
Ultimate Equipment, 62
Unsoeld, Nanda Devi, 48, 110
Unsoeld, Willi, 48
Ushaw College, 104, 105

Vitamin pills *see* Medical supplies

Whillans, Don, 20, 55
Wilkins, Bill, 62, 137
Wilson, Ken, 19
Wragg, Martin, 14

Yasu (porter), 37, 163, 164, 166, 167, 168, 170
Yeti, 62
Young, Geoffrey Winthrop, 106

PETER BOARDMAN was born in Bramhall, England, and began climbing on gritstone as a schoolboy; he was still only in his teens when he climbed the Matterhorn North Face. Before attempting Changabang, he made five first British ascents in the Western Alps, climbed in the Hindu Kush and the Caucasus, reached the Everest summit on the 1975 British Southwest Face expedition, and made the first ascent of the South Face of Mount Dan in Alaska. After Changabang, he and Joe Tasker took part in two abortive attempts at K2 and a successful climb of Kongur in China; and Pete and his bride-to-be, Hilary, completed a successful climb of the Carstenz Pyramid in New Guinea, an expedition described in his book *Sacred Summits*. He was National Officer of the British Mountaineering Council until he moved to Leysin, Switzerland, to take over there as the director of the International School of Mountaineering. He is survived by his widow, Hilary Boardman.

JOE TASKER's Alpine climbs included the north faces of the Matterhorn, Dent d'Herens, Dent Blanche, Nesthorn, Eiger, Grandes Jorasses, Eckpfeiler, and winter ascents of the north faces of the Lauterbrunnen Breithorn and the Eiger. He was a member of the successful two-man first ascent of Dunagiri's South-East Ridge in 1975. Until his death, in 1982, he was a technical adviser and sales manager for a climbing-book manufacturer, and lived in Manchester.

The Boardman-Tasker Prize for mountain literature was established in 1982 as a permanent tribute to the talents of Peter and Joe.